Books One-Three of the Ben Hunnicutt Series

Washtub Gold
Warhead
CrossKill

Excellent read...True to Alaska. Ben Hunnicutt uses skill, luck and intuition to solve a very intriguing situation. Step by step he gathers pieces of information (in the most unlikely yet realistic situations) which will lead him to an interesting finale. This book would make a wonderful movie...everyone would enjoy it, there is something for everyone from teens to seniors. This book has adventure, mystery, beautiful scenery, intrigue, partnership, surprise and a touch of romance. I highly recommend this book to anyone wanting to read a different yet very believable and interesting story.

The hero, Ben Hunnicutt, must search Alaska for the murderer. Carefully researched, this crime procedural is richly draped in Alaska history and landscape. It's a sweet read that kept me up way past my bedtime.

From the beginning, the story got my attention and it never waned. When I finished I knew I had to get the next book in line. Being from Alaska myself, I was familiar with the locations in this story which made it all that more interesting.

Excellent read! Alaska Cold War history, mystery, suspense. Author's first novel and first of a series. His Ben Hunnicutt series gets better and better - need to read Warhead and Crosskill also!

Excellent book! I read it with great delight and was impressed page by page and surprised by the ending. A must buy!

A Ben Hunnicutt Novel

The Last Kill

Don Neal

First Edition Design Publishing
Sarasota, Florida USA

The Last Kill
Copyright ©2019 Don Neal

ISBN 978-1506-908-61-8 AMZ
ISBN 978-1506-907-97-0 PBK
ISBN 978-1506-908-25-0 EBK

LCCN 2019939470

April 2019

Published and Distributed by
First Edition Design Publishing, Inc.
P.O. Box 17646, Sarasota, FL 34276-3217
www.firsteditiondesignpublishing.com

*This work is dedicated to the memory of
Janice Martfeld Wills,
1943—2017*

*Jan Wills existed to heal, to guide, to comfort, and to
teach. She excelled at all, and was a Big Sister to all
who knew her.*

Part One

KOREA

Spring
1953

CHAPTER 1

Hill 672

It was about 0330—I was well wrapped in my snug double sleeping bag, dreaming I was fishing in a quiet lake in the Talkeetna Mountains of Alaska, when the world exploded. The ChiComs started dumping artillery and mortars on us like they owned stock in an ammo factory. Our bunker, dug in and well sandbagged, was just down from the south crest of our hill, Hill 672 on the maps. Most of B Company was bedded down in similar bunkers, but our night guards and two light machine gun crews were outside, dug in near the summit with only their foxholes for protection.

I jolted upright and looked for Perkins, my Radio/Telephone Operator, but he was already way ahead of me. At the far end of the bunker, barely visible by lantern light through the dust that concussions were kicking out of the sandbagged walls, I could see him cranking away on the field phone with one hand and yelling into a radio handset held in the other. His first response must have been on the wire, for he slid the EE8 field phone as far in my direction as possible without pulling loose the wire connectors.

I jerked the sleeping bag zipper pulls to the top quick-release position, ripped the bag open, and threw myself onto the field phone.

"Fox Oboe Baker!" I yelled into the mouthpiece. "Fire Mission!".

"Send your mission." replied the ever-calm voice of the Battery Exec, Charlie Taylor.

"We're getting heavy artillery and mortar fire," I responded. "If this is like last time, they'll come in on us as soon as it lifts. We'll need to hit 'em quick."

The reply from the Fire Direction Center was blotted out by a ripping crash as two near-misses nearly tore the bunker out of the ground.

"Say again, over," I shouted.

"I say again, do you want Final Protective Fire, or Concentration Baker-2? Over."

"Final Protective Fire" was a phrase for bringing your artillery down on your own position, generally used to brush off the enemy prowling around your area while your own people sheltered in holes or bunkers. I hoped we weren't that desperate yet, but I knew in a small hidden place in my mind that it could come to that, depending upon how our next move played out.

"Concentration Baker-2, on my call. Shell HE, fuse Victor Tare. And Charlie, give me illumination—keep one in the air so we can see to shoot the bastards! Over."

"Roger," was the reply. "Call it when you need it. I'll give you a splash. Over."

Normally there was a precise protocol for requesting an artillery fire mission, data being exchanged between the Artillery Forward Observer (FO) and the Fire Direction Center (FDC) in a certain order to prevent confusion or transposition of numbers and information. Some Battery Execs (the Executive Officer usually trained and commanded the FDC) demanded strict adherence to the book, but I was lucky in having First Lieutenant Charles Taylor on the other end of the wire tonight. Charlie had been in my shoes often enough to know that speed overrode protocol when your ass was on the line.

"Roger, wait."

My name is Benjamin Hunnicutt, Second Lieutenant of Artillery, presently assigned as Artillery Forward Observer for Baker Company. I had been bedded down in the Company Command Post bunker so as to be instantly available to the infantry Company Commander, Captain James, if artillery support were needed.

The bombardment seemed to go on forever, mind numbing concussions painfully pummeling brain and body, many of us cupping palms over our ears and holding mouths open to protect our eardrums from pressure shock. The choking dirt and dust pounded out of the bunker walls gave a sense of suffocation. That, and my lifelong tendency toward claustrophobia, created a strong urge to claw my way outside before a direct hit buried us all alive. The Coleman lantern, which had earlier lulled me to sleep with its soft hiss, now danced on its hanger like a wild thing, throwing grotesque shadows which jerked and gyrated like the innards of a black kaleidoscope.

As bad as it was for us in the bunkers, it had to be more terrifying for the guys stuck outside, cowering in foxholes which crumbled a bit with every nearby shell burst. Luckily, all the incoming seemed to be point-detonating. When fused for a contact burst, a shell was triggered to explode when hitting the ground. However, in the fraction of a second between contact and burst, the shell would bury itself a foot or so into the earth, which would absorb much of the shock. More importantly, the lethal fan of hot shell fragments would blow up and out in a wide inverted cone pattern, often leaving untouched any soldiers lying flat or in holes or depressions more than a few yards away.

If they had fired shells fused for air-bursts, the GIs would be in a world of hurts—shells bursting overhead would drive their fragments downward into the foxholes, and into the bodies of anyone below. Spinning shards of hot jagged steel do not make clean wounds. Luckily, although the enemy now had more artillery on the line than our UN forces, he still lacked the skill and precision to use it to best effect.

After what seemed hours, but turned out to be about ten minutes, the shelling abruptly stopped. Waiting a few moments to be sure, I hit the butterfly on the EE8 handset.

"Charlie! Give me Concentration Baker-2 now! And give me time-of-flight and Splash. Don't forget the illumination! Over."

"OK, Ben—just hold on. You're getting battery ten rounds for effect. Time-of-flight, twelve seconds from... NOW!" I could hear the six howitzers crash out in the earpiece as Charlie spoke.

The captain had already scrambled outside. I joined him, pausing only to clap my steel pot on my head and snatch my carbine from the peg on which it hung. Despite the taste of hell which had enveloped the hilltop, the pre-dawn air was cold. The last skeletal survivors of vegetation on the hilltop had been blasted into shredded remnants; broken limbs, bare of leaves, lay far from the trunks that had sustained them. Smoke was curling up from the newly plowed earth as Captain James and his NCO's searched for casualties and survivors. The air stank of detonated explosives, and the torn earth was starting to reek of death and rot from newly uncovered bits of humanity left from previous battles.

"Skipper," I yelled, "we're getting Baker-2 in about nine seconds. Battery ten rounds, VT. Better get 'em ready!" I slapped the selector switch on my carbine forward to the full-automatic position and twisted the safety to "fire".

The Company Commander waved a "Roger" and hustled his men into position to cover the mouth of a shallow ravine which funneled from the low ground to our left front, uphill and into our position. He also placed a just-in-case Browning Automatic Rifleman and a machine gun to cover the steep bluff falling off to our right, though it was unlikely that an attack in strength would come from that quarter. The medic and his assistant were helping four wounded men into the aid bunker; other troops searched for more. I had been mentally counting off the seconds; just as I looked over to alert the captain, we both heard the rustling of shells passing overhead, instantly followed by the flash and slam of airbursts above the gully to our left. At the same time, a single shell popped high above Hill 672 and a dazzling parachute flare ignited and slowly descended. Its stark white light clearly showed us all, frozen into position and aiming our weapons toward the mouth of the ravine. Our six-gun 105mm battery fired ten rounds from each piece, the entire 60-shell barrage taking less than half a minute.

Within seconds after the first shells burst, the flare revealed running figures, Chinese in thickly padded brown uniforms, spewing out of the ravine, screaming and wildly firing long Russian Mosin-Nagant rifles and drum-fed PPSH 41 submachine guns in our direction. B Company was more than ready—the riflemen hunkering down and delivering a steady aimed fire which ground down the head of the attacking mob as though it was being fed into a giant pencil sharpener. The machine gunners were mostly firing in short accurate bursts, conserving ammunition and keeping their barrels cool. One gunner was obviously panicked or overexcited, freezing on his trigger until the tail of his ammo belt fed through the gun and it fell silent. After little over a minute of our deliberate and deadly fire, scarcely a dozen of the enemy remained standing. There appeared to be no leaders left to organize or direct them. They retreated in disorder in the direction from which they had come.

A second parachute flare popped high in the dark sky just before the first faded below the horizon, the timing perfect for maintaining visibility around the hilltop.

After the survivors had faded back into the gully, we very cautiously examined their casualties and found many that had already been badly chopped up by artillery shell fragments. It was easy to see why their attack had been piecemeal and disorganized—they had waited, crowded together in the draw, for their own barrage to lift, expecting to follow it up and catch us in our holes and bunkers. Trapped by the close confines of the gully, they were a prime target for our own unexpected barrage. Their charge up into our guns was probably as much a panic to escape our shellfire as an attempt to take the hill.

James and his Platoon Leaders combed the hilltop for more American casualties, finding two newly dead and five freshly wounded. I heard sporadic single rifle shots, an indication that perhaps some of the attackers had not been killed as dead as was deemed necessary. Perkins appeared beside me carrying the SCR 300 backpack radio, already in contact with the FDC so I could report on the situation, and on the results of the fire mission.

As I reached for the radio handset, a crumpled figure at the mouth of the gully suddenly stirred and raised itself to knee level. I saw no weapon, but a large cloth bag hanging diagonally across his shoulders marked him as the Chinese equivalent of a grenadier. He reached into the bag just as I dropped the handset, pivoted my carbine to a level position, and loosed a long burst from the hip. My bullets stitched a path across the intervening ground and into the twisting, jerking figure, still fumbling inside the grenade sack. Perkins had levelled his own carbine the instant he had seen my reaction, and his slugs mingled with my own. One of us hit the sack in a tender spot— the would-be grenadier and his explosive supply disappeared in a ragged eruption of smoke, noise, and body parts.

With the sound of the explosion, the captain and his people had hit the ground, assuming another artillery attack. Realizing what had happened, they sheepishly arose. Captain James, white faced, walked over to me and stared into my eyes for a few tense moments. Then he said loudly, "You damn' artillery people just can't do anything quietly, can you?"

With this weak joke, the tension broke and the grinning troops continued about their grisly chores.

I contacted Charlie at the FDC, reporting the results of the mission and requesting that he keep B-2 dialed in, just in case. Since dawn was starting to show, I terminated the succession of parachute flares that had lighted our targets so well.

For the dozenth time, I gave silent thanks to the genius who had devised the VT fuse used with our artillery shells on anti-personnel missions. Even gunnery experts have difficulty adjusting time fuses to explode the optimum distance above enemy troops to achieve maximum casualties. The projectile's time-of-flight had to be calculated as accurately as possible by the FDC, then the time fuse set to this interval minus the precise fraction of a second needed to explode the shell just before impact. Any shifting of fire would minutely change the shell trajectory, causing a burst too high, or in the dirt, and require a new setting.

With six or more cannon blasting away as fast as their crewmen can slam their breeches open and stuff in fresh rounds, a crewman on each gun cutting powder charges, and another setting the timing ring on fuses, it takes skill and cool heads to achieve speed and accuracy. Any error can kill one's own troops as easily as the enemy's.

VT stands for Variable Time, that term given it late in WW2 to conceal the nature of the system from the enemy. There was actually a tiny radio transmitter built into each fuse which sent out radar-type signals ahead of the outbound shell. When the signal bounced off the earth and returned to the fuse head at the correct interval, the fuse detonated. Thus the shell exploded at the desired altitude above the enemy without worries about calculations and setting of fuse timing. A very expensive little gadget which has been known to self-detonate while flying through thick clouds, but has saved the lives of thousands of American GIs.

CHAPTER 2

Meanwhile, Back at the Ranch

Hill 672 had changed hands three times before today. It was a lump in the terrain with no real tactical or strategic value, fought over solely to give whichever side held it extra leverage at the Panmunjom peace negotiations. I had been assigned as Baker Company's Artillery Forward Observer for a little over three weeks, and this was the second time I had defended Hill 672. I was thankful that I had never been required to attack it; the southern slope was bare and fully exposed to defending fire all the way to the top, if anyone made it that far. It was our good fortune that the northern slope, on the enemy side, was steep and nearly impassible, except via the sheltered gully on which we had carefully zeroed artillery concentration Baker-2. Whoever had previously taken 672 from Joe Chink had my undying admiration. The corpses being continually uncovered in the vicinity were from both armies, but former rivalries meant little to them now as they lay, intermingled and rotting, under soil that was alien to both.

That afternoon, as we cleaned up the fighting ground, I got a call from the Battalion S3 advising me that my replacement was on his way up the hill. My Battery Commander also rang up and instructed me to report to him as soon as I returned to the Battery Headquarters area. I didn't recall screwing up lately, but natural soldierly concern had me wondering how I might have unknowingly stepped in deep kimchee somewhere along the line. He also told me to pass on to Captain James that the enemy dead should not be disposed of, but should lie where they fell for the time being. An officer from Division Intelligence would arrive with my replacement, and would examine and search the corpses for any information of intelligence value. His final admonition, "Don't shoot him." puzzled me, but I decided to ignore it as a simple weak joke.

The reek of rotting bodies permeated the hilltop, filtering up out of the newly blasted soil; I was finding that it bothered me more each day. I wasn't sure if it was the unpleasantness of the stench, or the tragedies of hundreds of fathers, brothers, sons, and husbands, ripped from life for no particularly good reason. Either way, I longed to find myself someplace where the earth was clean, the grass sweet, and flowers blossoming.

My replacement arrived as predicted, much to my relief. I introduced him, a very young Second Lieutenant Burns, to Captain James. I oriented him on the important terrain features, the pre-planned fire concentrations, and the radio/telephone call signs he would need. His Radio/Telephone Operator was an old hand, so I didn't feel too bad about leaving Lt. Burns to the tender mercies of Captain James.

As Corporal Perkins and I turned to go, the Intelligence captain arrived and introduced himself. I immediately understood the Battery Commander's little joke; Captain Jack Ito was an oriental, a Japanese, I guessed, nearly as tall as I, and with the healthy filled-out look of the Japanese-American Nisei. His background and education became obvious as we chatted, he speaking the same sloppy slang-filled English as the rest of us. I liked him on first meeting, which was just as well—he and I were eventually destined to have a marked effect on each other's lives.

I shook his hand in parting, expressing gratitude that I didn't have to help him with his macabre duties in dealing with the dead.

"C'mon, Perk," I called. "We're heading for a bath and a beer, not necessarily in that order."

"Roger that, Sir, and not too soon, either. By the way, your carbine is still set on 'full'. Might want to put it back on 'single'."

"Right, thanks." I pulled the selector switch on my carbine back to the single-fire position and checked that the safety was on, chiding myself for not having done so sooner. It was practice, unless action was imminent, to keep M2 carbines set for single fire; in event of an accidental discharge in a crowded dugout, a single bullet would do a lot less damage than an eight or ten-round burst.

Perkins and I packed our gear and left Hill 672 in the hands of our successors. On arrival at the gun park, I sent the shuttle driver and Perkins on to the Battery Orderly Room and made my way back to the FDC bunker. Charlie Taylor was sitting in a folding chair gnawing on a hard chocolate disk from one of the left-over World War Two field rations we were being issued.

"Loo-damn-tenant Taylor," I began, throwing my arms wide, "like it or not, you just mighta saved my butt last night!" I grasped his face between my palms, bent down, and kissed him on top of his shiny black head.

"What the hell, man—what I ever done to you to deserve this kind of abuse? Next time you yell for help, I'm just gonna fire my 45 in your general direction and go back to sleep!"

"Well," I said, glancing at the enlisted FDC crew, who were sitting around the firing chart table watching the performance with amused interest, "your crew probably deserves more praise than you do. But if I kissed one of them, I'd be court-martialed. How about you set 'em up with a case of beer on me?"

"I'll do that, and I'll make sure it's the most expensive case you ever bought. Hey, weren't you supposed to check in with the Old Man first thing?"

"Oh, damn! You're right. I'd better go find out how I screwed up this time. But thank the gun crews for me too; they shot the perfect mission with no stray rounds, and they took out at least two dozen bad guys for us. Beer for them too, next time we're off the line."

I slogged over to the orderly room tent in the Admin area, stuck my head inside, and asked the First Sergeant, "Hey, Top—is the Old Man in?"

"Whaddya mean, Old Man?" came a voice from the back of the tent. "I'm only a year older than you, and a better man for it. Drag your sorry ass in here and tell me about that gun-fight you had on the hill this morning."

Captain Hamish Francis was, in truth, a good bit older than I. I had enlisted in 1947, a couple of years after World War Two, and served five years in the Infantry before being sent to Artillery OCS at Fort Sill. Francis, an enlisted Chief of Guns during WW2, had been commissioned in the reserves, was called up as a retread for Korea, shortly promoted to Captain and given a firing battery of towed 105's. He had also served a tour at Fort Sill as an OCS Tac Officer, which was where we first met. Francis had made my life as an Officer Candidate miserable for 22 weeks, and seemed determined to keep his hand in.

I recounted the action on 672, emphasizing that the speed and accuracy of the FDC and gun crews probably saved him from having to requisition a replacement second lieutenant, and definitely saved a lot of Infantry lives.

"Sir, I know you'll be rotating out pretty soon now, and it's not really my place to say so, but I'd sure like to see Charlie get the Battery when you leave. He trained the gun crews, he trained the FDC, and he's served his time as FO on several hills around here. He's earned it."

"I appreciate your thoughts, Ben, but I expect the Battalion Commander's gonna tell me who my replacement is."

"That's what I'm afraid of, Sir. I hear there's a new First Looie at battalion, a Pointer. The Colonel's West Point too. If somebody doesn't tell him different, that's who he's gonna pick. Taylor's earned the job by being shot at, and by putting together a helluva fire team in your battery. Put him in for a Bronze Star and push the Colonel in the right direction. They'll listen to you."

"Yeah, sure! Taylor's black—how many black Battery Commanders have you seen? And with a ring-knocker waiting to get his combat command ticket punched?"

"Do it, Skipper. He deserves it and you know it. Any black officer has to be twice as good as the rest of us just to break even."

Captain Francis just rolled his eyes at me, shaking his head in exasperation.

"By the way," I added, "Perkins was right in the middle of it on that hill, never lost his cool, kept me out of trouble, and took out a gook grenadier. I'd like to see him make E5 when you get a vacancy."

"OK, I'll take care of Perkins. And I'll try to help the Exec. Now, about why I wanted you to report to me right away when you came off the hill. Which you did not do, by the way!"

Francis' voice took on a stern note which I had seldom heard in the past—and which unsettled me a bit. I was frantically trying to recall how I might have screwed up, or which of my past misdemeanors might have been freshly uncovered. He continued.

"You ignore my instructions to see me immediately after getting off the hill. You take it on yourself to advise me how to run my battery. You're getting too damn uppity for a punk Second Lieutenant, at least in my outfit."

I hadn't had a chewing out like this, or at least not many, since I graduated from OCS. I pulled myself to attention, squared my shoulders, and tried to look suitably chastised. I hoped this wasn't a first sign that the Old Man was cracking up.

"So I guess I've finally got to do something about it. Second Lieutenant Hunnicutt, I'm officially busting you down to—First Lieutenant!"

The Skipper's face broke into a broad grin as he reached into his pocket and withdrew a pair of battered, scratched, and tarnished silver bars.

"Congratulations, Ben. These are overdue, but the system never hands out rewards as quick as it delivers crap. These were my bars, so they're well broken in. Take care of them and when you make captain, pass 'em on to somebody who deserves them."

He pinned a bar on each epaulet of my field jacket, shook my hand, and stepped back to enjoy the befuddled look on my face. When I finally got my thoughts together, I said the first thing that came into my mind.

"Skipper, if your bars and brass were always this messy, how the hell did you ever make captain?"

CHAPTER 3

A Paid Vacation

I held an impromptu promotion party in my tent that evening, but with one of our FO's out with the Infantry and another recovering from wounds in Japan, it consisted of me, the Old Man, Charlie Taylor, and the First Sergeant passing around a bottle of middling scotch. I promised a better party next time we were off the line, a concept which met with unconditional approval. The captain repeated my comment about the cruddy condition of his bars to the limited audience, implying that such impudence was bordering on disrespect to a superior officer. Charlie leaned over and carefully examined the bars in question. He straightened and solemnly rendered his opinion.

"Sir, if Ben stands the next formation with those bars in this condition, he should be restricted for a week and busted back to Second Lieutenant."

Captain Francis sat for a second, blank-faced, while he decoded the Exec's comment, then managed an unconvincing scowl.

"Mutiny, that's what it is. All my officers ganging up on me—it's worse than the Bounty. I oughta hang you all from the yardarm. Unfortunately, there aren't any yardarms within 40 miles, and I'm in no condition to walk that far."

He turned and leered at me.

"But I can get my revenge on you, ex-butter bar. I'll just forget to tell you that you've been approved for R & R to Japan next week. Then you'll miss the plane and I'll laugh my ass off."

"Cap'n, I'm not sure if it's Christmas or my birthday—or if I'm gonna wake up in a minute and find myself back in that bunker on 672. Did it really come through, or are you just getting revenge for my remark about your bars?"

"It came through, Ben. I look forward to having you out of my hair for a week, and you're probably looking forward to a clean, warm place to sleep—one with no 120mm alarm clocks. Nobody should be so lucky as to get a promotion and a shot at R & R in the same day. Maybe you should try a little blackjack while your luck is running!"

Lying in my sack that evening, I let my thoughts wander to my upcoming visit to Japan. Having been stationed there with the occupation forces right after the war, I recalled a population in shock and shame at having been beaten by the barbarians that they had been told were weak and degenerate. Compared to Europe, Japan was still relatively intact. Our bombs had largely been aimed at cities and military complexes; Japan's countryside was still fertile and beautiful to see, but often barren of food crops due to the absence of man-power to till and harvest. The Japanese were hungry then, and our government was just beginning to bring in food and the necessities of life. Towns and cities had been dull and joyless. I looked forward to seeing the refreshed Japan, somehow feeling a proprietary interest in the newly reborn nation.

R & R, standing for Rest and Recuperation, or Rotgut and Rutting, depending on the attitude of the soldier, had been initiated to get GIs out of the mud and battle of war-torn Korea and let them unwind for a week in safety—and in luxury, as a matter of fact. Far East Command had set up hotels, recreation retreats, and entertainment facilities in and around several US military installations in Japan. Guys could apply somewhere around mid-tour, priority being given in accordance with the stresses of their duties. Just the anticipation of such a holiday was often a factor in maintaining morale and sanity when life consisted only of a hole in the mud. I told myself that I didn't really need R & R as much as many other GIs, but nevertheless found myself daydreaming about the possibilities.

The following Sunday I found myself nervously standing in front of a Quonset hut at Kimpo Air Base, waiting to hear my name called. I was in a relatively clean field uniform, but one of the few. There were soldiers that appeared fresh from the forward outposts, combat uniforms torn and muddy, and some blood-spattered. Others wore rumpled clothing that was still impressed with duffle bag wrinkles. They looked naked without cartridge belts and dangling grenades, and some obviously felt insecure without rifles or carbines slung over their shoulders.

I felt a jab in my ribs and a voice said, "That's you, Buddy." I realized that my name had been called while I was daydreaming, and looked to see who among this group of strangers might have recognized me. I looked into the grinning oriental face of the Intelligence captain who had visited Hill 672 on my last day in the field.

"Go, Man. I'm next and we don't wanna miss this bird."

We quickly walked toward the boarding platform of the C-47 that waited impatiently on the tarmac. I stuck out my hand.

"Captain Ito, isn't it? I'm Ben Hunnicutt. Thanks for waking me up back there."

"Jack Ito. Call me Jack. I remember you from 672, but it seems you're either wearing somebody else's field jacket, or you just got a pay raise?"

"Promoted the day I left the hill." I said. "Found out the same day that my R & R came through."

"Well, we'll have to celebrate in Japan. If you want to hook up with me, I know the territory pretty well."

We climbed aboard the "Gooney Bird" and found seats—not exactly first class seats, but the canvas and aluminum folding benches that ran alongside the fuselage fore and aft. Obviously, the old airplane was rigged for cargo, not for comfort. I tried to engage Ito in casual conversation to decide if I wanted to commit to his company during what I expected to be a week of relaxation, playing tourist in Japan. At first, it was a little disconcerting hearing pure slang-filled American being spoken by one who resembled the Hollywood stereotype of a World War Two Imperial Japanese officer. When the big radials fired up, the rattle and roar of the venerable old workhorse effectively blocked any conversation that wasn't directly mouth to ear. There being no window to look out of, I settled into the semi-coma of GIs world-wide who have become accustomed to grabbing sleep at every opportunity.

There is something ominous about a sudden near-silence at ten thousand feet that demands immediate attention. I snapped awake, feeling for the parachute that I didn't have. Captain Ito waved a hand disparagingly.

"No sweat," he said, "We're on approach to the field. This crate's so damn' noisy that cutting back on the throttles sounds like dead silence."

The landing was so smooth it seemed the runway must have been greased. I mentally cheered the pilot, who was doing his job in an airplane that was probably older than he was, and was doing it well.

A shuttle bus hauled the two dozen or so passengers to a military installation, "Camp Fisher" according to the sign at the gate, and on to the enlisted and officer billets set aside for R & R arrivals. Far East Command had done a fine job of setting the place up to make the new arrivals comfortable. Luxurious compared to the usual barracks or BOQ, the tub baths and food available at any hour made the quarters resemble a resort hotel more than a military facility. But there were still rules aplenty, some handed out in writing, some posted in appropriate areas.

There were Japanese handling the usual desk and concierge duties, escorting GIs to their rooms, and answering their many questions. Japanese girls—attractive, crispy clean, and speaking good English—were behind counters selling souvenirs and personal items and dispensing information. Others were circulating about the lounge area fetching snacks and cold drinks for their GI guests.

One of the rules, heavily emphasized, was that all employees were strictly off-limits—no suggestions, no touchee-feelee, absolutely no tipping. About all that were allowed to be exchanged were conversations and smiles.

"But don't worry," said one of the deskmen, "Outside the gate you can choose from hundreds."

I took this with a grain of salt, but it later proved to be an understatement.

We were fitted with fresh khaki uniforms, and busy seamstresses sewed on the appropriate patches and insignia. Washed clean, wearing fresh clothing, and with no thoughts of coming under fire or digging foxholes, I sat in a comfortable armchair in the lounge and allowed the peace, quiet, and security to sink in. I had been told that there was an officers' club near the BOQ where food was of hotel quality and drinks were a pittance, but at this point I didn't want to be anywhere that I might hear shop talk. I had sat in a relaxed trance for nearly an hour when a familiar voice behind me said, "Hey, Buddy—I know just how you feel."

I looked around to see Jack Ito settling into a nearby chair. I pulled mine around so we could talk comfortably.

CHAPTER 4

Playing Tourist

"Hey, Jack. How does it feel to go from mud and blood to luxury in 24 hours?"

"I feel about the way you look," he said, "like I'm melting down into sinful comfort and, somehow, there must be something wrong about that. Nobody should feel this good when so many poor bastards are still where we were yesterday."

We digressed from that uncomfortable sense of guilt and began a general exchange of information about our respective backgrounds. Jack was from a Japanese-American family just one generation removed from the home islands. His father had extensive business interests in the Far East, and Jack, although American-born, had spent as much of his life in Japan as in the States. He enthused about the beauty of Japan, about its orderly politics, and about its people's sense of duty to the greater good of society, rather than to themselves. Thinking about the Japanese mindset that had led us into World War Two, I had some misgivings about their concern for "the greater good", but kept silent on the subject.

"Do you prefer it to our country?" I asked.

"Oh, hell no! Don't get me wrong. I'm not cut out to voluntarily become a small, well-behaved worker in this ant hill. I like being different, shooting my mouth off when I feel like it, even being rude to my elders on occasion. But Japan is the perfect place to relax and go with the flow when you get tired of the Stateside hustle."

I told him a little about myself, mostly about my last assignment before coming to Korea.

"Alaska hooked me good," I told him. "A fresh country, a new population, a million places where nobody but you has ever walked, folks whose jobs involve a little risk and some mental innovation—it's on my 'dream sheet', just in case the Pentagon ever really pays any attention to our preferences."

Ito looked at me pityingly, shaking his head.

"Ben, you're a gunner. How many artillery outfits do you think there are in Alaska? The sunset gun at the post flag pole is probably the only cannon in town! Don't hold your breath."

"I'm gonna get there, Jack, sooner or later. Maybe after I do my 20 and retire. But I'll see Alaska again. There's just too much I didn't get around to the first time."

"Well, more power to you. But what are you going to do about seeing Japan while you're here, sitting in the middle of it?"

I explained that this wasn't my first visit. I had been with an infantry division as an enlisted man during the early days of US occupation, back in '47.

"Of course, that was in northern Japan, on Hokkaido," I explained, "and I didn't see much except the top end of a shovel."

"Ben," he said, "northern Japan is about as much like southern Honshu as North Dakota is like South Carolina. And Kyoto, right outside the gate here, is probably the cultural center of the nation. When you get your fill of being pampered, let me show you Japan at its best. You might actually learn something."

He looked at me questioningly. "Unless you had planned to blow your bucks on booze and broads, like most of these guys?"

"Give me my day of being spoiled," I said. "Maybe by tomorrow I'll be ready for some self-improvement. Tonight, I think I'll just drop over to the O-Club and listen to some Glen Miller over a tumbler of good Scotch."

I did just that, pleased to find that the club had a nice little Japanese combo that concentrated on American big-band favorites. A great seafood combination dinner, some super-smooth sippin' whisky (which I could never have afforded back home, even if I could find it) closed out my day in fine fashion. I basked in comfort until nearly midnight, when a few over-enthusiastic second lieutenants began arguing too loudly about their plans for tomorrow.

I chuckled at myself for mentally disparaging the second lieutenants. Last week I was one; now from the lofty level of first lieutenant, they seemed hopelessly green.

I pried myself loose from the club and returned to the BOQ. Grabbing a handful of newspapers and magazines, I went to my room with thoughts of another soaking bath and an hour of reading. I flopped on the bed, still in my clothes, and began to plan the coming week.

Ten hours later I was awakened by a discrete tap on my door. I arose, still in my newly acquired but now quite rumpled uniform, and sat on the edge of the bed.

"Come!"

A young Japanese head poked in.

"You have shoes to shine? Press uniform?" He took in my unkempt state. "While you bath, I take care of all." He stood there respectfully, obviously waiting for me to shed my clothing so he could "take care of all".

I stripped, a little embarrassed until I remembered that I was now in the land of community bathing, handed him my clothes, and hit the shower. When I stepped out 20 minutes later, I found polished shoes (which, being new, didn't need it) and refreshed khakis waiting for me. The houseboy must have had a platoon of helpers waiting in the hallway to provide such quick service—and, I had been told, with no tipping expected or accepted.

I had heard that the entire R & R program had been initiated by General MacArthur, and that he had demanded maximum luxury at the least expense for the military people who were being accommodated. It was rumored that old Doug got his way in most of the things he wanted, and it was apparent that his wishes had been carried out in this instance.

I wandered down to the Dining Hall. It would have been called a mess hall in most military establishments, but in this case was definitely a dining hall—white table linen, chinaware and silver laid out in waiting, and attendants scurrying around to tend to all wants. Late breakfast or early lunch, at one's command. Real milk by the quart, real butter, fresh fruit, all the goodies that were missing from the Army's combat ration, were here at one's request. I wondered if I really wished to see beautiful downtown

20

Kyoto, or might prefer to just hang around the compound eating, drinking and sleeping out my R & R week.

As I was enjoying a final cup of coffee, Jack Ito entered, scanned the thinning diners, and spotted me. I waved him over, telling him I'd be glad to sit and chat while he had breakfast. Ito shook his head.

"Be glad to share your coffee, but I ate hours ago. What are your plans for the day?"

I admitted that, so far, my plans were to do as little as possible and enjoy it as much as possible.

"Well, if you want to see some of the town, I've laid on a taxi. Be happy to play tour guide if you're up to it."

My conscience began to nip at me at the thought, however pleasant, of wasting a day of the precious six by goofing off.

"OK, Jack. I'm all yours for the day. Split the cost with you, and give you a handsome tip if you're any good."

"Tell you what," he said. "If you don't enjoy it, I'll pay for the whole day and whatever you can drink tonight."

"Sounds like a deal! Of course, with yen at 360 to the dollar, neither of us is going to be hurting too much."

An hour later, we were rocketing around Kyoto in a Japanese cab, and I was beginning to wish I were someplace safer, like on top of Hill 672. Perhaps it was just the strangeness of rolling down the left side of the road and having the driver and controls located far over to the right, but it seemed that most of the other traffic was deliberately trying to Kamikaze us.

"Today is gonna be garden day," said Jack, "while the weather is good."

I had to agree about the weather. We had caught a day that might have been mistaken for springtime in Virginia—a soft breeze, caressingly short of being too warm, blue skies set off by small clouds like floating pearls, and the aroma of unfamiliar blossoms teasing the senses.

Never having been much of a gardener, perhaps due to the work involved, I resigned myself to a day of lazy boredom. Jack chatted amicably with the driver for a few minutes, and they apparently agreed on our schedule for the morning.

By the time we turned back for Camp Fisher, in the late afternoon, I had revised my ideas on the art of gardening.

Japanese gardeners working for the temples, shrines, and large estates had sculpted trees, plants, moss, and blooming flowers into scenes of living art. I had seen gardens entwined around tiny lakes and ponds so that they framed specific scenes and colors, with benches and large 'sitting rocks' precisely placed for the best orientation toward the desired view. There were walking gardens with paths routed to pleasantly surprise the stroller with sudden springs, ponds, waterfalls, or flowering trees as he rounded a corner or topped a hillock. Some gardens were obviously designed to encourage meditation or contemplation, and were successful enough that I found myself reluctant to leave them for the noisy world of streets and people.

All of the gardens we visited, and their related estates or shrines, looked as though they had been in place, untouched, for centuries, even though we knew that their keepers must put in many hours each day meticulously training and teasing every twig and blossom into the desired configuration.

When we finally returned to the compound and dismissed and thanked the driver, I turned to Ito.

"Dinner's on me," I said. "You done good! And to show you I'm not cheap, if you want to find a really nice restaurant off post, I'm willing to pay civilian prices."

He grinned at me with a "Gotcha!" look. "Just so happens, Ben, I do, and it won't be cheap. See you here at the gate at 1800."

On the way back to my room, I noticed a Japanese man fiddling with some papers at the front desk. His dress was formal enough that I guessed he was the person in charge of the BOQ, so stopped over to chat for a moment. Describing my day, I expressed my admiration for the effort the city of Kyoto had put into the preservation of the ancient structures and the gardens surrounding them. He introduced himself as Mr. Nagoya. And yes, he was the Director of the officers' side of the R & R camp. We talked a bit about the camp, and about keeping the delicate balance between relaxed luxury and uninhibited pandemonium.

"The enlisted facilities are exactly as lavish as yours," he said. "The main reason for having them separate is the obviously inhibiting effect that the presence of rank would have on enlisted people in the relaxed atmosphere we try to provide." He went on.

"You will see that we do not discourage any reasonable pleasures or recreation a battle-weary soldier might desire. We just try to keep them civilized. For instance, as you leave the gate in the evening you will see many young Japanese women in the vicinity. They will not be crowding the gate trying to solicit the young men. They will be chatting with each other, strolling up and down the block, and will not approach the soldiers. If a GI nods, smiles or catches their eye, they will titter behind their hand in the way of Japanese women."

"Sounds as though they are not very competitive," I commented. "How are connections made?"

"The man makes a selection; he approaches the girl of his choice. If he asks only for sex, he may be turned down or referred to another girl. These are not all professional prostitutes. Many are attracted to the excitement, dancing, and night life that lonely soldiers and their money can provide. Many GIs spend their six days drinking, dancing and enjoying a jo-san's company as a guide and companion, and never have sex with her." He smiled in a between-us manner. "This is not what he tells his friends back in Korea, however!"

"You're right—that doesn't tally with the war stories they bring back," I said. "But it makes some kind of sense. About half of my guys are small town boys that consider a date a resounding success if they get a hand on a boob. If a girl rolled over for them, they'd panic and not know what to do."

He laughed and continued.

"The best deals for all concerned are the package deals. A man usually comes in with two or three hundred dollars he has saved up. He sees a girl at the curb that he likes. Maybe she reminds him of someone special back home, or maybe she's just a knockout. He tells her he wants to spend his bundle on the economy—doesn't want to see the post gate again until the day he ships out. He gives her his wad, and she takes over. Arranges hotel rooms, restaurants, night clubs and shows, takes care of cabs, tipping, and admission for any place that requires it. He wakes every morning in a clean bed, to freshly cleaned clothing and shoes, and she'll even shave him if he likes. And she may be in the bed if he likes.

"It's mutually understood that she'll get a cut from all the bills she pays. And she hands him back any left-over funds when they say goodbye at the gate at week's end. It sounds crazy, but it works. Often he'll tell his buddies headed out for R & R to ask for Michiko-san or for Candy-san, or whatever name she goes by. The girls know this and strive for a good reputation. Many derive a steady income from the escort business."

He looked up at me. "Sorry, I guess I sound like a pimp. But I'm really a fan of a system that can benefit the guys and the business girls alike without either taking advantage of the other."

"Your English is better than mine," I remarked, "and it's Main Street, USA English. What's your story?"

"No real story." he said. "My family ran a small hotel in Seattle when Pearl Harbor was hit. We were interned. After the war, I decided to capitalize on the only real talent I had—being fully fluent in both English and Japanese. Came over here as a government translator, then jumped into the R & R hotel business when General MacArthur started this project. It's been good to me, and I work well with the locals."

I shook his hand. "Thanks Mr. Nagoya. You've given me a fresh view of things I never thought much about. And it looks like your talents have been put to good use here."

Jack Ito was as good as his word; his personal taxi driver delivered us to a nightclub which seemed to cater equally to Japanese businessmen and American officers. He was obviously known to the management, as we were immediately ushered to a table in a quiet corner, but with a view of a small stage and the four-person combo which provided background music for the clientele.

I noticed that about half the tables were of the western pattern, while the remainder were the low sunken tables preferred by native Japanese. Jack noted my interest.

"If you want to try the low tables, you'll have to eat alone. My knees and legs have never been able to readapt to my ancestors' posture—I could take a meal that way, but you'd have to find two strong men to straighten me out again."

"No, thanks. I'll stick with what I know. And I'll trust you to do the ordering for us both. I know damn' little about real Japanese food."

"Well," he said, "order American food. They serve as good a steak here as you can get in Kansas City, and have as good a selection of drinks as you could find in 'Frisco."

I hesitated, but finally gave in to my lust for the sorely-missed red meat that seems to be a necessary part of the American diet. I ordered a filet with all the fixings, feeling a bit ashamed at not taking advantage of the occasion to sample Japanese cuisine. I must have shown surprise when Jack followed suit—he reminded me, with a trace of guilt, that he had grown up on the same unhealthy grub that I had, and he missed it as much.

"But tomorrow we'll go Japanese all the way," he said. "I have some intelligence matters to take care of in the morning, but later we'll go native. You'll have an experience seldom granted to gaijin barbarians, and I hope you'll appreciate it."

Both the Kansas City steak and the 'Frisco booze lived up to his claims, and we returned to the Post sated and sleepy.

CHAPTER 5

We're Going to What Kind of House?

It was almost mid-afternoon when Ito interrupted my reading. I was in the lounge going through a pile of Stateside newspapers, trying to reconcile their version of the Korean War with my own. It appeared that I must be living in a world of multiple realities, but considering my present enviable situation, I had little reason to complain.

"Saddle up, Ben. We're about to visit what the Japanese call the Flower and Willow World."

I obediently followed him to the Post gate where we awaited yesterday's taxi driver. I noted the ever-present group of strolling, chatting ladies in the vicinity, some in western attire, many in traditional Japanese kimonos. They made themselves visible to any soldiers who passed through the gate, but made no overtures, speaking only if addressed, shyly tittering behind delicate hands. I was reminded of the conduct of American kids awkwardly trying to become acquainted at their first teen dance.

Our taxi arrived precisely at the appointed time, and whisked us away toward whatever adventure Jack Ito had dreamed up for my further education.

"Well, what now, Jack? Museums, or pearl divers, or possibly a sake distillery?"

"Ben, you just don't appreciate how lucky you are to have me around to introduce you to the wonders of the Far East. You're about to experience the exotic wonders of an Ochaya."

"A what?"

"An Ochaya. You might call it a glorified teahouse, or Geisha House."

"Hey, whoa-up, old hoss! I'm in this man's army for a career. And the last thing a career officer needs on his record is a visit to the pecker-checker. I'd as soon you drop me off somewhere— then you can go ahead with your evening."

Ito gave me a look of pity mixed with exasperation. His voice went cold as he replied.

"Ben, it's no wonder the Japanese refer to most whites as 'barbarians'. What you don't understand, you're ready to condemn. You haven't the slightest idea what a Geisha is, but you're ready to assume the worst if it fits your preconceptions."

I was taken aback by Jack's response and its unexpected hostility—I knew he was largely right, and I felt a twinge of guilt.

"Well, I'm sorry, Jack. I admit my ignorance on the subject— I've probably listened to too many old sergeants' tales about the wicked Far East. Educate me."

Somewhat mollified by my easy surrender, Jack shifted around toward me as much as the narrow seat permitted and began my education.

"You're right, Ben, in thinking that there is a professional class of prostitutes in Japan. They are considered a necessary segment of society, and a respected one. Your do-gooder commanders of the American Occupation Forces, or perhaps their wives, are pressuring the Japanese government to ban them.

"But the Geisha, or Geiko as they are called in Kyoto, are more like professional hostesses and entertainers. At around the age of 14 or 15, young girls who display grace, attractiveness and engaging personalities often aspire to become Geisha. Like American girls who try out to be cheerleaders, or to earn parts in school plays."

"If accepted by a Geisha and her Okami-san, who is sort of a combination house-mother and manager, the girl moves in with them. She may be alone, or there may be several apprentice girls. They are called Maiko, which loosely translates to 'dancing child'."

He turned and grinned at me.

"And if you think it's like a private school for pretty, well-endowed girls, you'll have to think again. Maikos live under a strict seniority system—almost a caste system. The newest are like 'buck privates' in the Army; they get all the scut work around the house, and act as assistants or servants to the more senior Maiko and the Geisha.

"As they mature, their dress and adornment change, and they watch, listen, and learn as their Geisha performs.

"Oddly enough, a gaijin seeing a Maiko and Geisha side by side would confuse the two. The Maiko is dressed in brightly colored, exquisitely patterned kimonos, and her very elaborate hair arrangement is decorated with flowers and ornaments. The Geisha, while striking in appearance, has few hair ornaments; her kimono is of a slightly different cut and more subdued in color."

I considered all this new information for a few moments.

"Maybe," I said, "they feel that the Geisha's beauty and talents offset the need to use bright apparel to catch the customer's eye?"

"Now you're beginning to get into the spirit of the Geisha world," said Jack approvingly. "The Geisha has learned to play several musical instruments, to conduct the tea ceremony and other rituals precisely as laid down by tradition, and to sing and dance in the classic ways. No tap-dancing or jitterbugging here!" he laughed. "You will see one Geisha where we are going, and one Maiko. You may meet the house mother, if she chooses.

"And I have to warn you," he continued, "your wine or sake cup will always be full, no matter how much you drink. And you are expected to drink, to relax—even to get a little high. But getting drunk or boisterous is a no-no."

As I started to remonstrate, Jack held up a palm. "Hold it, Ben. I know you too well to think you'd get out of hand. But I have to warn you because if that did happen, you'd never be welcome in this or any other teahouse in Kyoto. And you probably should know this—it is very rare that a 'round eye' is accepted in a Geisha house. My family connections, of course, gave me entry. And my word allows you entry. Once."

I sat silent, finally starting to realize that this was far more than a night on the town. And that Ito was sticking his social neck out for me.

And I kicked myself for not reading up on Japan and its history and customs while I waited away the days for my R & R to come through. I had assumed, having been among the troops who occupied Japan right after WW2, I knew all that I needed to about the subjugated nation.

Now, I began to feel like a teenager on his first date, so afraid I'd do something embarrassing that I couldn't really enjoy myself. I thought of another possible problem that I had better clear up with Jack Ito.

"Jack, how about the language situation? My Japanese is strictly tourist grade. Do the ladies know English?"

"Probably," he replied. "But they won't speak it. It is customary for only Japanese to be spoken in a Geisha house in Kyoto. But they do tolerate English from a foreign-born guest, and translation by another guest. But you'd better assume that whatever you say will be understood, so be tactful."

I had more questions, but before I could voice them, the taxi sidled up to a curb. My conversation with Jack had distracted me, and I hadn't noticed that we were now in an old-fashioned neighborhood of fragile-appearing wooden houses lining unpaved streets. As we exited the cab, Ito had a word with the driver, who nodded and drove off. Jack beckoned me toward a neatly raked path which led to the door of a small house centered in a tiny, meticulously tended garden. The lot was partitioned off by a delicately fashioned wooden fence obviously meant to capture the eye rather than repel trespassers.

As we approached the door, it slid silently open in the hands of a neat, but plainly dressed middle-aged woman. She smiled warmly at Jack, bowed low to each of us, and motioned us to enter. Inside the portal was a three-step rise to a main floor of polished wood. Jack bent and removed his shoes, leaving them on the center step. I followed suit and we were led down a short hall to another sliding door. Our guide motioned us into a medium sized room, sparsely furnished, and with a low Japanese-style table in its center. Much to my relief, the table was suspended above a sunken area which would accommodate our outsized American legs with a minimum of discomfort.

Opposite the table, at the far side of the room, a delicately featured Japanese woman in an exquisitely fashioned kimono knelt in placid silence. To her right, near the corner of the room, a second girl, much younger, also waited. The older woman bowed to us—the dignified bow usually accorded to an equal. The younger bowed, but much lower, and for a second longer.

My glance lingered on her; the intricately patterned yellow kimono nearly engulfed her slight figure, its colorful flowery design was striking, yet more joyful than flamboyant, and her elaborate hairdo was draped with ornaments resembling budding flowers. Her face was painted white and her lips painted red, but in a cherry blossom outline that ignored her natural lip line. There was dark eyeshadow with hints of red.

Her deep bow had revealed that the white paint was carried around to include the back of a graceful neck, but ended in a design which focused attention on the unpainted upward sweep of the nape. Jack Ito informed me later that to Japanese men, the nape of the female neck was as sexually attractive as breasts to Americans. Jack returned the bows, and I awkwardly copied his movements.

The older woman rose in a fluidly graceful motion and seemed to glide across the floor, stopping at the table and motioning us to be seated on the opposite side. She spoke to Jack, addressing him as Ito-san, bowed again, and spoke to me in Japanese. Jack replied in the same language, obviously introducing me, as I could pick out the words "Ben Hunnicutt". She turned to me with a welcoming smile and a sentence which seemed to include the words "Hoon-nei-cah-san". As she offered her hand, I responded with "Ben-san.", which brought a silvery laugh and another bow.

Jack spoke a little more in Japanese, turned and informed me that I was speaking with the honorable Geiko, Amami. Amami gestured toward the girl that I had first noticed, still kneeling silently to one side. Jack translated her introduction to the Maiko, Kioko, who smiled and repeated her bow.

I was beginning to fear that the entire evening would be taken up with formalities, and that we would remain thirsty and unfed until time for departure.

CHAPTER 6

Song and Dance

The conversation and its translations soon smoothed out, the three of us gathered companionably around the low table while the Maiko, Kioko, remained to one side listening attentively. Amami asked my home state, and seemed solemnly impressed when I responded,

"Virginia".

"Ah," she nodded. Jack translated, "First state, old state with old customs, like Kyoto. You must be proud."

As the conversation progressed, I found myself telling an abbreviated version of my life story. The two ladies seemed an appreciative audience, and the story took on new life when they found that I had played baseball in school. I was astounded at their range of knowledge of the sport, as shown by the many questions they asked. Jack Ito proved an excellent translator, maintaining the smooth flow of conversation between us.

Amami suddenly stopped in mid-sentence, covered her mouth with the tips of her fingers, and showed a sad, apologetic expression.

"She apologizes deeply," translated Ito. "She is very remiss in her duties as a hostess—she finds your story so interesting that she has not provided refreshments for her guests. Please state your wishes. If sake, would you prefer it cool or room temperature?"

"I've never acquired a taste for sake," I answered. "But back in '48, I ran into a plum wine that I enjoyed. Ask her if she has anything like that."

Before Jack could speak, she nodded enthusiastically and spoke a few words to Kioko, who rose and gracefully glided from the room.

"I am pleased that you prefer the plum wine," Jack translated. "It is a special favorite of my own."

Before Jack had finished, Kioko was back bearing a tray with shallow cups and several small, highly decorated flasks. As the ladies served us, I noticed that Jack received cool sake without asking—our hosts evidently making it a point to remember the preferences of their regular guests.

Amami filled my cup with the care one might bestow on a rare Napoleon brandy, murmuring approvingly in my ear.

"She says you have a cultured taste." He smiled knowingly as he spoke.

The plum wine didn't taste remotely like the cheap stuff I had tried years ago. It was full bodied and fruity, just a hair short of being too sweet, and with a pleasant, slightly spicy, aftertaste.

When I complimented her on the quality of the plum wine, she leaned toward me, took my cup and sipped, smiling as though we were kindred spirits sharing forbidden fruit.

Amami was not wearing the white makeup of the Maiko, and her kimono, more subdued in pattern and color, was of a slightly different cut. Her hair, while elaborately configured, had only an ornamental comb for embellishment. But Amami, by her manner and demeanor, was the one who immediately drew attention. Every movement exuded grace. Her voice, though higher in pitch than that of most American women, was rich, clear, and self-assured. There was no hint of subservience in her conduct or manner. I was already beginning to sense that we had a special rapport, and that this was going to be a memorable visit.

Jack, having sampled his sake, spoke a few words of praise to our host. After a short conversation, he turned to me.

"Amami will dance for us, if you like."

At my nod, she stood, moved to the doorway facing us and turned, framing herself before her audience of two. Kioko went to the corner to her left and lifted a shamisen which had somehow appeared there, awaiting her need. Although the shamisen resembled a long-necked relative of the banjo, it had a squared, angular configuration and only three strings. It was tuned, I found, to an odd register which seemed, to my non-musical ear, a little above that of a banjo or guitar.

Amami stood motionless, her hands raised to face level, one holding a fan which had appeared from nowhere. She spoke a few words which Ito translated.

"She says this is the dance of a willow tree in a spring breeze."

Kioko began slowly plucking the shamisen in, what seemed to me, random and somewhat discordant notes. Amami barely moved, a slight swaying, mostly noticeable in the motion of her flowing garments—the first stirring of leaves, heralding the coming breeze. During the next minutes, the breeze increased, Amami fluttering her fan, increasing the sway of her upper body, only a bit of movement in her lower limbs, and perhaps a slight twisting. The background sound of the plucked shamisen strings rose and fell as the breeze ebbed and surged. I watched with fascination as the sounds of the instrument, the minimal motions of the dancer, and my imagination, blended into a vision of a slender willow tree, moving and shifting and dancing to the invitation of a passing zephyr.

I sat, entranced, as the sound of the instrument died away and Amami became motionless. She sank to the floor, kneeling, and gave a low bow. As she rejoined us, she laid a hand on my arm and spoke a few words. Jack Ito translated.

"She says that dance was for me. She knows it was one of my favorites. Later, she will sing for you, if you like."

I assured her I would like. Before I could say more, there was a scratch at the door. Both ladies went to the door, slid it open, and returned with several small trays of various foods that I didn't recognize, but which triggered my appetite at first sight. I didn't really know how much wine I had consumed, because the cup was full every time I reached for it, so I reminded myself not to appear too thirsty or too greedy.

I recognized none of the delicacies placed before us. Some were obviously of a fishy origin, some thinly sliced meats, all either topped with a sauce or spice, or paired with a nearby bowl of the same for dipping. I wasn't sure which, if any, of the small bite-sized pieces was intended for fingers and which for chopsticks. Being clumsy with the latter, I questioned Ito on the subject. He translated my query to the ladies and smiled at the reply.

"They understand your puzzlement, and will take care of it."

Kioko delicately took a morsel in her fingers and devoured it, showing me that that particular item was considered finger-food. Amami plucked up another item with chopsticks and popped it into my mouth, startling me for a second, and quickly provided another when the surprise on my face turned into a delighted smile.

Under this close guidance, the meal progressed rapidly. I asked the Japanese name for everything I liked, diplomatically omitting a few items which I found excessively fishy or otherwise unsuitable to my southern palate. The plum wine was unobtrusively replaced with another wine—a white, which perfectly complimented the meal I was enjoying. My wine cup was ever full, and I found myself relaxed, comfortable, and willing to remain in place as long as I was welcome.

I could see that Ito was enjoying letting me have the spotlight and most of the attention. He would later have his fun with "I told you so's." In fact, I noticed that he was getting subtle personal attention from the Maiko, Kioko. Their interaction and whispered asides had nuances that led me to realize that they were far from strangers to each other. I resolved to ask Jack about this later— perhaps when I needed to divert his attention away from needling me about my evening.

When we had finished the meal, Kioko whisked away its remains, leaving the wine and Ito's sake. Amami turned to me and asked, through Ito, if I would like to listen to her sing. At my nod, she had a word with Kioko, who retrieved the shamisen and moved to her place to the right of the sliding door. Amami asked if I had any favorite Japanese songs that she might know.

"Yes, there is one I used to like when I was in Japan in the late 1940's. Do you know 'China Nights'? 'Shina No Yoru', I think, was the Japanese name."

Her face broke into a delighted smile. "You have very good taste," Jack translated, "It is one of her very favorites also. The song of a soldier, just returned to his homeland perhaps, who longs for the Chinese mistress he left behind." She took her former place, framed by the doorway, and stood unmoving. Kioko plucked the strings of her instrument tentatively, then played the introductory notes that I remembered so well.

The long, slender neck of the shamisen was smooth, with no frets to guide the fingers of the player's hand, skill and muscle memory being her sole means of striking the right notes. There was no strumming of chords—each note was individually plucked, either matching or harmonizing with the singer's voice.

Amami sang the plaintive ballad sweetly, and in the near-falsetto range typical of traditional Japanese vocals. When the last sad note had faded, she sank to her knees and bowed deeply, joined by Kioko. Upon rejoining us, she raised my wine cup on the fingertips of both her hands and put it to my lips. After I sipped, she moved it to her own and took a sip and passed it to Kioko, who gathered all the wine paraphernalia and carried it away.

"Ben-san, do you have a left-behind girlfriend somewhere? I know you do—you are a man of good appearance, and I think you are a kind man."

Jack smothered a grin as he translated this question. I vowed that he would hear about it later.

"No," I said, "No girlfriend, anywhere. A soldier should not leave his heart behind."

I was proud of coming up with such a profound and sentimental statement, but then had to wonder if maybe the wine wasn't stronger than I anticipated.

"Such a girlfriend would be lucky," she replied, placing her hand on my arm. "I would feel lucky."

The sliding door behind her opened slightly, and the okami-san bowed slightly and raised two fingers. Amami nodded to her; Kioko rose and went to the door, returning with a tray holding four sake cups and a delicately fashioned flask.

"Our time together has been good," said Amami, through Ito. "We drink to it, and perhaps to another time to come." We raised our cups. "Kanpai!"

It was sake, but I didn't mind at all.

35

CHAPTER 7

I Told You So

As we donned our shoes and exchanged compliments, Amami and Jack exchanged cards. She turned to me and extended a card, but I had none to offer. Jack quickly furnished one of his own. I wrote my name on the blank side and handed it to her, and she added a note in Kanji. We all shook hands, Jack seeming to add an extra squeeze to Kioko's delicate hand. He and I left in the taxi which had miraculously appeared at just the right time.

We rode in comfortable silence. The evening was young and there was considerable traffic, but for some reason I wasn't bothered by the close calls and near misses that formerly had me flinching and pressing imaginary brake pedals. At the post gate, Jack engaged the driver in some complicated monetary transaction as I strolled up the path to our quarters. He caught up to me in the lobby.

"See you for breakfast?"

"Sounds good," I replied. "About nine?"

Jack nodded and we went our respective ways.

Back in my room, I pulled the cork on a bottle of scotch that I  had liberated earlier, leaned back in the comfortable chair, and contemplated the evening. I mentally listed a number of questions to ask Jack Ito in the morning, and drifted off into peaceful sleep.

At 0905 I entered the dining hall, joining Ito who was finishing his second cup of coffee. We ordered our breakfasts, filled coffee cups, and sat in silence for a few minutes. Jack glanced at me across the table.

"Go ahead. Ask. I know you have questions about yesterday."

"Jack, I'm really curious about this 'Flower and Willow' world. When we left last evening, I felt relaxed, at peace with the world, and like I was someone special. Like the dance and the song were just for me. Like the ladies were waiting on me and spoiling me because they were—I don't know the word—attracted to me as a man?

"As I thought about it last night, I realized that it's what they do. It's their talent. If I were a smelly 70 year-old cigar smoking geezer with a pot gut, I'd probably still come away with the same sense of self-worth and inflated ego. They flatter without seeming to. They lead the conversations so you can mention your achievements without seeming to boast. They subtly flirt, compliment you without embarrassing you, and tease you with their unavailability. They're con-women."

"And...?" Jack queried, with half a smile lurking behind his coffee cup.

"And—I think we should import a couple thousand of them back to the States. They'd put the psychiatrists out of business in a year, change the attitudes of American womanhood in two, and run most of the bars broke in a decade!"

"Maybe you aren't such a gaijin barbarian after all, my friend. Your eyes have been opened to one of the subtle mysteries of Japanese culture. Now, maybe you're ready to shell out for your share of the festivities."

"Sorry, Jack—I hadn't even thought about it 'till now. How do we pay them?"

"I already took care of that." he said. The taxi driver was the middle-man. Money never changes hands in an Ochaya." He named a sum that, while respectable, was not outrageous.

"How do they calculate the charges?" I asked.

"By time and people. If it's a larger party and more Geisha are needed, it's more, of course. And the traditional time for a hosting such as ours is the time taken for two incense sticks to burn. The charge would be more for a longer time, but the ladies discourage longer sessions."

"Why? I could have stayed forever—or, at least I thought so at the time."

"Too long a session, more booze is consumed, which requires more food and performances. The sharp edge wears off, the encounter becomes more routine. The two-stick time standard is a tradition molded by several hundred years of experience."

"By the way," he added, "I forgot to tell you. Amami asked for your card, remember? That meant that you are now welcome in their Ochaya on your own. You won't need me as a chaperon any longer."

"I feel honored. Too bad I'll probably never pass this way again."

"You should feel exceptionally honored. A westerner being accepted in a Geisha teahouse is not unheard of, but it is quite rare. And it's a compliment to me, as your sponsor. Thanks for being such a good boy."

By now, my curiosity was really awakened—other questions were nagging at me, and this seemed as good a time as any to ask.

"You implied that Geisha, or Geiko as you call them, keep their personal lives separate from their professional. How do they handle marriage?"

"A Geiko is not expected to marry while engaged in her profession. If she falls into a romantic relationship, it's to be kept strictly apart from her Geiko life. If a Geiko chooses to marry, she's expected to retire from the Flower and Willow world. Some become Okasans and manage their own teahouse. Only about a third of the Maiko apprentices actually become Geiko—partly because the standards are so high, and partly because they become romantically involved before they 'graduate'."

He leaned forward, speaking earnestly and obviously becoming more wrapped up in the subject.

"Did you know that a Maiko has to sleep on her back with a padded wood block under the neck to preserve that ornate, and expensive, hairdo? She wears sandals with six-inch high blocks for soles to teach her to walk gracefully under any conditions. Her Obi, the ornate folded pad that hangs down her back, is worn very low on a Maiko to force her to walk with minimal motion and maximum grace. A Geisha wears a smaller one in the center of her back."

He shook his head.

"It's worse than a fraternity initiation, and it goes on for five years in the Kyoto district. Not every Maiko holds up until she is eligible to become a Geisha. But she watches her Geisha during all this time. She learns grace, male psychology, and the ancient traditions of music and dance. If she chooses not to take the final step, she has still become a very desirable prospective bride or companion for some wealthy businessman."

I gave him a chance to catch his breath.

"OK," I said. "Tell me what's up with you and Kioko."

"Huh?" he said, looking at me like I had dropped three kings against his two pair.

"Captain Ito, I don't know how you survive in the intelligence business. It was plain to everyone in that room that there's something special between you. Is Kioko going to turn down becoming a Geiko and attach herself to you? Or is this just a passing thing that'll cease when you ship out to the States?"

"Ben, just shut up! I don't know, and it's worrying me. I've had to visit Japan several times in the line of duty. I took advantage of one opportunity to renew acquaintance with Amami. My father had introduced me to her on a business trip years ago. During that visit, very much like ours yesterday, Kioko was the senior Maiko. We hit it off, and she sneaked out and we met later. Now, we don't know what to do. She's turning 19, and will become a Geisha in six months or so."

He looked at me questioningly, and I could see real pain in his expression.

"Ben, I like the Army; I'm good at the intelligence business. I want to stay for a career. Kioko likes her world and wants to become a respected Geiko, like her mentor. That's a special thing in Japan, where women don't stand that high on the social ladder. But we both want each other. We're pretty well jammed up. Greedy, maybe— we want it all."

"Cap'n Jack, I'm the last one to give advice on your problem— I've been riding in wide circles trying to avoid this kind of situation ever since I joined up. And, as much as I enjoy the company of women, I'm glad I never met one who got me so pinned down."

I buried my nose in my coffee cup, put it down again, and cogitated for a few seconds.

"Don't reckon you'd settle for letting her do the Geisha thing for a year or two, and you'd do the Army thing—then getting together?"

"Thought of it," he said. "If I knew I'd still be on this side of the world, that might work. But this war will end and I could be in Berlin, or in Timbuktu, next year at this time."

"You think it'll end soon?" I asked.

"Pretty damn sure," he replied. "And we'll probably have to give a little credit to the artillery boys, much as I hate to admit it."

I was a little put out by his comment. Never disparage a soldier's branch of service, even if he's in a Quartermaster Mess Kit Repair Company. We all have a job, and the job's got to be done by somebody.

Jack anticipated my reaction and raised a hand.

"Back off, Ben. Just a joke. In fact, if you can take a wide detour to your outfit when we get back to Kimpo, I'll show you something interesting. Make your little cannoneer's heart go pitter-patter!"

The conversation moved on into lighter subjects. We parted, Jack having more business to conduct with a local Intelligence agency, and I with the bartender at the Officers' Club.

CHAPTER 8

Ours Is Bigger Than Yours

I finished out my week of R & R in a pretty low-key manner, mostly reading, doing a little sight-seeing, buying some bottled goods for the guys back in my outfit, and keeping company with the club bartender.

Jack Ito visited the Ochaya at least once more that I knew of. When we met at the bus for the airport, he displayed the air of one who had made a decision and was determined not to second-guess himself. He didn't mention Kioko, nor did I, not wanting to re-inject myself into his personal problems.

As the returnees lined up to board the C-47, the loadmaster, a grizzled Master Sergeant with a face like a combat boot, addressed us.

"Now you guys know damn' well that the regs won't let you haul any booze back to a combat zone, right?" He waited, getting a few nods from the passengers, most of us just standing poker-faced.

"OK, as long as you know. Now when you come aboard, be real careful how you handle those AWOL bags. I don't want any busted bottles messing up my airplane. Load up!"

Captain Ito had a Jeep and driver waiting for him at Kimpo. I found a field switchboard and, after having been plugged through three more, contacted Baker Battery's First Sergeant.

"Hey, Top. This is Lieutenant Hunnicutt. I'm at Kimpo; be back as soon as I can bum a ride. Tell the

41

Old Man not to wait up for me. If he's in a good mood, that is; if he's not, you never got this call."

Ito and I left Kimpo at a speed which seemed suicidal on the chopped up local roads, but smoothed out a little when we hit the main route to Inchon. A Jeep only has room up front for the driver and one passenger. Since rank always gets the front seat, I cussed my way to Inchon, bouncing between two steel rear fenders and a canvas seat padded with nothing much. Ito directed the driver to an isolated wing of the docks and had him stop in front of a grungy little office building. Two business-like guards momentarily appeared, saluted Ito, checked his ID, and vanished.

When we entered the scruffy building, it was like Dorothy stepping out into the Land of Oz A clean, organized office, the walls papered with maps and artillery firing charts, and—best yet, a bubbling coffee pot and row of cups, all within my greedy reach. Ito made his way past a guard rail and into a small alcove in the far corner, while I filled a cup and took it out to our driver. When I returned, Ito was filling two more. He handed me one and a clip-on badge, and led us back outside.

Two minutes later, we pulled up at a guarded gate, showed our badges, and were escorted through on foot. Ito led me to an area masked on one side by a large docked freighter, and on the others by piles of stacked crates and cargo. Sitting in the center of the open area was the damnedest looking cannon I had ever seen. Its big square carriage was hanging nearly five feet in the air, supported on each end by a huge fork lift. Each lift had a high driver's cabin, both cabins facing forward, the entire assembly obviously intended to be driven like an old hook-and-ladder fire truck and steered at both ends. Sitting on the big rectangular carriage, the gun reminded me of one of Kaiser Bill's mammoth railway guns, designed to shell Paris from 75 miles out.

The gun tube was telescoped back into the carriage, and would be slid forward and locked in place for firing. I could see that it was designed so the carriage could be lowered to the ground by the lift trucks in a minute or so, the tube slid into position and, and the gun ready to fire within another few minutes.

"What the hell is that?" I asked Jack Ito. "It's as big as a railway car, and it must weigh fifty tons!"

"Actually," he said, "it's 85 feet long as it sits, and weighs close to 85 tons. The gun without transporters is about half that weight."

I just looked at him, not understanding how this monster could be of much use in Korea, or why he was showing it to me. We walked up closer to the gun and I circled it, working out in my mind how it functioned, how the power rammer worked, and how the 40 foot gun tube was slid forward into place and secured.

"Ben, this is a 'Gun, Heavy, Motorized, M65, caliber 280 millimeter'."

"OK?" I said, waiting for more.

"It happens", he said, "that the egg-heads at Los Alamos have finally been able to squeeze an atomic bomb into a casing 11 inches wide and a yard or so long."

"OK?" I repeated.

He looked at me impatiently. "And it happens that 280 millimeters is just a hair over 11 inches."

"Oh," I said. Then, "OH!" as the light dawned.

"This piece can drop a shell on a tennis court at 18 miles with a fresh metro. Now, if it could fire a nuclear shell of, say, 15 kilo-ton yield, our enemy wouldn't dare assemble any large troop concentrations near the front lines. His human wave attacks would be more like human ripples."

"What do you think he'll do when he finds out about this?" I nodded toward the monster gun.

"Oh, I'm pretty sure he's already found out about it. In fact, we leaked it on purpose. There's been a sudden increase in peace-talk activity, and it's possible that you might not ever have to climb Hill 672 again."

"But do you think we would really use nukes? The first nuclear war won't be the last."

"I don't know," Jack said, "but the enemy doesn't know either. We hope he won't take the chance. Come on—let's get you home before you go on the Morning Report as 'AWOL'."

"Roger that," I said. "And now I know why you spent so much R & R time visiting the G2 staff in Japan."

"Lieutenant Hunnicutt, I have no idea what you're talking about."

We walked back through the guarded gate and took the Jeep back to the project office to turn in our passes and return the coffee cups. A few hours more of back seat torture and Captain Ito dropped me off at B Battery's Orderly Room. We shook hands and I thanked him profusely for his company and for his part in educating me in Japanese culture.

"And," I said, "I'll probably never know how you'll work out the problem that's been bugging you, but I wish you the very best outcome, for both your sakes."

I stepped back and saluted him; he snappily returned my salute, jumped into the Jeep, and gave a casual wave as the driver gunned it around in a noisy U turn and sped away.

CHAPTER 9

The Shooting Stops —and Starts

It was late when I reported to Captain Francis, but he was still at his desk fighting paperwork.

"Hey, Ben," he said as he returned my salute. "Have a good time?"

"A fine time," I responded. "You ought to try it yourself. You haven't even applied for R & R yet."

"First Sergeant shootin' off his mouth again?" he grumbled. "Gonna have to tune him up one of these days." He pushed the paperwork to one side.

"Hell, why should I take R & R? Only time I can get any work done is when you trouble makers leave me in peace for a week. I'd send you off for another week if I could."

"Well," I said, "as a reward for all that dedication to paperwork, you're invited to a redo of my promotion party. Are we coming off the line any time soon?"

"Your timing is good, for a new first lieutenant. The whole  battalion is going on stand-down tomorrow at noon. Seems the peace talks are mellowing a bit, and we've been ordered not to pick any fire fights. We're keeping a pretty sharp eye across the line though— can't trust those bastards any further than I can spit ball bearings. They generally make one last ruckus before they settle into peace talks, just to look tough."

I shook the cargo pack I was carrying—the one we called an "AWOL bag". The clinking sound immediately grabbed the Skipper's attention.

"Reckon I've done enough paperwork for today. Come on over to my tent and you can tell me about your week while I check to see if you smuggled a girl back in that bag."

I had anticipated Francis' reaction. He drank little, but he loved good scotch and he hated to buy. The clink of an illicit bottle drew him as nectar draws a bee, and the chance of a free nip at the bottle transformed him into a supersonic bee.

The distant, but ever-present rumble of battle faded after noon of the following day, but never ceased altogether. Rumors of an armistice rattled around the unofficial grapevine, but no one got too far from his rifle. I spent the time cleaning up my gear, replenishing my carbine ammo, stripping and cleaning the long 30 round magazines we called "banana clips", and wondering how soon I might again need them.

I tried never to dwell on the hazards of my job as a Forward Observer. In theory, the FO stayed under cover as much as possible as he picked out enemy targets and directed the artillery fire required to destroy or repulse them. The Infantry protected him as best they could—he was the eyes of the guns that supported them. Without someone skilled in delivering artillery fire when and where needed, an Infantry company could be cut off and chopped to pieces by a mass attack. The Infantry had long been called "The Queen of Battle"; the Artillery, which inflicted by far the greatest number of casualties on the battlefield, was known as "The King of Battle." A somewhat ribald saying among the troops was, "The King's job is to put the balls where the Queen wants them." But ribald or not, that's what we tried to do.

Of course, the enemy was well aware of this and made it a point to target any GI suspected of being part of an FO party. The shelf life of most young Artillery Lieutenants was pretty short. A radio antenna in the vicinity of a man with binoculars would draw a barrage of mortar or artillery fire, if noticed. Or possibly, the undivided attention of an enemy sniper team.

In any case, the longer the lull in battle continued, the closer I was to rotation out of Korea. I had stopped listening to the rumors, reminding myself that the rumor mill had built up false hope too many times in the past. I was here as long as I was here, and that was all I needed to think about. I had reported for duty last November, had rotated between Battery duties and Forward Observer work through the winter, and was looking forward to a spell of not freezing my butt off for a change. Even serving on the line was bearable if one was reasonably warm.

I recalled one stint with an Infantry company which was blocking a pass the troops called "The Slot", between two rounded hills called "The Boobs". The ground was frozen so hard and deep that we couldn't dig foxholes—we blasted them out with Engineers' shaped charges. The soldiers on picket duty cut holes in sleeping bags for their arms and wore them like overcoats over their parkas. I shivered at the memory.

The only good thing that had come out of that detail was a chance to bring in all the artillery in the sector for a Time-On-target shoot. We wiped out most of a North Korean battalion in 15 minutes. Most FO's never get to call a TOT in their entire career, so I felt pretty good about that. The resulting Bronze Star felt pretty good, too. But not worth going through another Korean winter. Well, it was late July now. I shouldn't have too much more cold weather to contend with—I'd be off the line in October and on my way to the States.

My thoughts were rudely interrupted by the resumption of the battle noise that had served as a background for our existence for months. But this time, it had doubled in volume and intensity. I threw on my combat gear and trotted to the Orderly Room tent, expecting the worst. I found it.

"Saddle up and head for 672," Captain Francis barked. "The Chinks are hitting all along the line. Burns was hit and James needs artillery!"

I did a hasty about face and started toward the commo tent to pick up our radio. Perkins was ahead of me, as usual— a Jeep was barreling down the battery street toward me, Perkins and his radio in the back. I jumped into the front seat as the driver slid to a near-halt, cut a reckless U-turn and headed toward the front—toward that damn Hill 672 that we had hoped never to see again.

I turned and told Perkins what little I knew. He nodded and hung on as the Jeep bounced and jounced its way up the trail that led to the base of 672.

"Hey Perk," I added, after a minute or so. "You're still a Corporal, I see. I know you made Sergeant last week—get busted already?"

"Never got around to sewing the new stripes on, Sir. Might get it done shortly, if these Gooks ever give me a chance. Or if you don't get pissed at me and bust me back to Corporal."

"Perk, if we get this job done and make it off the hill, I'll sew your damn' stripes on myself!"

We reached the jump-off point and waved the driver back to the Battery—much to his relief. The steady crackle of small arms fire and the slam of shells bursting up on the summit told us that things were bad up there, but we reluctantly began the climb.

CHAPTER 10

Oh, Damn!

When I found Captain James, he all but embraced me with relief.

"Ben! Thank God! Get me some fire down the front slope. When Burns was hit, his radio got shot up too. I haven't been able to get hold of the guns to call in a fire mission."

Perkins was already on the radio with the FDC; we hunkered down in a shell hole which was still smoking and stinking of HE, and he handed me the mike. We had a pre-planned concentration plotted for an area halfway down the front slope of the hill. I gave Charlie the number and called for "Battery, ten rounds, shell HE, fuse VT." Perk and I then crawled forward to a knoll from which I could observe the bursts and adjust fire if needed.

Intensely concentrating on getting fire onto the steep approach slope, I had hardly noticed that we had our own firefight going on all around us. There were enemy inside our perimeter—GIs and Gooks were shooting each other at point-blank range. Several of our guys were slugging it out with rifle butts and entrenching shovels in hand-to-hand contests, most ending when a buddy took notice and blew their opponent away. Perkins was alert, calmly killing any enemy that appeared a threat to me, but was otherwise quietly waiting for orders.

The situation was bad. My barrage had temporarily stopped any Chinese reinforcements from entering the fight. Now it was on B Company to win the brawl on the hilltop. If they couldn't, we were cooked. No US forces, even if available, could arrive in time to affect the outcome.

Our barrage ended. Sixty high explosive 105mm shells had shredded the forward slope of Hill 672 in less than a minute. I could see 20 or more bodies scattered below me, most still, some moving, none a threat. Perk and I began picking targets from the ruckus going on around us, I still keeping an eye downslope against another attack from that quarter. Perkins dropped his carbine, picked up an M1 rifle and a bandolier of ammo, and hammered away at any surviving enemy, seldom having to shoot twice.

When it came to a small arms firefight, Chinese marksmanship was terrible. They tended to fire wildly, as though the noise and flash of their rifles would drive their enemy off. Even the burp gunners would be more apt to spray an area than to pick a single target and kill it. Their doctrine seemed to be, "If you can't shoot straight, shoot a lot." Which was OK with me, of course. But put enough lead in the air, and people will get shot. They put a lot of lead in the air, and we took casualties.

The gunfire trickled off as we ran out of targets, and in five minutes or so, the hilltop was clear of live enemy. I asked Captain James about Lieutenant Burns. He jerked a thumb in the direction of the row of American dead.

"Sniper. They had him spotted before the fight started. He was the first one down. His radio was damaged, so his RTO grabbed a rifle and fought it out alongside us. He was killed too."

Perkins and I stood in respectful silence. Neither of us had known Burns or his RTO very well—when we were on the hill, they were in camp, and vice-versa. But it hits a bit harder when it's someone you can identify with, who does the same kind of work you do. Because you know that, had the duty roster been set up one day differently, you and your RTO could be lying over in the KIA row.

The forward slope of 672 had a bulge about a third of the way down. Our artillery concentration was zeroed on that bulge, ready to flatten any enemy force as it came into view, and probably any reserve that was just out of sight just below it. However, from the crest, we could see nothing below the hump. There could be a whole regiment massing below, and we'd be unaware. There was another access corridor to the crest, a gully funneling up from our left. The Chinks had tried that recently, but our pre-planned artillery concentrations had turned it into a slaughter pen. Neither James nor I believed they would try that approach again.

"Captain, I'm worried about the blind area below the hump to your front. We can't see zilch on that lower slope. The Chinks are doing crazy things lately, and I wouldn't put it past 'em to try us again. I figure they think anything they can take just before a cease fire, they can keep."

"Hunnicutt, I can't see through solid rock any better than you can. You could be right, but I don't want to stick any of my people down there on lookout. They'd be cut off and lost in five minutes if the bastards attack again."

"Why don't I leave Sergeant Perkins here on your field phone— if you need artillery, he can call in a mission as well as I could. I'll take the radio and work my way down to where I can check out the lower valley. Anybody there, I'll call in the wrath of God on 'em. Just lend me a flak jacket to wear."

Captain James looked at me like I was crazy.

"Ben, if I wouldn't order one of my own men to go down there and put his ass on the line, why in hell should I send you?"

"Captain James, I'm your artillery adviser, and it's my job to call in fire when you need it. But you're not my commander. With all due respect, I advise a one man recon be carried out to check the valley bottom. And I recommend that it be done by an artillery observer so fire can be called in if needed. You see any other artillery observers around here?"

"Hunnicutt must be a southern word for 'stupid'. Go ahead if you gotta, but haul ass back if anything looks wrong."

He peeled off his own flak vest and handed it to me. I briefed Perkins on the plan and eased over the brink and down the slope before James could realize that he could, in fact, have given me a direct order not to go.

It wasn't long before I found myself working my way around the bodies of the victims of our last barrage. A few groaned and stirred, but posed no threat. When I reached the hump which blocked our view of the lower slope, I was very careful to ease my way forward, trailing the radio antenna low and behind so no sharp eye would see it silhouetted against the sky.

51

I was about to raise my head and survey the lower slope when I caught a glimpse of movement to my left. Thinking it just another of the severely wounded seeking ease, I rolled onto my right side to check it out. That was when the first bullet punched into my left thigh.

"Dammit!" I yelled, mad at myself for letting some Gook get the drop on me. My carbine was back on the crest, my pistol pinned in the holster on my right hip. I rolled all the way over on my back, freed the 45, and tried to spot the shooter.

It wasn't hard to do. A Chinese in an officer's uniform had pulled himself up on one knee and was aiming his pistol for a second shot. His face was bloody, but there didn't seem much else wrong with him. Of all the emotions which might have been running through my mind, I recall mostly outrage. 'That sunnuvabitch is actually trying to shoot me— me personally!'

He fired again, and I felt the slug pluck at my sleeve. A third bullet whacked into the flak jacket like a blow in the ribs from a Louisville Slugger.

'Oh, damn. I better kill this bastard before he shoots me again.' Somehow, with that thought, my 45 seemed to go off on its own. My enemy went down, then stubbornly rose again, levelling his pistol for another try. Mine erupted with a steady cadence of fire until the slide locked back behind an empty chamber. My last few shots were into a dead body, the first big 45 slugs having done the necessary work. I didn't recall aiming or pulling the trigger; I only remembered indignant outrage at the realization that some shit I didn't even know was actually trying to kill me; me, Benjamin Hunnicutt.

I reloaded and holstered the 45, turning my attention to the lower slopes of the hill. The wound in my thigh was starting to make itself known—I needed to finish my business here and get the hell back to B Company.

My first view of the lower hillside was puzzling. The entire slope was a muddy brown color, and seemed to be rippling like wavelets on a scummy stagnant pond. A second later, a nauseating flash of fear swept through my mind and body. The slope was alive with enemy soldiers. More enemy than I had ever seen in one place. More enemy than I could imagine being fought off by one battered Infantry company. More enemy than I wanted to . . .

An unseen burp gunner somewhere on my right sprayed my position with fire. The great mass of Chinese, holding until now to delay discovery, began moving uphill. They must have gone to ground at the sound of my gunfight; now realizing that they were discovered, they were rapidly closing on the hilltop. I desperately snatched the radio and began yelling into the mike.

Charlie's calm voice from the FDC responded, "What do we have, Ben?"

"A battalion in the open. From previous concentration, add 100. Fuse VT and keep 'em coming until I call it off."

I rolled into a handy shell hole left over from the earlier barrage and waited. During the ten or fifteen seconds before incoming rustled overhead, I tried to take stock. The thigh wound hurt, but wasn't bleeding much. I found that the burp gunner who had hosed me down had gotten lucky. My butt had taken at least one hit—I couldn't see if there were more, but I was beginning to feel serious pain.

The 105's came in with ear-splitting cracks and slams that had me involuntarily shielding my ears with both hands. The ground jumped and jiggled, pieces of rock, shards of steel, and clods of earth rained down; my body felt as though it had been pummeled by a pro heavyweight.

Finally I gathered the courage to grab another look at the enemy. They were hunkered down, weathering the shelling as best they could, but I could see that their strength was being whittled away by the unremitting fire. A substantial number, however, were outside the main beaten zone; six guns can cover only so much territory. I got on the mike again, urging Charlie to spread the sheaf to cover the Chinese that were bypassing the carnage. The shells that struck 15 seconds later were more spread to the sides, accomplishing what I wanted, but at the cost of thinning the concentration of fire in the center and allowing the leaders to rally their men and resume the advance. They were taking casualties, but doggedly moved upward toward the hilltop—and toward my position on the hump.

As they moved uphill, the Chinese were converging toward the crest, and moving into a tighter mass. I could see that by the time they reached me, they would be packed into a close enough formation to make the ideal artillery target, even for a six-gun battery. I thumbed the mike.

"Charlie, on my command, drop 100 and repeat fire-for-effect. Everything you've got. You can even stick your 45 out of the tent and fire it in this direction. And from here on out, take your directions from Perkins on the field wire. Over."

"Roger. Waiting your command."

The enemy had almost reached my position. Still hunkered in my hole, I held the mike in my left hand and my 45 ready in my right. When the Chinks spilled over the hump and were almost in my lap, I thumbed the mike and raised my pistol.

"Fire! Fox Oboe Baker, Out." I dropped the mike and braced myself.

A soldier carrying a long-barreled Russian Mosin- Nagant rifle appeared at the edge of my hole. He looked surprised to see me, then thrust his rifle in my face to shoot me. I slapped the long barrel aside and he fired into the dirt. When he stepped back to work the bolt and crank in a fresh round, I shot him in the face.

A burp gunner following him appeared in the same place, saw me, and raised his drum-fed chopper. Before he could pull the trigger, all hell broke loose and the world dissolved into fire, smoke, and noise. The gunner fell across my body. I could see that the top of his head was missing, and it somehow bothered me. I tried to heave him off; he was a little guy, but I couldn't seem to muster the strength to move him. The noise faded. Everything faded. It seemed a good time to go to sleep, so I did.

CHAPTER 11

Damn, Damn, Damn, Damn

I awoke with a savage headache and the sense that something very heavy was sitting on my chest. I tried to shrug it off, but with no success. When I put up my hands to pull it off, I felt some sort of a framework cage. An immovable cage, apparently. I really wanted the weight gone so I could roll over and go back to sleep; I forced my eyes open so as to fight it on equal terms. A firm hand pinned my arms to the bedside and secured them. I was helpless, so I decided 'What the heck.' and went back to sleep.

I woke again, this time to nearby voices. One was a pretty voice. I liked it, so I listened to what it said.

"The bullet wounds were no problem," said the pretty voice. "Pistol or PPSH 41 slugs. We got them out OK." 'That's nice.' I thought. 'Bullets no problem.' I was happy to know that. I could quit ducking when my dream enemies shot at me. I faded into a sleep where people were shooting at me, but I laughed at them. I saw the officer with the pistol and the bloody face. 'You're no problem.' I told him. 'Go away.' He hung his head and walked away down the hill.

The pretty voice was saying, "We should get him out to the Haven. He's in good enough shape to fly."

I thought about it. "No," I said aloud. "Can't fly. Can't move my arms. Don't think I can fly."

"He's with us," said the pretty voice. The voice moved closer. "Can you see me, son?"

55

With an effort, I forced my eyes open. I saw my mother; she was leaning over me wearing a nurse's uniform with a Major's gold leaf on the collar.

"You don't have to worry about flying," she said. "We'll let the helicopter take care of that."

"You're sitting on my chest," I said, "and you're not my mother."

"I'm whatever you want me to be," she said. "You just hang tight. We're going to fly you out to a hospital ship. You'll be fine there."

My eyes swept the surroundings—I saw the usual medical paraphernalia, and I saw that the ceiling was made of olive drab canvas. I saw the nurse who was a major. My senses began to register, and to synchronize with my brain.

"MASH?"

"Yes. We got you patched up, but your chest and ribs are pretty banged up. We need this bed—you're going out to the Haven, anchored off Inchon. It'll be like a vacation on a cruise ship."

"OK," I said, and went back to sleep.

The next time I woke up, I was under clean sheets in a regular hospital bed. A young guy in whites was changing my bandages. Seeing that my eyes were open, he smiled.

"Welcome back to the world. I'm Frank, your corpsman for now."

"Where..." I began.

"US Hospital Ship Haven. We're anchored off Inchon harbor. You'll be here a while, then either back to the States or to a hospital in Japan."

"Can't, just now," I said. "We're way short of FOs. Get me well enough to go back to my outfit and I'll be OK."

"I doubt that, Sir. You were pretty banged up when they got you to the MASH. The Doc will be by in a while—he'll tell you more." He finished his work on my wounds and took off down a corridor.

I lay there trying to put my fragments of memory into some sort of pattern, and to recall just why I was here. Suddenly, my bloody-faced Chinese officer was with me again. The one I had killed with my 45. I ignored him, and he again disappeared, walking downhill, stepping on the bodies of his command. I wanted to yell at him, 'Don't do that. Those are your men. Respect them.' But he was gone and someone was poking at my wounds and bruises.

I opened my eyes and found myself staring at another white-garbed figure, this one now examining the chart hung from my bed post.

"Hey!" I began, "When am I gonna get outta here?" I noted the silver eagle on his collar and belatedly added, "Sir."

"Lieutenant, we patched three bullet holes in your tough hide, and had to rearrange a bunch of ribs and innards where your flak vest stopped a half-pound chunk of American steel. Were both sides shooting at you? You must really be popular."

"I'm not sure how I got here, Sir. I keep trying to put things together in my head, but I'm just getting bits and pieces. I think I got caught on an open hillside and artillery came in. And I think I shot a Chink officer. But I don't know. I just know my outfit is short of officers, and they need me."

"Well, maybe I can help you find out how you got here. A couple of officers from your unit bummed a ride out here on an LCI for a visit, if you're up to it. They've been waiting a couple of hours. Should I let 'em come in?"

"Hell, yes!—Sir."

The Colonel left, and I waited with impatience for my visitors. The fog I had been living under was starting to dissipate; my mind was becoming clearer, but I still couldn't recall much after Perkins and I had checked in with Captain James on Hill 672. And I had no idea how long ago that was, or how long I had been in custody of the medics.

A shadow darkened my bedside, and I looked up to see Captain Francis and Captain James standing over me, both wearing crisply starched fatigues, and without battle gear.

"Sirs. Welcome aboard. Looks like I've been drafted into the Navy." I stuttered to a halt, wanting to remain flippant, but wanting more to fill in the blanks in my memory.

"Thanks for taking the time to visit," I continued, "I know you've both got troops to look after, but please tell me how I got here—and how long they're gonna keep me."

Francis glanced over at James, who appeared reluctant to speak. Finally, James reached down and shook my hand, then patted me on the shoulder.

"Ben," he began, "what's the last thing you remember from our time on the hill?"

"Sir, seems to me I went down the hill to recon the part of the slope we couldn't see. Found a big bunch of Chinks below and called in fire on them. I think I remember shooting it out with an enemy officer. The main body kept coming, so I adjusted fire. A couple of Chinks found me in my hole. About that time, a bunch of shells came in and the lights went out. What happened after that?"

"OK", he said. "Here's what we saw from the crest."

"You did have a shoot-out with a Chinese officer. We had binocs on you from the time you started downhill. You both got off shots, he went down. You spotted the mass attack coming up below your position—the people we couldn't see. You called in fire, which seemed to stop them for a bit. Then they resumed the climb; when you were about to be overrun, you called fire on your own position. When the shit hit the fan and we lost sight of you, you were wrestling around with a couple of enemy soldiers."

He paused and took a deep breath. "Now for the part you don't wanna hear. You left Sergeant Perkins on the wire with FDC. He was watching you the whole time through your binoculars. When the air cleared after the last 105's came in, we could see a bunch more bodies and wounded scattered around the hump you were on. And we could see what we thought was your body, still in the shell hole with a Chink body draped across it. It hit Perkins hard. He was about to break down, when somebody saw you move an arm or leg.

"He dumped his battle gear and ran down the slope before we could stop him. He reached you and started dragging you up the hill. The Gooks had left a few people to cover their retreat. They poked their heads over the hump and started shooting. We tried suppressive fire, but they were stubborn. Perk had you three quarters of the way home when they hit him. A dozen of my guys scrambled down to help, and got you both back up the hill."

He paused again, but I knew what he was going to say.

"Sergeant Perkins didn't make it. He died before we could even get him off the hill."

Every curse word I knew welled up in my mind, but my voice could only say, "Oh, damn, damn, damn, damn."

CHAPTER 12

The Party's Over

After a minute of silence, while I let Captain James' words sink in, Captain Francis spoke softly.

"We put him in for a Silver Star, Ben. I think he'll get it, posthumously. It was a brave thing he did, and it was witnessed by the entire outfit.

"It was a dumb thing," I murmured, "but he'd better get that Star, or ..." my voice choked out, and I lay there trying to see through eyes filled with tears.

"And you're in for the DSC for calling in artillery on your own position to save my company." said James. "There are enough witnesses that you'll probably get that to go along with your Purple Heart."

"Damn," I said again. I turned to Captain Francis. "What Perkins did was way beyond the call of duty—he deserves the Star. I was just doing the job they pay me for; this Distinguished Service Cross business is pure bureaucratic bull shit." I rolled my eyes up to the ceiling. "I'll be so damn glad when this stinkin' war is over!"

The two Captains looked at each other in surprise, then back at me. Francis spoke.

"Didn't you know, Ben? The war is over. They called a 'cease fire' back on the 27th of July. This is the August the 4th.

"How the hell long have I been here?"

"You were hit on the 25th. It's taken us until now to find you, what with all the "stand down" procedures, and the catching up on records. And," he added sadly, "the letter writing."

After my visitors had left, I just lay in bed retracing my time on earth with Corporal Peter Perkins. I knew he came from the tiny town of Oberlin, in Ohio. Oberlin was a college town, stuffed full of teachers and professorial types according to Perkins. He was not scholastically or socially inclined, actually preferring to bicycle out of town and do part-time work for local farmers and dairymen, rather than bag groceries or deliver papers in town. He soon cured his classmates of giving him the nickname PeePee, and was called just Perk thereafter.

Perk, like me, had enlisted for lack of anything better to do and, like me, found the Army a satisfactory substitute for home and family. He was assigned to me early on as a Radio/Telephone Operator, and we had learned to survive Korea together. He had learned enough of my job that I could trust him to call in fire when it was needed—learned well enough that I had been encouraging him to apply for OCS, to earn a commission, and to make the Army his career. 'Now', I thought, 'he'll have no career. Hell, he never even got to sew on his sergeant's stripes.' The service had lost a good man, and I'd lost a good friend.

Perkins had no family that I knew of, other than his parents. Captain Francis would have written them already, but I made a vow to do so myself, and to visit them when I next went home on leave.

I knew my emotions would catch up with me later, but for now I pulled a mental curtain across the entire painful subject and went to sleep.

Frank, the medical corpsman, was right. I lounged around the ship with six or seven hundred other patients until she had a full load. Then I was choppered to Kimpo and freighted off to Japan. There, the docs messed around with my upper body, trying to get everything back in place. Constant pain told me that the jigsaw puzzle wasn't fitting together very well. Finally, the head doc told me that they were going to quit trying. I was healing up with some internal parts still in a bind, and they were afraid they'd do permanent damage if they kept fooling around. All this in medical terms, of course, but I got the drift. I would be put on a plane and airlifted, along with other complicated cases, to Letterman Army Hospital in San Francisco. I remembered San Francisco as warm and green, so that sounded like as good an idea as any.

The flight was as pleasant as one could expect a medevac flight to be— and a lot more so than the packed troop ship that had carried me to Japan last autumn. I was able to make my way to a window as we approached the Golden Gate, and I'll never forget the lump in my throat as we passed over that beautiful, graceful bridge, its glistening white city spread out beyond.

I was able to walk from the bus through the entry into Letterman Hospital, although stiffly, and with pain accompanying each step. We were warded according to our injuries, so I found myself quartered with a dozen or so other walking wounded, all officers. Some of the medical personnel were military, others civilians. This was convenient, as the civilians often had little patience with military protocol, and worked in a much more relaxed manner. The military people, not wanting to seem hard-ass in comparison, ran a looser ship than usual; we soon learned to work around both groups.

Letterman Army Hospital had a reputation for being the most advanced of any Army medical facility. We found this hard to believe at first—Letterman was built about 1898, and the basic structures looked like props in a western movie. We soon found that it was quite up-to-date, and that the people working there really believed in looking after the troops. To the point, in fact, that we took shameful advantage of them.

My own troubles were soon addressed, much to my discomfort. The docs said that nothing in my chest appeared to have been ruptured or severely damaged, but that some parts had been pulled or torn away from their assigned locations. The solution seemed to be to open me up, replace the AWOL organs where they should be, and close up. But this couldn't be done all at once, so would require several entries and exits to put everything back in place.

Given the necessary healing time between fixes, this meant that I'd hurt a lot after a procedure, and the docs would know I was ready for the next when the pain from the last finally went away. I became expert at hiding the lack of pain, just to get more rest time between procedures.

After several weeks of learning the ropes and getting to know the hospital staff, life began to get boring. At the time, no passes were given until one became nearly well and was close to being discharged. We became more restless, finally falling into active rebellion. There was a Lieutenant Yokum in the ward who had lost his left arm at the elbow, but swore all his other parts would work fine if he'd ever be given a chance to use them. He had previously served in the Presidio area, and was able to tell us the precise route that led from Letterman to the Presidio Officers' Club. This information was not helpful to many of the patients, as the Club was about a mile and a quarter from our ward. Not everyone was in shape for such a journey. Those of us who were, or thought we were, decided to slip out after a midnight shift change and engage in a little R & R. The first part of the operation went as planned. But like most carefully concocted battle plans, things fell apart pretty quickly. Evidently, we were far from the first Letterman inmates to hatch such a caper. The Club staff, seeing white gowns, pajamas, and bandages, phoned the hospital; ten minutes later we were rounded up and hauled back to the ward, nurses shaking fingers at us like we were naughty school kids. We, of course, took the incident as a challenge and made up our minds to beat the system at any cost. What could they do? Restrict us to quarters? Cut off our booze ration? We initiated Plan B.

The chief civilian nurse on our floor was a big strapping blonde gal from Pierre, South Dakota. She had shown a certain sympathy toward our efforts, as revealed by a half-hidden grin while the head military honcho was fuming and spluttering at us.

I managed to corner her the following day and casually asked where our uniforms were stashed. I mentioned that I was worried that I may have left some personal items in the pockets, and they might be stolen while we were helplessly penned up in the ward. Janice, which was how she was labelled by her name tag, thought for a moment.

"Your gear and clothing are in a storage room in the basement. The room's always supposed to be locked, except when someone is discharged or asks for access to look for personal stuff." She walked me out to the nurses' station and showed me a row of keys behind an apparently locked glass-fronted cabinet.

"The gear locker key is the one on the last row with the red paint daubed on it. Of course, you can't get to it unless the cabinet is left unlocked—which it often is." She reached up and pulled on a knob. The cabinet swung open.

"See," she said, "that's downright carelessness. I'll have to speak to someone about that one of these days." She closed the cabinet and left it, still unlocked, to escort me back into the ward.

CHAPTER 13

Plan B

The following Friday night, those of us fit to travel infiltrated the storage locker at various intervals and secured the uniform items needed to appear as legitimate thirsty soldiers.

By 2315 we were making slow headway across the Presidio in the direction of the Golden Gate Bridge. The left turn and climb up the hill to the Club was challenging to some of the more sorely wounded, but good old American teamwork, plus the near proximity of an alcoholic bonanza, carried us to our goal.

The least obviously wounded of us invaded the bar, sometimes roughly displacing sitting patrons. The least fit took over the tables, gratefully resting their overtaxed bodies.

We only stayed about 45 minutes— which was the time it took for suspicious servers to contact the Club Officer at his home, for him to arrive at the Club and ask embarrassing questions, and for the hospital to send a convoy of ambulances to retrieve us. During that 45 minutes, a considerable amount of booze was swallowed by troops whose capacity had been diminished by a long period of unwilling abstinence. The Club regulars wisely departed, and our crew of sick, lame, and lazy, flush with unspent money, spent it.

When the tongue lashing came the next morning, we took it with either wide grins on our faces, or with flinching misery and throbbing heads. Our uniforms were confiscated, and the key to our personal gear storage disappeared from the key cabinet. Although we had lost the skirmish, we managed to salvage a bit of consolation from the evening. Lieutenant Yokum had rigged his half-arm in a sling, the bottom of which was filled out by rolled newspapers to resemble a forearm. During the action, he had managed to slide a full bottle of scotch inside the newspaper and bring it back as a very palatable souvenir. A portly Engineer Captain who had dressed in a full blouse, rather than just a khaki shirt and tie, managed to tuck two bottles of bourbon under his belt before being hustled out. Several others managed innovative ways to hide their liquid loot and return it to the ward undetected.

We carefully rationed out nightly medication within the ward for some time to come, and it seemed to relieve many of our more persistent symptoms.

For the next weeks, two guards were strategically placed outside the ward to prevent any further night excursions. Since the hospital had no personnel available for a security detail, it had to request the guards from the Post Commander. Sentries were customarily on post for two hours, then given four hours off for rest and sleep. Therefore, one guard post normally required at least three or four men, depending on its location and duration. The Post Commander finally demanded to know the purpose of this daily drain of his scarce manpower. Upon being told, he summoned his staff car and was driven straight to Letterman. A subsequent stormy session in the Hospital Commandant's office was overheard by everyone in the vicinity, including Nurse Jan. As she related to me later, it went something like this:

"Colonel, are you telling me that you are restricting combat-wounded officers from going about the post like normal soldiers?"

"In a way, Sir, yes. We have to make sure that they don't do anything that might hinder their recovery."

"And you don't think that a bit of relaxation and a drink or two might actually help their recovery?"

"Sir, an excess of..."

"Colonel, a gentleman named Mark Twain—whose common sense I hold in high regard—is supposed to have said something like, 'Too much of most things can be bad for you. But too much whisky is just barely enough.' And recalling my days in the combat arms, I tend to concur. If these men had the freedom of the post, or even of the city, they wouldn't need to do anything to excess. After all, anything that's available at will doesn't need to be taken by force."

"Sir, I am still responsible to do everything possible to help these men in their recovery. I cannot allow a person to do something that I think might harm him."

"Colonel, I cannot tell you how to run your hospital. But I would suggest that each patient be evaluated on his own particular condition. And if there is no reason to believe he cannot safely be out on his own, cut him loose! Then, if he screws up, shut him down.

"And you're not getting any more of my troops to imprison wounded officers!"

And that's about what happened. Most people in our ward, and in some others in the facility, were deemed qualified to be loosed onto the local scene. A few overdid it, of course, and paid the price. Those who were not considered well enough for a pass seemed to work harder to cooperate with the medics and thus hasten their freedom.

Jan and other medical staff who lived off post began a free taxi service. When they went off shift and left the hospital for their homes, they offered rides to patients who wished to be dropped off at the Club or PX, or to hit the city. It may be wishful thinking, but it seemed to me that healing and recovery came about more quickly with the change of policy.

It may have changed my outlook, also. I had always leaned toward conformity to the rules and customs of any authority under which I worked. But after the rebellion of the Wounded Warriors succeeded in inflicting common sense on hospital protocol, I experienced an inner revelation.

It was actually possible, by persistence, for us little cogs to change the way the big wheels run things! 'Keep that in mind, Hunnicutt,' I told myself. 'Maybe everything in the Army isn't written in stone after all.'

CHAPTER 14

The Dam Breaks

My upper works began to improve, so naturally I was given more exercises that hurt even more. I was assured that, if they were not done, I'd really hurt, and for the rest of my life. So, kicking and screaming, I went along with their program. I was now allowed the freedom of the Presidio, so explored it thoroughly while getting my outdoor exercise. The old fort under the south entry to the bridge was fascinating to me because it had not yet been restored. Somehow, I had always preferred untouched historical sites for carrying me back in time. Slickly "restored" sites always left me with the idea that I was seeing someone else's version of their original appearance—I rather enjoyed letting my own imagination fill in the blanks.

The old post of Presidio was beautiful and relaxing compared to most Army installations. Huge eucalyptus trees shaded dignified old buildings that had served the soldiers of half-dozen wars. The two ornate antique bronze cannon flanking the entrance to the Officers' Club had been left by the Spanish, then ceded to the United States by Mexico when this part of California became American

I was told by the curator of the post museum that there were many old coastal fortifications on the Marin Headlands near the north end of the Golden Gate Bridge, so I bummed a ride across on one balmy fogless day. I spent the full day exploring seacoast gun positions dating from the Spanish-American War through World War two. As an artilleryman, trying to determine the types of cannon, their field of fire, and the means of directing their fire, was a fascinating puzzle. Coast Artillery was an entirely different game from Field Artillery—your target was a distant vessel moving in an imprecise direction at an unknown speed. Your shells could take a full minute to arrive at their target. Once you observed a shell's impact, you had to second-guess the ship's Captain and shoot where you hoped he would be when your next shells landed.

I sat on the wall of a 1900 vintage gun pit, soaking up the warmth of a welcome sun and admiring the city across the bay, glistening white against the green hills beyond. In my mind I viewed the gun position as it might have been at the turn of the last century, and mulled over the gunnery problems inherent in anti-ship cannoneering. I wished Perkins were here to help me think out the details.

'Perkins!'

I hadn't allowed any thoughts of Perkins to linger in my mind since I left Japan. I couldn't forget him, but I could, and did, successfully draw a curtain across my mind whenever his memory intruded. I tried to pull that curtain now but Sergeant Perkins lingered, refusing to be driven away.

I realized that I was about to cry, looked about, ashamed I might be seen by some passer-by, and broke down completely.

I buried my face in my arms and let the anguish, guilt, sorrow, and grief flood out like water over a dam. I don't know how long I sat there, eyes streaming and shoulders shaking with emotion. Eventually, a tentative voice from behind brought me back to the moment.

"Are you all right, Sir?"

I looked around and saw a young couple standing on the pathway a dozen feet away. Of high school age, they were standing in the afternoon sun, watching me and holding hands. They weren't much younger than Perkins had been on that day when he...

"Yes," I answered. "Yes, and I appreciate your concern. I was just remembering a very bad time—a day when I lost a friend. But I'll be OK now." I smiled as I dabbed my cheeks with my pocket handkerchief. "Sometimes, old guys have to cry too."

They nodded a farewell, embarrassed to have witnessed such emotion in a grown-up stranger, and moved on up the slope.

My mind returned to Perkins, but more calmly now. I had lost friends on the battlefields of Korea before, but none had affected me this way. I was beginning to realize why. Perk had lost his life saving me, and I wasn't sure I was worth it. And I'd never know whether I would have willingly done the same for him. I could never be sure, because I'd never have a chance to prove it, one way or the other.

And I now recognized and accepted the fact that I would have to live with that pang of guilt for the rest of my life. The sorrow would heal, the grief would fade, but the tinge of guilt, of not knowing, would always be there.

I stood, dusted off the seat of my pants, and made my way back to the hospital.

Eventually I was deemed in serviceable condition and ready for whatever else the Army had in store for me. I phoned the Artillery Officer Assignments Office in Washington to learn where my next post would be. I was cheerfully informed by a Major Vaughn that I had been selected for assignment as an instructor at the Artillery School at Fort Sill, Oklahoma. I not-so-cheerfully informed him that my assignment preference request plainly stated that Alaska was my first choice, and that perhaps my battle time and my wounds entitled me to some say in the matter.

This shameless attempt to capitalize on my Purple Heart received exactly the consideration that it deserved.

"Lieutenant, I have several thousand Artillery officers that now have no war to fight. I have to find places to put them. Some we have involuntarily taken off active duty, but there are still too many to send each where he wants to go. The mission of the Army, when there is no current war, is to get ready for the next one. The best way for me to do that is to put the most qualified and combat-experienced people in slots where they can train the less experienced."

During the silence that followed, I remained quiet.

"By your lack of a rebuttal," he resumed, "I take it you agree with me?"

"Sir, I'd love to be able to disagree, but logic says you're right. At least there's no war in Oklahoma—unless the Apaches have left the reservation."

"No Apaches, Lieutenant. In fact, I think they're mostly in Arizona now." His voice took on a less official tone. "Tell me, Hunnicutt, what's so special about Alaska? You're not the first to bust a gut trying to get there."

I spent the next five minutes trying to put into words the hold that the Territory had on me after my six months of duty there. The Major listened patiently—and sympathetically, I hoped—but with no indication that his decision would change.

"Well, son, you can look for a three-year tour at Sill, teaching what you know. And maybe a chance to help devise new tactics and weaponry for our next war. If you do, remember that we always seem to fight every war in a different climate. We'll probably fight the next one in the jungle, and the following one in the desert—keep that in mind with your new guns and gunnery."

The Assignments major was correct in sending me to Fort Sill, of course. And much later in my career, I found that he was right in his guess about the next war being a jungle fight. And I did spend three years at Sill instructing young officers on the delicate techniques of bringing death and devastation to the enemies of our nation.

My next move was to Germany for three years in an Armored Division, staring across Cold War borders at the Russian and East German armor which faced us. I was becoming a well-educated traveler by now, able to order a beer in four languages (if I included English). My next transfer to Fort Bragg, in North Carolina, added to this specialized education. My southern accent meant that I could seek out certain civilian purveyors of illicit local liquids well enough to be designated the official Battalion Bootlegger (nick-named 'Captain Moonshine' by my companions). We could get all the alcohol we needed on post, of course, but clear corn whiskey from a hidden still seemed to have a special flavor all its own—probably because it was illegal.

Subsequent assignments and moves pretty well used up the years between my leaving Korea in 1953 and reaching 20 years of service in 1967. And, despite keeping Alaska on top of my assignment preference list, it remained a distant mirage. I wore out a half-dozen Assignment Officers during those years, but the "good of the service" always seemed to preempt my personal desires.

When I hit my 20th year I was wearing the gold oak leaves of a major and became eligible for retirement. Ironically, I was informed that my next duty station would be in Washington, DC, at which place I would assume the duties of Artillery Branch Assignment Officer. This meant that, in another three years, I could reassign myself to Alaska if I chose—but, until then, I would be locked behind a desk in a town I hated.

I quit! I forwarded my retirement request with same speed and accuracy that I had previously delivered artillery fire on target. There was some discussion of a national emergency due to the Vietnam mess, but I parried this threat with three bullet holes, and a Distinguished Service Cross (yes, the recommendations of Captains James and Francis had borne fruit), and was allowed to retire.

Feeling completely free for the first time since my teens, I packed my gear, sold my little 1966 Pontiac GTO, and flew north.

PART TWO

ANCHORAGE, ALASKA
1972

CHAPTER 15

You Remember Her From WHERE?

My return to Alaska, now a full-fledged state instead of a mere Territory, was not quite the joyful homecoming I had anticipated. New streets and roads had been built, towns and villages had expanded, and the "Last Frontier" had definitely become more civilized. Much more so, in fact, than I preferred. But, civilized or not, I seemed to keep stumbling into situations that were anything but.

During the year of my return, I accidentally uncovered a string of murders of some of the former Stay-Behind Agents that I had recruited and trained in the early 1950's, before Korea. Sorting out that mess had involved stress, fear, and danger, but had somehow left me with a beautiful but feisty girlfriend—who also happened to be an agent of the FBI. Agent Elise Nichole, whom I called "Liz" because it sometimes annoyed her, generally managed to keep me out of trouble, more by the power of her personality than by her badge of office.

 Then in 1969, an exception occurred when I bumped into my old Battery Commander from Korea, Captain Hamish Francis. Francis was now a Lieutenant Colonel, and commanded the Nike Hercules Air Defense Missile Batteries which defended the Anchorage area and its nearby military installations. He had been alerted to expect some sort of move against his missile units by an offshoot

branch of the underground Weathermen faction, and had somehow conned me into working as a temporary counter-terrorist agent. Another messy affair, it nearly cost me my life. In the end, justice somehow triumphed despite my going a bit rogue in handling some of the insurgents involved.

And then, to top it off, I stumbled into a murder while on my annual caribou hunt in late summer of 1971. As usual, I couldn't keep my nose out of the investigation, really ticked off the killer, and somehow created a situation in which the killer and I were taking turns chasing each other. Strangely, this killer touched off the same attitude of indignant outrage triggered by the Chinese officer trying to shoot me in Korea those many years ago. When this struggle also became up close and personal, my Korean luck held and my adversaries ceased to be a threat.

Now, back in Alaska for nearly five years and bumping up against my 44th birthday, I was sitting in the bar at the Anchorage International Airport waiting for the 727 that was bringing Liz back from a three-week investigation in Fairbanks. I was actually enjoying the wait, the martini that accompanied it, and the anticipation of seeing Liz again. Absence may make the heart fonder, as in the old saying, but it also stirs the imagination as to the nature of the reunion.

Liz strolled into the bar about five minutes after her flight arrival was announced, drawing the attention of most of its male customers. A tall lady with dark hair, worn longer these days I noticed, high cheekbones, dark eyes, and a challenging demeanor that cooled the ardor of most casual suitors. Liz was nearly my age, but much more pleasing to the eye. She was dressed in FBI conservative mode, but the businesslike suit couldn't hide the fit and filled-out body beneath it. I could never understand how added years could give her added mystique and attractiveness, but only made me more leathery.

I waved her over to my table, carefully chosen for its view of the Alaska Range on the western horizon. Two fresh martinis were waiting. It was early May and the sunsets were becoming more spectacular with each lengthening day. If we lingered for a drink or two, the thin clouds to the west should furnish a vivid light show of orange and red. Liz came to my side of the table and we shared the chaste kiss of couples who tended to avoid public displays of affection. The deeper feelings within weren't obvious to onlookers, we hoped, but a few male observers seemed to abruptly lose interest.

"Well," I asked, knowing the answer, "how did it come out?"

"Boring," she replied. "Typical financial fraud case. You know what was done, but you spend days on the paper trail trying to nail down how they did it. Guy and a woman took their boss to the cleaners to the tune of a quarter-million over a couple of years. They'll probably get three years each, and be out in 18 months."

"Almost worth it," I said. She rolled her eyes at me.

"Not for you, it wouldn't be, Ben. Being cooped inside on a rainy afternoon drives you up the wall. A year in the barbed wire hotel and you'd be gnawing on the bars like a mad beaver."

At this moment, a slightly built woman in a JAL flight attendant's uniform made her way to our table. She appeared to be in her early thirties, quite attractive, and probably Japanese or Japanese-American.

"Excuse me, but you are Ben Hunnicutt, are you not?" Surprised by the fact that she asked about me by name, I hesitated, then merely nodded in affirmative.

"You do not remember me." She smiled. "It is not surprising. When you last saw me, my face was covered in white paint." I stared at her, trying to put things together in my mind and memory. Suddenly recollection kicked into gear. I shook my head unbelievingly.

"You're Kioko, Jack Ito's friend from Kyoto. We were on R & R and I met you and Amami in the Geisha teahouse. I apologize for not knowing you, but that was over 15 years ago—how did you ever recognize me?"

"Because I was looking for you. Also," she tittered, "we were trained in our work to tell one round-eye from another. You gaijin all look alike to most of us, you know."

About this time, I noted an extreme drop in temperature across the table. I turned to introduce Kioko to Liz and found myself impaled by the glare of a pair of gun-barrel eyes. I had seen that look before, but never directed at me. My mind reverted back to a rustic uncle who, during my youth, had had several occasions to stare at me and say, "You inna heap a trouble, Boy."

There was no doubt but what, at this moment, I was in deep trouble. I opened my mouth to explain the Geisha situation, but knew full well that I needed more time than I was likely to get. Liz tossed back half her martini and, I suspected, was ready to take sudden leave after the final swallow.

Kioko moved around the table and grasped Liz's hands in her own.

"This must sound strange to you—you please let me explain."

I don't quite know how Kioko managed it, but she was able to keep Liz seated and listening for the five minutes that it took her to explain what Jack Ito needed 20 minutes to explain to me, back in 1953. I listened, nodding occasionally, but afraid to break the spell by opening my mouth. Kioko spoke colloquial English, correctly pronounced and mostly grammatically correct, her word order sometimes reverting to that of her native Japanese. I had suspected she understood English during our session in the teahouse. She was doing quite well now.

"So," as she turned to me, "Jack and I were caught between his duty and my duty. You see, I had been Maiko in that teahouse for many years. If I quit to marry Jack, the mama-san and Amami have to train another. Amami gets older, wants to live a simple life, but she cannot quit with honor until another Maiko is trained to be house Geisha. Jack is afraid if he wait to marry, he will get moved to a place we cannot be together."

"Yes, I know. Jack told me about your problem, Kioko. What did you decide to do?"

"I became Geisha when I am 19," she said proudly. "I stay two years and some months. We get new Maiko and start training her, so I can go." She smiled. "The new Maiko is very good, very smart, very quick, so Amami told me I could marry and have a happy life with Jack Ito."

Liz was listening with an expression of wonder and puzzlement as I discussed this extraordinary subject with apparent understanding.

"Jack was in Germany," she continued. "He took a long leave and we were married in the teahouse by an Army Chaplain, and also in a Japanese ceremony. There was much trouble in your Army when Intelligence Officer wanted to marry Japanese national, but Jack had patience and Army finally said OK."

"And now you are a hostess for JAL? A waste of talent, I think."

She broke into modest laughter.

"What was I trained for, Ben-san? What I do now is what I trained for as a Maiko. I make people comfortable, I serve and entertain them, make them feel good. Just as I did for you and Jack that afternoon in Kyoto."

"Are you and Jack still together?" I asked, immediately regretting the question.

Her face took on a grave expression.

"We are together. We have no permanent home—just what we can find between moves. I took job with JAL to keep busy while Jack travelling doing intelligence work." She looked me directly in the eyes. "Jack is now Colonel Jack Ito with Army Intelligence. He spent much time in Vietnam, in Thailand, Cambodia. Find out some bad stuff about Vietnam government."

She paused to catch a breath, and, I suspected, to rein in her emotions.

"He always kept track of you, Ben-san. He liked you. When he learned you were hurt just before the cease-fire, he wanted to visit. But he was very busy with cease-fire things, and could not."

I had to ask, "Where is Jack now?"

Her reply was less than enlightening. "I have a long message from Jack. Nothing written on paper. He had me remember it for telling you in person. If you will allow, I will visit your house," she nodded at Liz, "this evening and explain."

Liz started to offer to pick Kioko up at her hotel and drive her back later, but Kioko was shaking her head.

"No more public contact between us. I can walk. Jack gave me your address. Then I walk back to hotel—tell others I am shopping."

She stood, saying clearly for the benefit of any who might hear, "I am so glad you enjoyed your flight. Please consider using Japan Air for your future travel—it is our pleasure to serve you."

CHAPTER 16

Great Expectations

Kioko arrived at Liz's apartment shortly after six. Liz insisted that she dine with us, to which Kioko hesitantly agreed. I felt that she was reluctant to begin her story, and perhaps a little embarrassed at thrusting herself upon strangers.

During a rather good, but somewhat silent meal of quickly thawed halibut steaks, Liz and Kioko exchanged trivial bits of personal information and background. I could see that their relationship was thawing, largely due to the fact that Kioko was using the same tactics on Liz that she used on males during Geisha hostings in Japan. Soon, they were talking together like long-time special friends, both far more relaxed than they had appeared at the airport.

After the meal we all relaxed with a decent white wine, Liz and I anxiously awaiting Kioko's story.

"Jack was given job of what you call general troubleshooter for Vietnam war zone. He sees all intelligence reports, keeps lookout for suspicious stuff. The war is not going so well; many Vietnam high-up people are starting to plan for maybe they lose. Jack is watching for anybody who looks like maybe changing sides, or helping the North."

She took on an expression of intense concentration.

"I don't know much details. He talk to me sometimes to help him think things out."

I had noticed that her consciously correct English began to slip when she became tense or stressed, and it was showing now.

"We are living in Tokyo now—good for me with JAL job, good for Jack because easy to get anywhere in Asia he need to go. Last month I come home from flying and find note from Jack. It say he will be in Saigon for ten days. I hear no more for 20 days, then he comes home with much worry. He tells me how to find you, and says to tell you these things. And he show me your picture—from Army records, I think. That is how I recognize you in airport. Good luck for me. Saves time trying to find you at your home. Or hers." she added with a smile.

Kioko took a deep breath, screwed up her face in deep concentration, and began.

"Jack kept track of you while you were in the Army, and after you retire. His job let him do such things. He knows about your finding stolen gold after Operation Washtub ended, and your helping when the terrorists steal nuclear bomb from missile unit. He even dug out story of your helping in Berglund murder case.

"Now he needs help in different kind of problem. And since many intelligence people on other side have a dossier on Jack, he needs somebody who has never been on record as ever knowing him before. You and Jack have never seen each other except one week in Japan during the Korea War, and no records show you know him."

She stopped a moment to gather her thoughts. She enumerated on her fingers;

"You will probably not have to leave Alaska.

"Jack has much money at his disposal for such things. He will pay you $10,000 a month for any month you do any work on his project.

"He will pay all expenses.

"You will meet with him one time at a remote place to learn details.

"If you are in any way injured, pay doubles.

"If you die, one million dollars will be paid to person of your choice.

"Everything is Top Secret until you are told otherwise."

"There," she said. "I think that is all. Except he said to tell you that you would probably be dealing with American nationals,

80

maybe some Vietnamese. Language should not be a problem." She looked at me, probably searching my face for some indication of how I would react to such an outlandish proposition. I remained silent.

"I will be back to Anchorage on the same JAL flight in one week. If you can be seated near the same place as today, I will pass by you on the way out. If you are interested in Jack's offer, wear your watch on your right wrist. He will send more instructions. If you are not interested, wear it on your left wrist. I will tell Jack; he will try to find someone else, but he will be very disappointed."

She turned to Liz. "Since you are FBI, Jack trusts your silence on this matter. If you feel obliged to inform your Bureau immediately, Ben should decline this offer at once and you will hear no more about it."

Kioko stood, performed a shallow Japanese bow, collected her belongings and left the apartment. Liz and I saw her out, shifted our attention to the martini flask tucked in the freezer, and settled on the sofa with glasses in hand and questions in mind.

"Wow, your buddy Ito doesn't expect much from you, does he? You guys must have formed one helluva friendship during that lost week in Japan." She looked at me suspiciously.

"Are you sure he doesn't have something on you that he can use for blackmail? Maybe that Geisha house wasn't so innocent after all."

"Liz," I said, "if I ever did anything that might subject me to blackmail, it sure wasn't during that week in Japan. Ito and I did hit it off, right from the start; I'd still call him a friend even though I haven't seen him for a decade or so. It's just that way with some people." I pondered for a few seconds. "I think I'd ask him for help if the situation was reversed, and if there were no one else that could handle it. And," I added, "he actually did me two favors back in '53. He searched a pile of freshly shot-up bodies for intel info, saving me from having to do it, and he made my R & R week interesting and educational."

I could see Liz forming her next remark, probably having to do with my definition of "interesting and educational", but she mercifully withheld it and remained silent.

"Actually, the offer comes at a pretty good time for me," I said. "I had a respectable nest egg in the bank when I retired. But getting a couple of new vehicles and buying Frank Hooper's house for cash wiped out most of it. Be good to have ten or twenty thousand in the bank again."

"Yeah," she responded caustically, "and maybe you could manage to break an arm and double it. Or better yet, get killed and have a whole million in your account."

This conversation was not going the way I wanted; Liz obviously thought I should steer clear of the whole affair. But I was pretty damn curious about the proposition, almost ready to agree just to find out what it was all about.

We temporarily abandoned the subject, turning to the enjoyment of our martinis, and to the natural culmination of a three-week separation.

I marked the day of Kioko's return on my calendar, hoping I could make a firm decision during the intervening days. On the evening of the sixth day, I was still waffling like a kid caught between chocolate pie and a plate full of brownies. Liz had not contacted me at all, and I thought it was probably because she didn't want to be seen as influencing my decision—or perhaps just didn't want to share the blame if I chose the wrong one.

It was about an hour after supper when I heard a car in the driveway. There was a tap on the door and Agent Liz slipped inside, closed the door, and took her accustomed place on the sofa.

"Well? What are you going to do, dammit? Are you keeping me in suspense on purpose?"

"Liz, I hadn't really made up my mind." I paused, thought again. "No, I take that back. I'm realizing right now that I made up my mind a week ago, and just didn't want to admit it."

"You're gonna do it."

"I'm gonna do it."

"Benjamin T. Hunnicutt, you are either stupidly stubborn, or stubbornly stupid to step into something like this without the slightest idea of what's involved. And don't try to tell me it's the money—I know damn well that it just sounds exciting to you, and you want to get into the game."

I could find nothing to say; Liz could be right on all counts.

I was sitting in the bar at the appointed place and at the appointed time when I saw Kioko enter. She walked to the window and looked out, shaking her head in disgust. It was a nasty gray day, clammy and with wind-blown rain. I couldn't blame her. Her last landing had probably been in Hawaii under balmy blue skies, and the contrast must be depressing. She turned and left the bar, passing my table just as I raised my right wrist and checked the time. I caught a slight smile on her lips as she passed into the lobby.

CHAPTER 17

A Wilderness Vacation?

I heard nothing from Kioko or from Jack Ito for two weeks. June was my favorite Alaska month, having the longest days and nearly continuous daylight. June was the month we Alaskans made up for the confining winters of near dark and constant cold. We fished until midnight, chatted and told lies around the campfires until the early dawn, and slept-in well toward noon. I was impatient, anxious to begin my strenuous summer routine of doing as little as possible for as long as I wanted, but felt that I should be available for Ito if his mission was as serious as Kioko had led us to believe.

The mailman delivered a fat oversized envelope to my roadside box one Friday afternoon. I opened it, feeling like a kid on Christmas. Inside was a large color brochure describing the delights of something called "The Kivchak Luxury Fishing Lodge". The photos in the brochure showed a large building constructed of peeled and varnished logs, and equipped with a full front porch complete with rustic-appearing rocking chairs and small serving tables. Other photos showed small cozy guest cabins and several out-buildings, all of the same varnished log pattern. Two Cessna aircraft and a Super Cub, all on floats, were tied up to a small dock on the bank of a river which I assumed was the Kivchak. Several small boats were also present, and it occurred to me that nobody staying there planned to do a lot of walking.

The brochure went on to describe the conveniences of the lodge, stressing the fact that one would be waited on hand and foot, fed by a famous chef, and sleep in warmth and comfort.

'How nice,' I thought. Then looking at the cost, I thought, 'It'd be even nicer if there's a handy gold mine nearby to help defray the $4000 per person, per week rate.' I had barely noticed the rate, which was mentioned in very small print near the bottom.

And there was! Well, maybe not a gold mine, but certainly a giant nugget. Out of the brochure there fell a large receipt showing that I was paid up for one week, the reservation covering the second week of July. There was also a notice that Red Buckner's Flying Service, which operated out of Lake Hood in Anchorage, had been paid in advance to haul me to the Kivchak and to fetch me back on the appropriate dates.

There wasn't much doubt that Jack Ito had set the trip up as a means of getting me briefed with no chance that we would be observed, or any connection made. My guess was verified by a small unsigned note which was taped to the inside cover of the fancy brochure. It read, "I will be hanging around with a small group of Japanese businessmen. You've never met me. We will go out fishing together, do a little drinking, and have a lot of chances to talk alone. Burn this, NOW." I did.

When I next saw Liz, I showed her the brochure and filled her in on the details, at least, as far as I knew them.

"Ben," she said, in her FBI-Agent-Elise-Nichole voice, "this has to be some kind of scam. How the hell can Ito get away with spending so much money just for a quiet meet? You could meet in any bar in town, or on the Russian River on a weekend."

"You're just jealous," I said, "because the FBI doesn't have the imagination to come up with a fine plan like this." Seeing her hackles begin to rise, I went on in a more serious mode.

"If Jack's a Bull Colonel of Intelligence, his counterparts in every civilized nation on earth have a dossier on him, and on everyone he has ever been connected with. And you can bet they have observers on him also. If he's seen contacting anyone outside of his normal routine, the other side would start trying to guess why, and begin connecting dots to try and figure what he's up to. Agree?" Liz reluctantly nodded.

"I'm not known as ever having met Jack, and there's no reason I should be connected to him. No enemy agent could reasonably be expected to show up at a remote wilderness lodge. If one does, tailing Jack, I'd just be one among a group of total strangers who like to fish, and who were randomly thrown together at the lodge."

Liz was silent, considering the plausibility of my explanation. She must have bought the concept because she expanded upon it.

"Yes, I can see your point. And if his problem is Alaska-related, you'd be the perfect guy, the one person in the world, probably, that he can trust, and who has no known connection to him or to the intelligence community, but is already embedded in Alaska." I saw the beginnings of a smile.

"But come on, Ben—first he leads you into an exclusive Geisha house in Kyoto, now to a luxury fishing lodge getaway in the wilds of Alaska. I'm beginning to think you boys have something going." Having no ready response to her jibe, I sensibly said nothing.

During the month of June, I fell into my usual use-up-all-the-daylight routine. The retired pay of a major wouldn't have supported a family, but it served nicely for a single man with no responsibilities to anyone but himself. I lived on it easily, saving just enough to pay cash for a new truck every three years or so. I was permanently unemployed and had every intention of remaining so. I bummed around South Central Alaska visiting old friends, asking and answering the traditional Alaska query, "How'd you winter?" And, as usual, the answers ran from "Just barely." to "Just fine." with a few abstaining, having moved on to unexplored territories.

I dip-netted my allocation of 20 Copper River red salmon at the dying town of Chitina, and sport-caught some nice silvers from the banks of the turbid gray waters of the Klutina. I had stopped on the Chitina road where I knew there was a deep wooded gully where the packed winter snow turned to ice and did not melt until late July. I climbed into the gully, hatchet in hand, and retrieved enough ice to pack the now-full fish coolers. I drove casually across the Denali Highway watching the land finally come alive after its deep frozen winter. The "Highway" part of the road's designation must have been an inside joke by the old Alaska Road Commission; the 130-odd mile highway was rutted dirt, wash-boarded and cut by snow runoff and flooded creeks. I reached Cantwell on its western terminus having had to use both my spare tires, and with a violent wheel shimmy that indicated serious front end problems.

After limping south to Anchorage, taking care of my fish, and leaving my truck at my friendly Ford dealer, I called Liz at her office and bummed a ride home. My home, for the past year or so was a small single story frame house just off the upper reach of Rabbit Creek Road. It had been hand-built by an ex-friend of mine who had chosen the perfect location, a scenic lot hidden from the road by a fringe of evergreen trees and alder thickets. The view from the small stone patio built behind the house took in a sweep of Cook Inlet and the Alaska Range which defied description. The "friend" had turned out to be a serial killer, and had attempted to add Liz and me to his list. After his plan misfired and his luck turned terminally bad, the house had stood empty for several years. Since his building skills were first-class, and I thought the location and view perfect, I bought the house and moved in. And, I must admit, I found a lot of satisfaction in enjoying the place that my friend-turned-mortal-enemy had worked so hard to build.

Liz decided not to go to her apartment that night; I got myself scrubbed down and cleaned up and we dined on what we could scrape together. It was too warm for a fire, but we staked out the empty fireplace and lay around sipping wine while I described my week on the road.

Liz was unusually solicitous, generally waiting on me and catering to my whims. We hadn't mentioned the forthcoming meeting at the Kivchak lodge, but I suspected she was genuinely worried that I was getting into something I might not be able to handle. When we finally eased into the subject, she showed her concern and once more tried to convince me to cancel out.

"Liz, you know I can't back out now. In the first place, I gave my word; in the second place, Jack has jumped through a lot of hoops to set this thing up—I can't let him down."

"I know, Ben. I knew it before I opened my mouth. But I had to try—I have a bad feeling about this job."

"Heck, Liz—you never worried about me before. Or if you did, you never let me know about it. What's so different about this operation?"

She was quiet for a few moments, puzzling out what she wanted to say, or how she should say it.

"I guess that's what's worrying me, Ben. The fact that I never worried too much before, and this time something's eating at me. Maybe it's a 'cop thing', but I just have a bad feeling about it."

"Well," I said, "I have to respect your intuition. I've seen you clear FBI cases with damn few clues and lots of intuition. Why don't we just wait and see what Ito throws at me before we get too worked up. If it's something really hairy, he can't blame me for rethinking the matter."

I decided to change the subject to one more soothing to us both.

"In the meantime, why don't you take next week off and we'll do a little sightseeing and camping while the weather holds. My camper seems fine now that I fixed the damage from the Eureka fire. The truck doctors say the front end will be repaired by tomorrow evening. And we won't even have to do any fish cleaning—I brought back enough to last through the summer."

Liz considered the suggestion, smiled, and nodded agreement. The remainder of the evening passed most pleasantly.

CHAPTER 18

He Could Fly

The day arrived when I had Liz drop me off at the Lake Hood headquarters of Red Buckner's Flying Service. I wasn't carrying much gear, as the lodge claimed to furnish everything except the clothes one wore. I did pack my 45 service pistol and the little 38 snub-nosed revolver which had pulled me out of several scrapes in the past. 'Better to have it and not need it,' I thought, 'than to need it and not have it.' My outdoor clothing was minimal; if the weather got too nasty for the leather jacket and heavier wool trousers that I carried for cool weather backup, I'd just stay inside the fancy lounge, sip fine wine from a chair by the big picture window, and watch the rain come down.

"Howdy," said a deep resonant voice behind me. "I'm Buckner." I spun around on the dock, putting out my hand in preparation for meeting a strapping backwoods bush pilot built to match the voice. I had to lower my gaze and my hand to locate him. "I'm Ben Hunnicutt", I said, shaking the hand of the very short but compactly built individual facing me. I'm a medium person, often accustomed to looking up when speaking to my tall friends. For

once, however, I found myself towering above a new acquaintance. Red Buckner couldn't have been more than five feet three, and weighed possibly a hundred forty pounds. And his hair wasn't red, it was iron gray. He took in my expression and laughed.

"Don't worry—I can fly."

"Well," I replied, "all I ask for is an equal number of successful take-offs and landings."

"Can't promise that, Ben. It'd depend on your definition of successful. I've broke a coupl'a airplanes in my time, but walked away from 'em."

"OK," I said, "I can handle the walking away; just keep in mind, though, I can't swim worth a damn." He chuckled and led me over to the plane we would use. It was a Cessna on floats with side-by-side seating and plenty of cargo room behind.

"No more gear than you're taking," he said, "I guess I could've used the Super Cub. But now I can fill the extra space with cargo for the lodge and save a supply trip. And you'll enjoy the flight more 'cause you'll see better from up front. Give me another twenty minutes to load the lodge stuff and we'll be ready to go."

He waved an employee over and began instructing him as to the cargo change. I wandered over to the water and watched the steady stream of landings and take-offs by a dozen different types of float planes and several Grumman amphibians.

"What do you do in the winter," I asked, "when the lake freezes?"

"Most of us just unbolt the floats and mount skis or wheel-skis. Private pilots who don't fly off-season have their planes hoisted ashore and tied down for the winter. The amphibs park on the hardstand."

"Sort of entertaining when we get an early thaw," he added. "Pilots scrambling around to get back on floats before the ice melts and their planes break through and sink. There are sometimes a few that are too late."

I reckoned it might be entertaining for spectators, but not so much for the owners.

A half hour later we were winging our way westward over smooth air and under clear skies. Red, now sitting on a level with me due to a very thickly padded seat cushion, pointed out points of interest, at least to him, and maintained a continuous stream of chatter through the provided earphones. Air traffic was heavy, single engine craft and an occasional twin dotting the sky, all seeming on different courses at varying altitudes. I asked about traffic control, and what kept pilots from colliding with each other, especially on days with bad visibility.

"Common sense and concentration. Plus, it helps if everyone in your plane keeps his eye open for traffic. Don't be afraid to call out other planes to me if they seem to be getting close. I may be concentrating on one plane and overlook one coming up from the other side." From that moment on, my head seemed on a swivel and I lost interest in any conversation that didn't deal with flying the airplane. It had been a long while since I had flown over uncivilized Alaska, and there had been little traffic back in the 1950's to distract a flyer. The braided rivers and hundreds of scattered lakes below were as fascinating as ever, but it was startling to note the number of planes passing between them and us. Some of the gravel bars along the rivers had small aircraft parked on them. I gave Red a questioning look and he replied with one word—"Fish".

I commented on the probable cost per pound of fish that had to be hunted down with light aircraft. He replied with a question.

"How much do you reckon this fishing lodge going to cost you, per fish?" I decided not to answer; Red grinned and piloted us on our way.

A little over an hour after take-off, Red circled a rustic lodge that I recognized from the brochures as the main house of the Kivchak Lodge complex. It seemed to live up to its bragging, at least from 500 feet up. As the Cessna settled down and skimmed the surface of the river, it hardly seemed to slow. Then, as the floats lost their lift and settled deeper in the water, there was a sudden deceleration to about walking speed. Red fed power and eased the plane over to the short dock, cut the engine, and startled me by climbing out and standing on a float while the plane was still moving.

He loosed a light rope which I hadn't noticed and lobbed it to a helper standing on the dock.

In a matter of seconds, the aircraft was secured and lodge employees were unloading supplies and gear, hauling it all up to the main building.

A tall bronzed man dressed in semi-cowboy fashion strode down the path and grasped my hand as though he were afraid I might change my mind and get back in the plane.

"I'm Rick Norton," he said, "I ramrod this place during the season. You're Ben Hunnicutt, I reckon?" I nodded, trying to conceal the struggle I was having trying to free my hand.

"Welcome aboard. You're next to last one in. Looks like we're gonna have a smaller bunch than usual, but that's OK. More guided fishing time for everyone, and no worries about running out of booze."

"Not that we ever have." he added hastily, as though he feared I might cancel out if the possibility even existed. As though to reassure me, he led me up the hill and straight to the ornate bar in the main hall of the lodge. Once a glass was settled comfortably in my hand, I asked what kind of clientele was on hand for the week.

Rick maneuvered himself so he straddled the bar stool like a saddle and sat with his Marlboro Man profile silhouetted against the big picture window overlooking the river. I could swear he looked to see if I had a camera trained on him, but that may have been my imagination.

"We have a couple of Jap businessmen here—they're on the river now—and are expecting a third. And a Virginia peanut farmer, complete with daughter. You have to wonder how a peanut farmer came up with the bucks to stay in a place like this. One Hollywood cowboy; somebody said he's been in movies with John Wayne, if you wanna believe that. And you. What do you do, Mr.Hunnicutt?"

"Retired soldier—do as little as I can get away with."

"Hey, that's great. We like people here that can tell good stories when the evenings get mellow. See any action?"

"Some."

"I sure wish I coulda' joined up. Bad feet, you see. Bone spurs. Can't walk far, or carry much load."

"Too bad," I said. "We coulda' used a big strapping guy like you. War mighta' ended a lot sooner."

"Yeah," he began, "but I..."

I signaled for a refill, took it out onto the wide front porch and found a rocking chair which sat apart from the others. He didn't follow.

I sat in the sun until it eluded me by swinging down toward the horizon and disappearing around the corner of the lodge. By then the breeze had dropped and the mosquitos were forming up for a raid. The barman came outside and lit several coiled segments of vile smelling incense which seemed to keep the mosquitos at arm's length, so I decided to enjoy the view for a few more minutes, or until the odor of the burning coils drove me inside.

A buzz on the river caught my attention and I spotted a small river boat working its way toward the dock. When the boat had been secured, the group moved to the front steps. I saw a fishing guide and two Japanese men, neither of whom matched my memory of Jack Ito.

The clients posed on the steps holding a string of good-sized trout while the guide took pictures. The guide then took the fish around the building to be cleaned while the fishermen headed to the bar for a celebratory libation.

I joined the company at the bar, a little annoyed that Ito was still absent. A free fishing trip was welcome, of course, but I had worked my curiosity up to where I was almost anxious to take my part in Jack Ito's game, whatever it might be.

As I was wondering if a third drink would be wise, the sound of an approaching light airplane made itself heard, its engine dropping to a flutter as the pilot cut the throttle for a landing.

Buckner had departed an hour ago; I glanced out the window to be sure that he hadn't had to return for some reason, but this was a different aircraft. I found a comfortable lounge chair and picked up a fishing magazine, simulating interest while I waited for the passenger of the newly arrived airplane—who I hoped would be Jack ito.

CHAPTER 19

The Lodge

I was flipping disinterestedly through Field and Stream when the pilot and Ito joined the group, Jack immediately being cornered by the Marlboro Man and, I assumed, given the same spiel that I had received. There was no doubt that it was Jack; older by a good bit, and wearing a small neatly clipped gray moustache that made him look quite distinguished. The "Ram Rod" scanned the group, obviously wishing to make formal introductions, but decided that he was missing too many guests. He retrieved a telephone from behind the bar and spoke quietly into it for a few moments, then hung up and suggested drinks all round.

Jack had gotten into an animated discussion with the two Japanese fishermen, listening with seeming awe as they made casting and reeling motions, finally holding their hands about six inches farther apart than the lengths of the fish I had seen. Rick Norton was handing drinks to those interested; I decided on a beer, at least for the time being.

 The other guests showed up, summoned, I guessed, by Norton's calls. Norton asked us to introduce ourselves. The farmer was Sam Galloway, who spoke with an accent I would call educated southern. His daughter, Helen Galloway, was more educated than southern—I suspected she had spent a lot of time north of the Mason-Dixon Line. The Japanese men appeared to be 50 or 60 years old, older than Jack Ito, who was bowing and scraping, clearly acknowledging

them as having superior status. I missed their names, but was surprised when Jack used his own.

Thinking about it later, I realized that if Jack were under observation, use of a fake name would make it obvious to his watchers that he was on an official mission of some sort. Using his own name lent credence to the illusion that he was on a personal vacation.

My own name evoked no comment. The Hollywood cowboy called himself Chuck Richardson; I recognized him, as he had indeed been in a number of films with John Wayne. He made no mention of the fact, so I assumed he was here to fish, and I decided not to mention the movie business unless he did. His attire was less western than that of Rick Norton, whom I had already classed as a "drugstore cowboy". The Japanese were decked out in expensive new sporting attire, probably purchased in Anchorage at Mountain View Sporting Goods, where most outfitters seemed to take foreign clients to be rigged out.

The Galloways were in country-comfortable clothing, Chuck Richardson in California-comfortable, and I in loose jeans, plaid shirt, and my old leather flying jacket. Rick Norton, in his drug-store cowboy outfit, was the gaudiest person present.

The Galloways had been assigned rooms on the second floor of the lodge, as had the Japanese. Chuck and I were each given a private cabin beside the main lodge, which suited me well, and I guessed suited Chuck also if he were really trying to remain low-key. We were all briefed on the facilities, cautioned about the bears, told how to obtain drinks or snacks 24 hours a day, then turned loose until dinner, which was to be furnished at six PM.

I went outside and around the main lodge to examine my home for the week. There were four cabins, mine being number four, last in the row. Further around, behind the lodge, were a generator building, equipment sheds, and several freezer units. The freezers were needed for lodge groceries, and for storing those fish the clients considered worth taking back home for bragging purposes.

The generator shed emitted a muffled chugging sound—much quieter than I would have thought. I opened its door, curious to see what kind of power plant was used, and was nearly blasted off my feet by the roar of a monster Caterpillar diesel, its back-up twin standing silently in the shadows at the rear wall. I quickly slammed the door, changing the lion-like roar back to a cat's purr. Some acoustic engineer had done a masterful job of designing an efficient sound-insulating building and routing the high-tech exhaust muffling system out the back wall and away from the lodge. The constant noise of the electrical generating system was hardly noticeable within the lodge, and scarcely more so in the guest cabins.

As I turned to walk back to my cabin, a puffing Rick Norton galloped around the side of the Lodge and slid to stop.

"Sir, was that you opening the door to the power house?"

When I answered in the affirmative, he relaxed with relief.

"Thought it was a bear. They know we keep meat and fish in these storage sheds, so they'll try to bust into any that aren't secured. One big brown knocked out our power one evening—broke into the generator shed, and we think the blast of noise startled him. He swatted the instrument panel once and took off. The swat tore up the panel and killed the generator for a few days."

He looked at me pleadingly. "Please don't open any of these buildings. They should be locked anyhow." We walked back to the door I had opened; the padlock was loosely hanging from its staple. Rick muttered something about stupid seasonal help and snapped the lock into place.

"Hey, Rick," I asked as he started back toward the lodge, "Do the bears try to get into the guest cabins too?" I wasn't really worried about it, but wanted to hear what he'd say. All I heard was a mumble about not leaving any food inside, as he disappeared around the building.

The cabins were small, but well-furnished and clean. A small refrigerator was provided, freshly stocked with soft drinks and several kinds of beer. My gear was on the bed, still packed, but ready at hand. There was an actual plumbed bath, much to my surprise; I had expected a washbowl and pitcher, with a trip to a privy for more serious business. I was beginning to understand why hunting and fishing lodge vacations were so expensive. The cost of getting men, materials, and heavy equipment to such a remote location must be enormous. Having flush toilets, good water, heat, lights and engine fuel on hand for the rich and fastidious must require first class planning and logistics. I

wouldn't have touched it with the proverbial ten-foot pole—
except as a guest, of course.

Dinner was all one could have hoped for—the best of steaks
and a side of New England lobster with good wines. The lobster
appeared to have been freshly flown in, and was without the
rubbery texture and slightly used look of the average "surf and
turf" tourist specials found in Anchorage restaurants. After pie
(several choices) and coffee, the lady excused herself and went
out to the front porch and sat alone, watching the Kivchak River
flowing past. The three Japanese engaged in a private
conversation in their own language, while Sam Galloway and I fell
into idle talk about the great Commonwealth of Virginia, its past
and future.

Chuck Richardson, the real cowboy, had been keeping an
interested eye on Helen Galloway throughout the evening. Not in
any obvious or rude manner, but I could see that he wasn't
missing much. I couldn't blame him; Helen was medium to short,
had blondish honey-colored hair, and was wearing inexpensive
country-store jeans and a plaid shirt. She filled them both nicely.
Finally, Chuck left the table and went outside to help Helen watch
the river.

Later in the evening, Rick called us all together in the main
lodge to assign fishing areas and guides for the morning. The two
Japanese who had fished together during the day got the same
guide, and were to be taken to a different fishing area on the river.
The Galloways elected to fish together, and were assigned a guide
named Lance, whom I had not seen before.

Lance was as slender as his namesake, and towered above
Helen by a foot and a half. Since Sam was about my height and
built like a barrel, the trio would make an odd sight as they
drifted down river.

That left Jack Ito, Chuck Richardson, and me. It was obvious
that we would either have one guide with three fishermen, or two
guides, one with a single client. I knew Jack wanted some time
alone with me, but figured it best to let him pick the time and
place, so I remained silent and let the others sort it out. The
younger of the two guides, a rangy Texan who had a week's
beard, a big hat, and bad B.O., made it plain by his expression that
he didn't relish nurse-maiding a Jap. I could guess that the Jap was
of like opinion, but Ito kept a poker face; he had never revealed

that he spoke more than the crudest broken English. He smiled and nodded at anything that Tex said, no matter how insulting. I inwardly smiled also, anticipating the comeuppance Tex would eventually face, and hoping I would be there.

Tex ended up with Chuck; Jack Ito and I with the remaining guide, a taciturn old timer with a remarkable resemblance to the character actor, Gabby Hayes. Ironically, he was also nick-named "Gabby", not because of the resemblance, but because he hardly ever spoke.

The muffled drone of the big Caterpillar generator lulled me to sleep that evening before I even had time to think about Jack and the forthcoming mission he had conned me into. I was still wondering when we all gathered for breakfast in the morning.

CHAPTER 20

Fish On!

The weather was perfect; blue skies with just enough breeze to deflect the mosquitos that were sure to come. Gabby went to the tackle shed and brought our fishing rigs and a lure box, then to the kitchen for our lunches. He led us down to the dock, pointed to a boat, and waited for us to board. Ten minutes later, we were chugging upstream under the blue sky, dodging occasional rocks and small islands as we followed the tricky channels formed by the unpredictable braided river.

Gabby took us a few miles upstream to where a tight oxbow had cut a deep channel and left an adjacent deep but quiet pool. We beached the boat; Gabby checked the area for bears, then rigged our lines while we climbed a small knoll and looked over the countryside. There was heavy brush along much of the river bank; islands and small peninsulas had been formed by the river changing course and cutting across its own path over the years. There could be dozens of bears fishing or sleeping within a quarter mile of us, and we'd never know—but if we never knew, then we had no problems, and that was OK with me.

 The surrounding terrain was mostly small rounded hills, bare of trees but with islands of brush and tanglefoot dispersed over a grayish alpine-like dry lichen that crusted over dirt and gravel, crunching crisply underfoot. This was high country, though not mountainous, and the vegetation was almost alpine in appearance.

Gabby stationed us on opposite sides of the deep pool. His instructions were simple enough; cast into the moving water above the pool and let the current carry our lure into it. He told us to expect a strike pretty quickly after the lure sank into quiet water, to let him net the damn fish rather than trying to do so ourselves, and to avoid falling into the pool and spooking the fish.

This all seemed pretty reasonable to us so we complied, each catching a dozen nice rainbow before noon. When we both decided to release our fish after they were netted, Gabby's mood mellowed considerably.

"Good to see folks who don't want to catch or kill everything in Alaska. That lodge has enough chow now to feed half the state. Guys that want to bring all the fish back generally just want braggin' rights—their fish are probably gonna be wasted after bein' showed off."

This being more words than Gabby had spoken all day, we gave him our attention and waited for more. The only words he uttered during the next hour were, "Ready for lunch?"

After lunch we half-heartedly fished for an hour. As we were pretty sloppy about it, we caught nothing. I asked Gabby if it would be OK to motor up the river a few more miles to let us see the country, and perhaps some wildlife.

"Sure," he said. "Saw three bears upstream while you were fishing this morning. Should be able to get a close look at em if we're lucky."

"Why didn't you tell us then?" I asked.

"Well, I didn't know you then. Thought you might either want to go haulin' ass up there and spook em, or you'd get so bear-skittish it'd ruin your fishing."

We packed our gear in the boat and Gabby eased us upstream, well past the brushy point where he had seen the bears. Then he shut the motor down and we sat for half hour before casting the craft loose and drifting back downriver. During our quiet waiting period, a large female grizzly and her two cubs had emerged from the bush and were beachcombing the river bank. She noticed us as we drifted into sight from around a bend, and watched us carefully. When Gabby skillfully and quietly used a paddle to keep us near the opposite bank, the sow decided we were no immediate threat. She tugged the desiccated remains of a large fish out of the gravel and dragged it toward the cubs, who immediately began a tug-of-war over the fascinatingly smelly carcass.

After we drifted out of sight of the bear family, Jack suggested we continue drifting all the way back to the lodge. We were apt to see more wildlife, we really didn't need any more fish, and the quiet would be welcome. Gabby seemed pleased with the idea, so we had a leisurely trip back to the lodge, managing to see another bear, a fox, and the aft end of a retreating wolverine on the way.

The day had been satisfactory in many ways, but I was burning with curiosity over the mission that had spurred Colonel Jack Ito to summon me to this place. I knew I couldn't fully enjoy the remainder of the holiday with this uncertainty weighing on my mind. I decided to confront Jack today and pull the story out of him one way or another. But, as usual, Jack was several steps ahead of me. After we checked into the lodge and collected a beer each, he suggested we go down to the dock and enjoy our brew in the warm sun. That would have been a fine idea under any circumstances, and I readily agreed. We found a nice spot where we could lean back against the cut bank and relax; if not for the questions pulling at my mind, it would have been the perfect place for an afternoon nap.

As I opened my mouth to demand some answers, the Colonel in Jack Ito took over.

"Ben, just hush and listen for a while. This may all seem overly melodramatic to you, but there are reasons for it. And there are reasons why I picked you as my Alaska operator. I was counting on your curiosity and your tendency to confront trouble. My contacts in Alaska are limited, and there is no one else I could go to—that I could trust."

He looked at me in silence, waiting for a comment.

"It's dangerous?" I asked.

"It's dangerous," he replied.

I shook my head, wondering why his answer didn't upset me all that much. Actually, it seemed to whet my curiosity. Strange how well Jack could read me, considering that he and I had spent a total of one week together, and that nearly 20 years ago. Maybe that's what it took to become a Colonel of Intelligence.

"OK," I said. "Spit it out."

"Ben, this isn't a chase after some two-bit black market operators or weapons smugglers. There's a massive theft going on

101

that involves people high in the government of Vietnam, and it could be traumatic enough, politically, to sway the way the war ends. Or, to delay its end."

I was silent, suitably impressed. My duties during my final years of service had kept me clear of the Vietnam mess, for which I had been thankful. And I had no real desire to get mixed up in it now, but if there was something I could do to help that didn't involve leaving Alaska, I was willing. Ito continued.

"Right after the 1968 Tet offensive, which hit us a lot harder than we were willing to admit, peace talks were begun." He gave a half-smile. "You remember that after the peace talks began during the Korean War, more people were killed than ever. Each side had to try and appear tougher and more relentless than the other.

"Well, we reduced our total force in Nam, at least on paper, but we went into Laos and Cambodia, bombed the heck out of whoever we were mad at, at the time, and shot up the villagers at My Lai, in South Viet Nam. The other side increased its activities likewise. In short, nobody really knows who's gonna win that damn war—but the smart money is on the North Vietnamese."

"I'm not up on the facts," I said, "but I hear the North is pretty dedicated to its cause, and the South is pretty corrupt, most bigwigs looking after their own welfare. I'd bet for dedication, bombing or no bombing. Remember the Battle of Britain."

"I slant your way," he nodded, "The high-ranking folks in Saigon are already setting themselves up to abandon ship. And that brings us to the point where I need your help."

CHAPTER 21

Gold? Not Again!

"The treasury of South Vietnam possessed between 15 and 20 tons of gold at last count. Gold isn't plentiful in that country, but it's probably the most trusted means of exchange. The value of government-issued currency flops all over the place, depending on who's in charge, how the war is going, and how much the US has pumped into their economy lately. Historically, in that part of the world, when things are going badly for a country, the big wheels look for ways to cache a good chunk of the treasury out of the country and in a place they'd like to live. Later, they move there. When the public finds out, it loses faith in the government and the nation crashes. Nobody wants to fight for a government it can't trust."

"I take it that there have been moves in that direction?"

"Off and on for years," he said. "But I've stumbled into something that looks really big. Someone has started a continuous draining of the gold reserve treasury on a huge scale."

"How would that involve me, or the state of Alaska?"

"I think—and I could be very wrong—that Alaska is somehow being used to 'launder' the stolen gold so it can't be traced back to Vietnam. Or to any place else, probably."

"And you expect me to be able to sniff it out just because I was lucky on another case involving gold? Colonel, you gotta be outta your mind!"

"Just cool it and listen for a change, Ben." I opened my mouth for a sharp reply but he waved me silent and continued. "I know—I've no authority over you and no right to give orders. But the amount I've offered to pay you for just a few months' work should earn your attention for a minute or two, if nothing else. You get $10,000 just for showing up here!"

I had to admit the truth of that, so remained silent and gestured him to go on.

"My Saigon network uncovered an on-going operation that was draining the nation's gold reserves with almost industrial efficiency. It was enabled by a couple of upper tier officials in their government that were getting ready to bail out, but most of the leg work was being done or ram-rodded by a group of renegade Americans."

"How much gold are we talking about?" I asked. "And in what form?"

"I can only estimate," he said, "The Vietnam government is damn closed-mouthed about the whole subject. About the only thing they want to discuss with us is, can we get it back for them. They don't trust their own people—afraid anybody that finds it will disappear with it." He thought for a moment. "Possibly as much as four or five tons, probably a lot less. But you have to remember, gold is over two and a half times as heavy as iron. A ton won't take up a lot of room.

"The high-level Vietnamese involved in the thefts who were caught were quickly executed. The Americans went to ground before they could be identified, along with some local Vietnamese who had been helping them. I came across some info that makes me suspect that the Americans had at least one ex-CIA and two or three military deserters in their group. The gang seems small considering the value of the loot they managed to steal, but their Saigon connections opened a pretty wide door for them."

We were both silent for a while, contemplating the problems before us. Just as I was about to ask more questions, a voice from behind rasped out, "Hey, whatta you guys doing down here, tellin' dirty jokes?" The voice and the rank odor that followed it immediately identified Tex, the Asia-phobic guide.

"No," I responded, "I was just trying to teach Mister Ito here a few words of English. He's not very swift."

"Hell, I coulda told you that. I can't hardly understand a word of American, the way he talks it, and he sure can't expect me to learn Jap. We won the damn' war, and they should all be talking American anyway."

Jack gazed at Tex, put on a toothy smile, bobbed his head a few times.

"Ah, so. You Tex-ass, yes?"

"Yeah. I told you yesterday, remember? I'm from Texas, but we don't pronounce it 'Teks Ass'. It's 'Texus', dammit!"

"So sorry. Tex-ass, you say?"

"No! I said... Oh, screw it!" He turned and stomped up the river bank to the lodge.

I turned to Jack.

"You boys are really helping international relations. You ought to consider joining the Diplomatic Corps."

"I wanted us to have time to finish this talk. Tomorrow, I've arranged to have a radio-phone message sent requiring me to return to my job on an urgent matter. You can stay the whole week and get one last taste of high living before you start working on this case."

"Well hell," I said, "You'd better give me a lot more to go on—I don't even have a place to start."

"You can start with the fact that two of the Vietnamese principals— ones who have now expired—had recently acquired interest in a small factory that produces mining machinery. The plant is located in Long Hoa, and is called Terracoupe Ltd. It was left by the French, and the Vietnamese government let it continue to operate because it brings in a few bucks from exporting second class equipment to small mine operators world-wide. It's not really suited to arms manufacture, but could produce some spare parts for heavy vehicles."

"What makes you think that the company is involved in this gold theft business? Did they dig a tunnel under the vault, or some such movie trick? Why not just shut 'em down and search the grounds? And how does any of that connect with Alaska?"

"Slow down, Ben, and let me finish."

I held up my hands in surrender and gestured for him to continue.

"The plant is being watched by some of my local undercover people. I couldn't get anyone inside, so they could be doing anything in there. Raw materials of a dozen kinds came in, of course. Steel, plastics, alloys of many types, most in crude form that would allow gold or anything else to be mixed in unseen. They were receiving the gold well before the government became aware of the theft. Now, they've gotten all they're gonna get. We believe they're somehow smuggling it out with the mining machinery they sell."

He paused and gave me a sharp look.

"The only change in their shipping habits after the gold went missing was the addition of several customers in Alaska."

"You certainly must have checked the shipments," I said. "No bullion hidden in fuel tanks or tires?"

He shook his head. "Not that we could find during our quick and dirty checks," he said. "We didn't want to let them know we suspected, or they'd just lie low for a while and we'd have to start all over later."

"And I'd guess that you're going to give me a list of the Alaskan companies that Terracoupe deals with, and you want me to check 'em out from this end."

He started to nod, then broke into a chatter of Japanese, ending with, "Japanese word for damn' fool is 'bakatare'."

I looked up to see Tex approaching us again, an annoyed expression on his face.

"Hey, you guys 'sposed to be in the main room for social hour. Don't have to, but it's the way we do things around here."

We heaved ourselves to our feet and moved up toward the lodge.

"Sorry," I said to Tex, "Just trying to learn a little Japanese."

"If he'd learn a little English, you wouldn't have to." he grumbled.

Ito looked at him and repeated, "Bakatare!" In colloquial Japanese, it sounds more like "Baka-toddy!"— I had heard it many times during my tour on Hokkaido, often directed at me. It did indeed mean something like "stupid damn' fool", or in this instance, perhaps, "Texas Fool".

CHAPTER 22

More Than I Wanted to Know

The social hour wasn't all that social. The Japanese formed their own exclusive group of non-English speakers, Jack still playing the subservient one, bowing and nodding as though in the company of royalty. Chuck Richardson was tucked away in a dark corner chatting with the Galloway girl, who seemed entranced by his conversation. Sam was dutifully ignoring them. He glanced over at Rick, rose as if to join him, then, spotting me alone at the bar, veered over in my direction.

"Do ya' mind?" he asked, indicating the next bar stool. I waved him aboard.

"What'll you have?" I asked. "Bourbon and branch?"

"You called it, Son," he replied with a big mellow grin. "Generally don't drink much hard stuff around my daughter, but she seems pretty-well occupied at the moment."

He stared at the couple in the corner for a few seconds, then turned his attention to the glass that had appeared before him. After an appreciative sip, he turned back to me.

"Know that guy Helen's talking to—or rather, listening to?"

"Don't know him. Know of him."

"Oh? What do you know?"

"Works in Hollywood. Helps make westerns. Stuntman and double for a few of the big stars; plays small parts too."

I'll be damn'. I thought it was just a line to pick up women. Is he a tomcat, or pretty straight?"

"Well, I don't know your measure of 'straight'. From what I've read, I'd probably let him date my daughter." I swiveled around to face him. "That's assuming I knew my daughter had her head screwed on tight. The guy's good looking, works a glamour job, and probably never has to sleep in a cold bed unless he wants to. But he came in here low-key, hasn't done any Hollywood bragging, and seems to like your gal. I were you, I wouldn't do any worrying until you're sure you've got something to worry about."

He nodded, appeared to think my comment over, and soon returned his attention to his drink. I mentally kicked myself. What business did a bachelor have giving Ann Landers-type advice to a gentleman half-again his age who's been a father for at least a quarter-century?

And, as if to make me out an instant liar, the couple in question got up and strolled out to the front deck and, by the sound of their footsteps, down the slope toward the river bank. I swung around toward Mr. Galloway, wondering if he had noticed. He was gazing toward the front door, a trace of a grin on his face.

"I brought her here to give us some together-time, and to rinse her mind of a certain slimy bastard that I probably should'a shot. I reckon I shouldn't complain now that she's found a distraction." He turned to face me and asked, very sincerely, "Did you know there are states up north where they'll put a man in jail for protectin' his daughter? I had to plead guilty to assault and pay a helluva fine to stay outta the local hoosegow. Hope Alaska ain't like that."

When I had to tell him that it was starting to get that way, he shook his head in wonderment and turned his attention to his bourbon and branch. I tried to imagine the big old guy grabbing some sleazy punk and bouncing him around like a basketball. I found it an attractive thought and nursed it along for a minute or two. Old Sam was middle-aged and running to fat, but he had a farmer's strength and slugging him would be like driving your fist against an oak tree. I never did learn any more about the situation that had faced Sam and his daughter, but I admired his down-to-earth approach to settling it.

I stayed at the bar for a few more minutes, then wandered out onto the front deck and settled in the vacant rocking chair, wondering if Ito would join me and fill in the information I'd need to do his dirty work for him. Chuck Richardson and the Galloway girl were sitting together on the small dock, not quite touching, but clearly engrossed with each other. I was willing to bet they'd sit a mite closer before the evening was over.

I had given up on Jack Ito and gone to my cabin out back of the lodge when I heard a scratching sound at the front door. Recalling my conversation with Rick Norton about bear problems, I pulled my 45 automatic out of my pack and awaited further developments. I didn't rate the 45 all that highly for bear work—the short stubby slug just didn't have the penetration to dependably punch through the tough shoulder bones and muscle of a large bear and get into the boiler room. A pissed-off bear can do a lot of damage before it finds out it's been fatally shot. But, as Alaskans were prone to say, any gun is better than no gun.

The point became moot when the next episode of scratching was accompanied by a mutter, "Let me in, dammit." I tossed the 45 onto the bed, the safety still on, and opened the door for Ito.

"Hell, if you'd just knocked like most civilized visitors, I'd have opened up. Making like a varmint isn't too safe a way to get invited in."

"Ben, I didn't really want to announce to the world that I was visiting you." He glanced at the Colt on the bed. "But if I'd known you'd go all 'cowboy' on me, I might have done differently."

He settled himself in the only comfortable chair in the room, leaving me to find a straight chair, twist it around, and straddle it backwards.

"I'll get an urgent call to return home just as we finish breakfast tomorrow morning, so we've got to get our stuff straight right now. Gotta' beer?"

I unwound from the chair and fetched him a can of Bud from the mini-fridge. He opened it, took a long swallow, and set it on the bed stand where it remained untouched for the remainder of his visit. Before he could begin, I congratulated him again on his long-ago marriage to Kioko.

"When we were vacationing in Japan, I could see that you two had big decisions to make. Decisions involving both your careers. I was hoping you'd do what you did—she'll always treasure her time as a Geiko, and I think she loves you all the more for letting her have it."

"Ben, you've got yourself to thank, too. You knew of our quandary; even though you didn't say anything, I could see you hoped we'd take the course we did. For some reason, after knowing you only a week, I trusted your judgement. It helped our decision."

"Kioko mentioned that you kept track of me through the years. Why would you do that when we never even met afterward?"

"A hobby of mine," he responded. "When I met a person I liked, or who seemed special in some way, I tried to follow their career. It got easier as I moved up in the intel field." He smiled wryly. "After all, what good is power if you don't abuse it a little?

"Now, for our project."

He produced a slip of paper and handed it to me. I could see three names; "Katy Bee", "Little Nel", and "Debby Lee". I moved to hand it back.

"Race horses," I asked, "or call girls?"

"Just about as risky as either," he answered, motioning me to keep the paper. "Gold mines. Memorize the names and burn the note. Those are the Alaska mines which have received shipments of equipment or parts from our friends at Terracoupe, in Vietnam, since the gold thefts were discovered."

"And you think one of them is somehow getting gold bullion mixed in with the mining equipment. Can't you just look over the customs inspectors' shoulders while they check it out?"

"We have," he responded grumpily, "and all we got was greasy hands from handling all those heavy chunks of machine parts. Thought maybe we were beating around the wrong bush, but our people at Long Hoa swear there was gold flowing into the Terracoupe factory and it's somehow being smuggled out."

The nature of the mission Jack was setting me on began to take shape in my mind.

"Jack, you're setting me up against an international gang with infinite resources and competent trigger men. I'm to go sneaking around isolated gold mines looking for millions of dollars in stolen gold. How am I supposed to feel, dangling all alone there outside the wire. You and Liz'll be the only human beings that know I exist, and I don't see you galloping back from Nam, or wherever, to rescue my sorry butt!"

He seemed surprised at my reaction—I was, myself. The trace of anger may have sprung from the touch of fear I felt. And there was more than a trace of unease, I had to admit. My pairing up with Liz was probably the key to this newly discovered timidity. I now had something to lose, something I treasured—which had not previously been the case when I casually exposed my body to armed angry men. Life had an added value when there was a person with which to share it.

Jack must have guessed at the nature of the thoughts running through my head; he remained quiet until I settled down and motioned him to continue.

"Ben, I've had an official letter sent directly to the Special Agent-In-Charge of the Anchorage FBI office. It requires—not asks, but requires—him to support you in any way that might be needed. It allows you, and him, to keep Agent Nichole informed of developments, and to use her as liaison if appropriate. It requires him to keep the entire matter under 'Close Hold', not even revealed to his higher ups." Jack smiled. "That'll load-test his loyalty to the Bureau, for sure.

"And," he added, "this letter is from an authority so high in our government that he'll probably never question your or Agent Nichole's credibility again."

"Jack, this'll be interesting." I had calmed down a bit more after hearing about the letter. I wasn't to be hung out as expendable after all. "Agent Montgomery Churn can't stand me, and I don't think a helluva lot of him."

"Well," he said, "you know how to get on the good side of any supervisor in a government agency. You find a way to make him look good, put it in an official report, and let him take the credit. He'll love you forever."

"Easier said than done, Jack, but I'll keep it in mind."

"And one last thing." He reached into a jacket pocket and handed me a thin folder with an odd looking plastic ID card and a laminated blue card displaying one long number.

"This ID won't be much good in dealing with civilian police— they probably won't know what it is—but it'll get the attention of any federal people. Don't use it unless you have to. The number on the blue card will get you to an operator who can contact me 24 hours a day. The numbers are random to anyone but you. But add each digit of your old enlisted serial number, in order, to the corresponding number on the card and you have the number to call."

"I'm supposed to swallow these if I'm captured, I suppose. That plastic might go down hard."

"Well, you can if you're really hungry, but I wouldn't advise it. Just a touch of a match or a burning cigarette, though, and they go up in one big hot flash. Sorta like a thermite grenade. Be careful with 'em!"

"See you in the morning," he added, standing and walking out the door.

I sat for a few minutes, trying to absorb the information he had provided and wondering how many essential questions I had forgotten to ask.

CHAPTER 23

A Place to Start

As we were all finishing our breakfast coffee and making plans for the day's fishing, the office manager came into the dining room with a radio message for Mr. Jack Ito. Jack read it, regretfully announced that he had been called back to civilization on an urgent matter, and that a plane was in the air to return him to Anchorage. Polite murmurs of disappointment rippled through the gathering, the most genuine from the guides. It being the custom at such posh resorts to lavishly tip the guides on departure, those who had worked with Jack were understandably wondering if such a short stay would result in a short tip.

Jack walked over to Gabby, thanked him for an excellent experience, peeled off three one-hundred dollar bills and presenting them to him. Tex, watching from the stairway, immediately descended and hurried over to where Ito stood.

"Ito-San," he began, "we much glad you come our lodge. Hope you have big fun visit. You maybe come next year again— I makee catch many big fish!"

"Mister Teks-Ass," Jack replied, in slow perfect English, "I  would like to thank you for the lessons in Texas manners that you so kindly provided; I was so taken by your friendly treatment of us Japanese guests that I have given you a nick-name that future Japanese fishermen will understand and appreciate. Just introduce yourself to them as 'Texas Baka'." He dug into his pocket and came up with a wrinkled two-dollar bill that he dropped into Tex's eagerly outstretched palm. He then mounted the stairs to his room, leaving a red-faced Tex staring at his tip.

"Reckon maybe he understood American better than you thought?" I asked as I looked around for a coffee refill. When I looked back, Tex was leaving in the company of Rick Norton, who had a black look on his usually jovial features, and questions in his eyes.

Jack flew out an hour later, and I began four days of relaxed fishing under the tutorage of Lance or Gabby, often with big Sam as a partner. Tex seemed to have been assigned duties keeping him around the lodge—duties such as cleaning fish and doing a bit of grounds-keeping. As on the first day, I conned the guides into spending more time drifting and watching wildlife than in fishing. They appeared to enjoy the relief from the "catch more and bigger" pressure that they normally experienced. I pushed the gold retrieval project out of my mind and reveled in the pampered life of a guest of a luxury fishing lodge.

The attachment between Chuck Richardson and the Galloway girl seemed to ripen satisfactorily. Sam had been properly introduced to Chuck and was often invited to join the couple on a day's outing, a sign of honorable intentions to my way of thinking. I was also invited to socialize with them several times, and probably made a bore of myself asking Chuck a hundred questions about stunt work and the making of Hollywood westerns—a subject which had fascinated me since my boyhood afternoons at the Saturday matinee.

On the last day, I managed to tip the two guides generously without showing too much pain. I had already decided that the tips were going down as reimbursable expenses when I had my final accounting with Jack Ito.

When I arrived home after another flight with Buckner, one which happily involved neither walking nor swimming, I found my small hillside home lit up and warm. Scotch and glasses were on the living room table, and a very agreeable lady FBI Agent at the kitchen stove stirring an oversized pan of beef stew.

"Let it simmer a while, Liz, 'till I tell you about my trip."

She turned the burner down and came to greet me— thereby turning mine up. About 20 minutes later, I began talking.

When I finished, she confirmed that Agent-in-Charge Churn had gotten the letter from the powers above. At first he had basked in the glory of a communication from the hall of the gods, then grew angry that I, whom he barely tolerated, could be considered so important by those same gods.

"And even worse, for him," she said, "he was told that he was not privy to any information about this project except that which he might need if he is required to assist you."

"Well", I said, "Jack named you as liaison to the Bureau, so I assume he wants you read in on everything I'm up to. At least, that's the way I'm going to interpret his words. Anyhow, I'm gonna have another scotch now; I guess you can turn the heat back up on the stew."

"I'll do that—you're sure your own burner has cooled down?"

It must have, as I dropped off into an extended nap after finishing my scotch.

My first task, obviously, was to locate the three mines that Jack wanted me to investigate. This wasn't too hard, considering all the paperwork that the government required for filing a mineral claim. A trip the next morning to the Federal Building in Anchorage led me to an office that contained mining records going back to the territorial gold rushes at the turn of the century. As there was still considerable interest in prospecting and mining in Alaska, the office was active, a half-dozen men and women poking around in the files.

With the help of a clerk, I soon had the information I sought. A trip to another office secured (for a small fee) the maps I would need to visit the mines Jack had listed.

Deciding to try and accumulate all the preliminary information I needed in one trip to town, I made a run to a Terracoupe dealer whose ad I had seen in the phone book, finally locating the place on Post Road, jammed between a dingy auto repair shop and a scrap yard. I entered the tiny customer service area—a counter tattooed with coffee cup rings and greasy spots, and currently unoccupied. The door to the back shop was partly open, so I picked up a loose bolt and rapped on the counter, hoping to get someone's attention. A minute of waiting brought no reply, so I went around the counter, stuck my head through the open door and yelled "Hello, the shop!" Still receiving no answer, I had taken a deep breath to yell again when the door of a smaller room at the rear of the shop opened and a bushy head poked through.

"Just a damn' minute!" it shouted, and disappeared.

I went back into the chairless entry room and propped myself against the counter to wait. The bushy head, this time with body attached, entered and perched on a rickety stool behind the counter. The head seemed mostly coarse black hair covering ears and neck, with a big dome of forehead overhanging eyebrows so bushy that they seemed to shade the pale gray eyes. The attached body appeared hardly big enough to carry the outsized head, but was, in fact, quite sturdy and hinting of compact strength.

"What can I do for you?" he asked in a tone that hoped the answer would be 'Nothing.'

"Me and a coupla guys are starting a mining operation, need a small, cheap dirt mover of some kind. I heard that you handle a French-made rig that might fill the bill."

"Yeah, that would be the Terracoupe, only it ain't really French. Being made in South Vietnam. With all the crap that's going on over there, delivery time ain't certain, though—maybe three to five months."

He reached under the counter, fished out a dingy brochure and handed it to me.

"It's a small machine," he said, a bit more voluble with the possibility of a sale. "But If you're figuring on a small operation or week-end recreational mining, it might suit you—but they're pretty damn' crude."

"Small operation," I replied. "Keeping start-up costs to a minimum. I hear the machine is small and cheap. Easier to haul into the bush than a D-8 Cat, and if it breaks down, we haven't lost much."

I looked at the brochure. It was cheaply printed and showed a very small full-tracked machine with a front blade and a rear bucket arm. It resembled a pre-war American farm tractor with an uncomfortable-appearing reversible steel seat on a pedestal, no overhead shelter at all, and a four-banger engine that resembled that of an old Ford Model-A automobile. It was hardly larger than a golf cart. The tracks were assembled of linked iron cleats which appeared to provide enough traction to climb a pine tree if you didn't mind the tree being chewed to shreds in the process. Rubber stamped in a blank space was "WOMACK BROS" and "Mining Equipment Bought and Sold"

Looking at the illustrations, I couldn't visualize any practical way to smuggle gold—or anything else—that wouldn't be in an obvious place for a customs inspector to check. The fuel tank maybe, or inside the engine crankcase or transmission housing, but the customs people, especially under the urging of Jack Ito, would certainly have checked those places.

"Delivery time wouldn't be a problem," I said. "We won't be starting up until next spring. What's the deal on parts and repairs?"

He admitted that parts would likely take as long to deliver as the machine, but he could do any repairs that might be needed.

"Do you have one here I could look at?"

He jerked his head toward the shop in the rear, and I followed him through the door and into a shop that might have had ten machines hidden among the piles of junk and parts. He tossed aside a piece of corrugated sheet metal to reveal a beat-up Terracoupe which appeared to be bleeding, obviously dying or already dead, and motionless on the shop floor.

"That one's waiting parts," he said. "Blew a hydraulic line."

I realized that the reddish spatter and stains were not really Terracoupe blood, but were hydraulic fluid. The first impression, a live thing wounded unto death, stuck uncomfortably in my mind until I thrust it out. The machine was crudely made, no doubt about that. Welds were lumpy and not ground down, sharp angles and corners were not beveled or rounded, and the paint, or so much as remained, was runny and uneven. I was surprised— craftsmen in the Far East usually paid a lot of attention to appearance, even though the design itself might be inferior.

"Thanks for your time, Mr. Womack. I'll let you know in plenty of time if this will suit our needs." I took the brochures, and retreated to my hillside home to think on what I had learned, if anything.

I mulled the matter over in my mind, assisted by a number of cups of black coffee that didn't help a bit. Later in the day, I tried a different combination of beverages—with the same result.

It was becoming obvious that I needed a starting point, some factor that would let me put priorities on the three mines that were under suspicion. If I just went down the line in alphabetical order, I might get lucky on the first try—or I might get caught. Or I might spook the smugglers if the word got around that an investigator was nosing around small mining operations. Or more than one of the mines might be involved and identifying one would tip off the other. It finally seeped into my brain that the first step should be to find out what parts each of the three companies had ordered from Terracoupe after the estimated date that the thefts took place. A package containing a replacement fan belt was unlikely to include an ingot of gold. However, a new hydraulic cylinder could conceivably contain several, and stand out only because of its excessive weight. And what layman would know how much a 4 by 16-inch hydraulic power cylinder should weigh?

I called Liz at work and asked if she could contact someone in customs and find out if there was a record kept of the contents of any shipments from Terracoupe to the mines in question. Some hours later her call interrupted a late afternoon nap that had somehow inserted itself into my busy day. She sounded irritated—and was.

"Here I am stealing time from other cases to get you started on your boondoggle, and you're snoozing away the afternoon."

"Well, I've about run out of places to go until I get more info... and how would you know I was napping?"

"Ben, I've awakened you enough times to recognize that dumb mumble you always come up with before you get your brain in gear. And I'm mad anyway, so I might as well take it out on you."

"OK. Who'd you stir up this time?"

"A Customs Supervisor. A big badge-heavy SOB that was happy to inform me that there was no way they could record the contents of every shipment and every mailed parcel that flowed into the country daily. And I was about to agree that my request was probably unreasonable, when he spent the next ten minutes telling me in no uncertain terms that the Customs Service didn't work for the FBI, and that he had more important things to do than cater to some agent with a badge and a pretty face!"

"Is he still in intensive care?"

"He might'a been if he hadn't mentioned the pretty face. Anyhow, on the way back to the office I got to thinking. When we were trying to trace the Washtub gold, you went to a gold buyer to see who might have been selling the stuff. It didn't get us the answer, but it narrowed things down quite a bit. Couldn't you check with the gold dealers and see if any of them had bought refined gold from any of our suspect mines? Might shortcut the whole search."

I wondered why I hadn't come up with that idea.

CHAPTER 24

Nothing's Simple Anymore

The next morning, I called Cambridge Assay and made an appointment with Gene Pond, a young man who had previously given me some solid advice regarding gold and its mining in Alaska.

"Yeah, Ben. I remember you. What kind of puzzle are you trying to unravel now? And if it takes more than five minutes, it'll cost you lunch at Gwennies. I hear they're serving a helluva beer-battered halibut."

Gene was right—the halibut was outstanding. The information I received with it, however, was not as definitive as I had hoped.

"Most medium and smaller mining operations don't refine and pour their gold on site. Smelting can get complicated and assaying the result can be tricky. It's easier for them to haul the raw stuff to a specialist who smelts it to a specified purity and pours ingots to order. The ingots are marked and certified as to content, all doubts settled."

"So," I asked, "you wouldn't expect to be offered cast ingots by most mining operators?"

"Unlikely, but not impossible. Some miners try to do everything themselves, and the stuff they bring in is pretty crudely done. Mostly impure, so has to be done over to get properly valued.

"But there are a few big operations in the state, one foreign-owned, who smelt, refine, pour ingots, and ship them out. I wouldn't see any of their product though; they stick it in a light airplane and whisk it out through Canada. Let's just say, they have simplified all the problems of red tape, taxes, and international trade complications."

"Then you've never bought refined gold ingots from miners."

Gene thought about it for a half minute. Then refilled our coffee cups and thought for another half minute. Finally, he looked up at me.

"Ben, we're getting into the neighborhood of confidential information now. I've been giving you generalities—if I get specific, I could be violating customer privacy, at least in my own mind. If there's criminality involved, I wish you'd get a court order."

"Then", I said, "let me give you a hypothetical. And this is to be forgotten as soon as our coffee is cold. Suppose someone was trying to 'launder' stolen gold. Big chunks of gold, maybe ingots. He somehow smuggles the stuff to an Alaskan mine."

Gene slowly nodded in understanding.

"If the chunks are melted and recast into more ingots, it wouldn't be possible to determine their origin, right?"

"Right." he answered. "All the characteristics which help identify the origin of placer, ore, or other naturally found gold are lost with the first melt."

"OK, how would you go about making the stolen gold untraceable? You'd only have a small crew—maybe two to four men. The mine would be a small operation, maybe one acquired just for the occasion. You'd want to keep it low key. You might have a cheap little Terracoupe earthmover, but not much else in sophisticated equipment."

Gene was slow in responding, obviously giving the matter some serious thought. I gave him time, concentrating on my rapidly cooling coffee.

"Ben, I'd first get hold of a purpose-built electric furnace designed to melt metals. It would have to heat up to at least a couple thousand degrees Fahrenheit, and the retort should hold at least two kilograms to pour ingots with any efficiency at all."

As he warmed up to his subject, I topped off my coffee cup again and sat it down to cool while I listened.

"To power the furnace I'd have to have a source of commercial power, or a reasonably hefty generator. And if the gold that's being transformed is in bars or odd-sized chunks, I'd want an electric power saw with metal-cutting blades. I'd have to cut it down to pieces two inches or smaller to fit in the melting chamber. Using a hand-held hacksaw would get old pretty quick. And I'd need molds to form the ingots—sizes depending on how I planned to dispose of the gold."

In answer to my questioning look, he explained.

"If I wanted to be able to conveniently convert it to cash, I'd cast small bars or ingots worth 500 or a thousand dollars each—saleable at most jewelry or precious metal dealers. If you cast big bars, when you need to cash it in, you're like a guy trying to change a ten thousand dollar bill in a hamburger joint. Your only option is a metals buyer, and he'll likely take notice of large unmarked, un-serialed, home-cast ingots."

I nodded in understanding.

"So," I said, "nothing would really stand out if I walked into a small mining operation. The casting equipment could easily be in a small tool shed, or something similar, and the generator a reasonable size to power a camp. No big smoking blast furnace or stinking fumes to give the process away?"

"That's about it. You'd be looking at other factors. If the operation looked pretty dead, but you knew bar gold was being produced, that would be suspicious. But how would you know, unless the operator was caught moving or selling bulk gold?"

"Gene, you're not making my job any easier. I had hoped for a magic set of circumstances that would zero me in on the bad guys. Now, seems like I'll have to visit each suspect location and poke around until I stir something up."

"Yeah," he said, "and that could be like poking around a grizzly's den to see if the bear's awake. Better you than me!"

When I relayed the results of my queries to Liz that evening, I saw her jaw tighten.

"Don't tell me—let me guess. You're thinking of taking off into the bush, sneaking into those mining operations—illegally, of course—and stomping around 'till somebody takes a shot at you. That's your version of scientific crime detection, is it?"

"Well, it might not be so illegal. I'd have to check on that, but I think the person who stakes a mine only has mineral rights; they can't keep people from walking through as long as the mining operation isn't disrupted. But if I'm wrong, I guess I could get embarrassed."

"Or dead!" she snapped.

We were in her apartment, so it was unlikely that she would walk out on me, but I could see she was really steamed.

"It's not really that bad, Honey," I said, walking over, gently grasping her by the shoulders, and hoping to smooth things over with a touch of manly togetherness. Liz jerked away, faced me, and pointed to a chair.

"Sit!"

I sat.

"When we first met, you damn' near got us both killed with a wrong guess—or was it just a wrong wild-ass unscientific hunch—as to who had killed off those Stay-Behind agents for their gold. I couldn't bitch too much because I'm a trained agent, and I stepped right into the middle of it.

"When you took off looking for that stolen nuke warhead, you didn't bother to tell me where you planned to be. I bought off on it because you were working with the Army, and I assumed you'd informed them. Then, after you were captured, no damn' body knew where you were. If the lid hadn't blown off that warhead can, we'd still be looking for your body."

I raised my hand to try and inject a word or two, and she slapped it down.

"Then, you take off up the mountain after a sniper packing a scoped rifle. You drag along a half-witted hunting guide and your antique buffalo gun. I'm sitting at home or at the office with no idea what's happening, and no way to help if you get in trouble. You lucked out on that one, but you still didn't learn.

"Then, after Dean was killed, you use yourself as bait on that winter Eureka hunt. Didn't think it important to tell me your plans—what the hell, you can handle it!"

I opened my mouth to justify myself and she slapped a palm over my lips.

"Don't say it! I don't wanna hear it.

"And at the very last, when we have the killers pinned down in the middle of the Hurricane Gorge Bridge, when I finally get to be on the scene and can maybe keep you out of trouble..." she was crying now, "you ignore me and everybody else—you go galloping out onto the bridge trying to convince two stone-cold contract killers to give it up and come to Jesus. She damn' near nailed you with that 44 ..."

I finally realized that my best and only reply was silence. Liz was sobbing openly now, and I moved to comfort her, keeping my big mouth shut at last. She accepted my embrace and cuddled in closely, the sobs diminishing over the next quarter-hour. During that period, I tried to assess my behavior during the incidents she had recounted. I began to understand a little, trying to put myself in her office and her out wandering around in the bush alone, chasing bad guys.

'But she would never let herself be caught in such a situation,' I thought. 'She'd have back-up, she'd have constant communications. She would... but that's different. She's an FBI Agent with an organization and protocols. I'm just a guy. I have to make do with what I have.'

I shook my head in frustration.

'No, it's not different. You could keep her informed. You could do more just-in-case planning. You don't because you like being independent, because you don't want to be tied down, and because you figure nothing can happen to a nice guy like yourself. And, mostly, you just never think about anybody but yourself.'

When her weeping had run its course, and my own feelings had somewhat settled, we remained on her couch, cuddled close. Morning found us there, still clinging to each other, having slept the night away in emotional exhaustion.

CHAPTER 25

Duty Calls

"Ben, I'm sorry. Letting my emotions run wild, like last night, doesn't help either of us get our jobs done. We'll talk later."

She said this as she was leaving her apartment on her way to work. I, being more or less what old-time cops would call a "vagrant", had no job to go to. I sat at her breakfast table stabbing viciously at an innocent-but-evasive strip of bacon.

"You wanna talk tonight?" I asked.

"Give it another day," she replied, "I'll call you. And maybe I'll tell you why you walk so close to the edge of every cliff you come to." She closed the door before I could question her last remark.

I half-heartedly finished my breakfast, cleaned up after myself, and departed for my own little place up on the Anchorage hillside.

I occupied myself during the remainder of the day studying area maps of the land surrounding the three gold mines I expected to visit. In every case, there seemed to be a reasonable means of access—at least, according to the maps. Whether the access roads and trails shown were really roads, or washed out gullies, I wouldn't know until I tackled them.

I happily noted that one mine, the Debby Lee, was located north of Montana Creek, near Talkeetna. A good friend lived on the banks of Montana Creek with his small family. They lived off the grid due to a serious misunderstanding with the law a few years back, but seemed to be thriving through winter trapping and panning gold out of stream pools after the spring runoff. Knowing Gordon Hitch, I doubted that much could be happening in his neck of the woods that he wouldn't know about. What better excuse to visit an old friend and his very young son, Benjamin Theodore Hitch—my namesake?

Happy that the first mine would probably present few problems, I moved on to the other two.

The Katy Bee was shown to be south of Moose Pass, on the Kenai Peninsula. The map locations were confusing—a claim called Falls Creek No. 1 was nearly overlapping the Katy Bee. Both were shown at the spot where Falls Creek changed from a quiet stream in a high shallow valley to what was probably a gushing torrent, plunging down the mountainside until it quieted and passed under the Seward Highway and out into the vastness of Kenai Lake. The closeness of the contour lines on the map predicted a long steep climb from the highway to the level ground high in the valley. That mine could wait until I was in the right mood.

The Little Nel was located north of the Glenn Highway, beyond Eureka. My maps indicated a lot of mining activity in that area, most of it probably dating back half a century or so. I marked the Nel down as number three to check out. It should be a pleasure to travel that country during the relative warmth of summer, considering that my last visit to Eureka had been during a blizzard in the dead of winter.

I didn't feel much like eating my own cooking that evening, so decided to drive off the hillside and check out the pies at Peggy's Restaurant just across from Merrill Field. Peggy's had been a hangout for pilots, sportsmen, and plane lovers since the late 1940's, and there was always a good chance of running into a friend or acquaintance to chat with.

I didn't know at first whether it was good luck or bad, but the first person I noticed when I grabbed a stool was Mike Gearhart.

Mike had once served with me during the organizing and training of the Alaskan Stay-Behind agents, back during the Cold War days of the 1950's. He was now a hunting guide and an avid outdoorsman. His knowledge of the Alaskan mountain and bush country had helped offset my ignorance in the past, probably saving my hide on several occasions.

Mike was also rude, opinionated, and more than a little arrogant when it suited his mood—I braced myself for the worst, but evidently, Mike had had a good day.

"Hey, Ben—c'mon aboard! The specialty tonight is your favorite, Dutch apple."

Peggy's was known all over the state for its pies. Most of its customers, being aviation oriented, had a different view of distance than we groundlings—it was nothing for a pilot working out of Valdez to land at Eureka for a hot-roast-beef sandwich for lunch, dip on down to Anchorage to pick up needed spare parts, have supper at Peggy's, and carry three or four whole pies back to Valdez for family and friends.

Personally, I had always considered flying as challenging fate. I flew only when there was no other feasible option. No matter the arguments and statistics offered by my air-oriented friends, I maintained that the surest way to avoid being in a plane wreck was to avoid being in a plane. I might fly someplace to pick up a thousand dollars, but never just to pick up a pie.

But, as Peggy's Dutch apple pie was almost as good as Helen Gwin's, down at Cooper Landing, I sat.

"Haven't seen you much since that Hurricane Bridge business," said Mike after I ordered. "Where you been hanging out?"

"Frankly," I said, "that action scared the heck outa me. Plus, Liz got all over my case for gallivanting around south-central without telling anybody, getting my boot-heel shot off by that hit-woman, and generally doing stupid stuff with no backup."

"Did you?"

"Yep."

"Well, maybe you better refine your technique. Ladies don't like to trade in their shot-up boyfriends every year or two, like we do our beat-up trucks."

I ignored him and ordered coffee. When it came, I poured and asked what he was doing to fill up his time. Five minutes later, Mike was still answering my question.

By the time the pie came, the coffee was cold and I was up-to-date on all the game Mike had harvested last season, and on the fish that he had hauled out of the many Alaskan streams and rivers. He was still living alone in his hand-built log house high on the north wall of Eagle River Valley, still driving a monster Ford

250 that sucked gasoline like a thirsty mule, and still running off anyone near his property with a 12 gauge double.

Mike finished his one-sided conversation about the same time I completed the destruction of an omelet and a generous slice of pie.

"And what are you doing to keep yourself out of trouble?" he asked.

Mike Gearhart was a lean, lanky, leathery lookalike for the movie star, Gary Cooper, complete with Cooper's laconic "Yep", "Nope", manner of speaking. Until now, I had not seen him so talkative or so interested in anyone's business but his own. Since I felt I still had a lot to learn about gold mining, I decided to pick his brain while the moment was right.

"I'm on another project," I told him, "and, as usual, I'm having to educate myself on it. I don't know my butt from third base about gold mining."

"Like I told you before," he said, "I have a few claims I work seasonally for walking around money. Maybe I could help. Does this involve getting shot at, like the last gig you talked me into?" I ignored the question.

"Can't talk here. Wanna drive up to my place and kick it around?"

"We could," he responded, "but I've got a lotta maps and such up at my place, plus my last hunting client tipped me a bottle of hundred-dollar single malt. You could help me sample it?"

Since my friend was obviously depending on me for a serious evaluation of his newly acquired gift, I considered it my duty to honor his request. We convoyed out to Eagle River and up the valley wall to his log home.

CHAPTER 26

The Bear Facts

Mike's place was as I remembered it—a skillfully built log building, the logs peeled and varnished, the furniture hand-made and rustically styled, the rooms remarkably devoid of animal trophies and plastic-appearing fish. The only exception was the very large brown bear rug before the stone fireplace. Mike had told me during my first visit that the bear had nearly killed him, so he thought it deserved a warm place near the fire.

"Besides," he had added with a grin, "the ladies like it."

While he was digging out a bottle and glasses, I wandered over to the hearth and hunkered down on the bear rug, absent mindedly stroking the massive head. Suddenly, I knew why the usually-grumpy Mike Gearhart was in such fine fettle this evening.

"Hey, Mike. What was her name?"

"What was whose name?"

"The name of the lady you shared this rug with last night."

He silently carried a bottle, two tumblers, and a small pitcher of water to the table by the window.

"It wasn't last night; it was two nights ago. And how the hell could you know?"

I lifted a handful of rug to my face and inhaled deeply.

"I've never known a bear to use this kind of perfume." I said.

As I sat down at the table, Mike poured three fingers of whiskey in each tumbler, trying to keep a steady hand and a straight face. Finally, he broke into a broad smile.

"She was something else," he said. "In town from Trapper Creek. Met her in Great Northern Guns while she was shopping for a new moose rifle. She wanted a Winchester 338, but was holding out for an old model with controlled feed. 'Course, you can only get 'em used; they quit making 'em back in '64. I told her I had a spare one, since I switched to a Weatherby. I could bring it in to town for her to look at if she wanted." His smile widened, if that was possible.

"She said she wasn't in town for long. Wanted to go straight to my place and check it out. We did. Took us all night."

I nodded toward a rifle leaning in the corner.

"She forget to take it with her?"

"No, she wants me to help her mount a scope on it. She'll stop by Joe's at GNG and pick up a Leupold on her way in next weekend. Says she might as well spend the whole weekend here; we can go to the Isaac Walton range at Birchwood and get it zeroed in."

"I reckon," I said, "being the kind hearted soul you are, you'll save her hotel costs and allow her to stay here? Maybe I should drop by and meet her."

"Ben Hunnicutt, if I see that truck of yours anywhere on my road next weekend, you'll be driving it home on four bare rims!"

I sat down at the table and turned the whisky bottle to see what a $100 whisky label looked like. The words "Laphroaig", "25", and "Islay" immediately captured my attention, and it seemed a very good time to become more diplomatic and not tease my friend too much—at least, not until we had explored a part of the bottle's contents.

"Mike, I'm into another one of those things I can't talk much about. But it has to do with gold mines, and I need to learn something about them. Are your claims placer or hard rock?"

"Placer. Hard rock's too much work, needs a bigger crew and more equipment. It's a really big deal." He offered water. I splashed a spoonful into my glass to dull the initial burn, and to free-up the flavor. The heady aroma of peat smoke was evident before the first sip, and the mellowness of 25 years in the cask was a treat I hadn't enjoyed since I was last attached to a British Highland Regiment.

"Can you think of any reason why a small placer mining operation would smelt and cast placer into ingots instead of just selling it as-found?"

"Maybe, if they were sniping it off somebody else's claim and wanted it unidentifiable. Or, maybe were caching it and wanted it in easily portable form for a getaway to avoid taxes or the law."

That made sense to me, and probably made my task a lot harder. Just the existence of smelting equipment wouldn't necessarily indicate that a mine was processing stolen Vietnamese gold. We could have our own homegrown thieves and cheaters muddying the waters for reasons of their own.

I asked Mike about the maps he had mentioned back at Peggy's; he went to a closet and returned with an armful of rolled up maps, maps that showed much more detail than the ones I had obtained at the Federal Building. When I asked for sheets for the three locations of interest, Mike peeled them out, recharging our glasses while I examined them. When I asked if he were personally acquainted with any of the three areas, he examined the maps and replied in the negative. Then he snapped his fingers and pointed at the map showing the Little Nelchina section.

"I did put in a little time hunting in the Nelchina watershed. There are a bunch of mines up there, mostly old and worked out. I do remember that getting in there was a bitch. There are some old tractor trails, pretty torn up and with some messy detours, but that's how the miners get their equipment up to the workings. Gimme your glass."

After further study of the maps, I borrowed the few that I thought might add to my knowledge and we turned our full attention to the fine product of the Isle of Islay. Whether it was the company, the cabin, the bear rug, or Mike's high spirits, I'll probably never know, but fine whiskey had never tasted so fine, and I cast aside any thoughts of moderation. The bottle was larger than the US standard, so by the time Mike and I had split it, a drive down the mountainside was out of the question. Since nobody would miss me—Liz had put our talk off until tomorrow—we agreed I'd just stay at Mike's overnight.

We talked until after midnight, Mike spinning tales of the Alaska bush and of characters he had known, I doing the same using the military as a backdrop. We argued about rifles and knives, about trucks and boats, and, with some caution, about women.

Mike was obviously smitten—just the concept of a woman, a good looking woman, who hunted, who knew a good rifle when she saw one, and who tolerated his bristly ways, was too much for him to believe. And I wondered myself if it were possible for a woman, any woman, to smooth Mike's rough edges, tone down his arrogance and his disdain for city types, and introduce him into polite society.

'Of course', I thought, 'when (or if) I met her, she might turn out to be as rough a woman as he is a man.' I thought not, however, as the perfume I had detected on the rug was not the choice of a Tugboat Annie, or of some barfly. It was the kind of scent that Liz might have chosen. Which made me even more curious.

I was out of shape for extended drinking, mostly due to the civilizing effect of a steady girlfriend—a girlfriend who packed a badge and couldn't let herself be seen in the company of a drunken bum. I informed Mike that I was more than ready for bed; when he stood to show me to the guest room, I refused. I walked unsteadily over to the hearthside, lay down, and rolled myself up in the bear skin, luckily avoiding claws and teeth. I inhaled the still-evident aroma of fine perfume, sighed, and went fast asleep.

CHAPTER 27

Tea Without Sympathy

Mike and I slept away the effects of the bottle of single malt, and by the time I got up, he had put together a breakfast that took us another hour to eat. He talked at great length about the new love of his life, and seemed happy to have someone to open up to. Although Mike seemed to know everyone in every pothole village in Alaska, when it came to his personal life, he was a loner. Now that he felt the need to talk, I was his chosen man.

Her name was Neeta and she was an artist who had become disgusted with California and had moved to Alaska for peace, quiet, and painting. She purchased a cheap Springfield rifle left over from World War Two and learned to use it, learned the rudiments of bush life, and settled down in a barely habitable cabin near Trapper Creek. The painting went well, but, after a year, the peace and quiet had eventually become overpowering. Somehow, during the course of an evening at the local roadhouse, she connected with a young man also fleeing California and quite willing to partner up.

After a very short acquaintance, she learned that his incentive  to leave Los Angeles was largely due to his interest in certain bizarre and brutal sexual practices. This revelation, followed by an overt attempt to demonstrate, led to the young man's leaving her cabin trailing blood and missing a number of teeth. The State Troopers, notified by the EMT's who had wired up the victim's broken jaw and taped a few cracked ribs, easily traced him back to Neeta's cabin.

Their questions elicited only stony silence; their subsequent queries to the victim achieved the same result. Not that he was apt to be too eloquent, considering a smashed jaw and broken nose. The Troopers checked out the victim's California background, then revisited the scene of the possible assault. They carefully examined an old army rifle with a shattered stock that they found there, but which seemed to be surprisingly devoid of any traces of organic matter. Concluding that perhaps justice had found its own path in this matter, they returned the victim to the proper authorities in California and closed the case.

Since then, Neeta had borrowed a neighbor's rifle on those few occasions when she needed meat. Last week, an encounter with a foul tempered bull moose while on her way to the outhouse had reminded her that she needed to replace the Springfield, and had led to her meeting with Mike at the gun shop in Anchorage.

I thanked Mike for his whisky, his hospitality, the hearty breakfast, and the use of his bearskin rug, and let my little red Ford pickup idle its way down the switchbacks to the valley floor. I picked my way through Eagle River and onto the highway toward Anchorage, thankful that it was a Saturday and there was little traffic. It was nearly noon when I pulled up in front of my own little place up on the Anchorage hillside. Seeing Liz's car parked in my usual spot, my spirits sagged a bit. I hadn't expected her until evening, I didn't look forward to the renewal of our ongoing argument about my excessive risk-taking, and I somehow felt guilty for enjoying the previous booze-saturated evening so much.

Liz was in the kitchen alcove building sandwiches and gathering the ingredients for iced tea. I knew she had her own lunch in mind—iced tea had never made my hit parade of favorites. At my entry, she smiled a warm greeting and moved closer for the usual hello kiss. About three milliseconds before contact, I detected a tensing of body and attitude; the kiss turned into a mere lip bump, and suddenly a full-fledged, on-duty FBI agent stood before me.

"Where the hell have you been? And who was she?"

"Stayed the night with Mike Gearhart. And there wasn't any 'she'."

"Mike must be wearing pretty strong perfume, then. Did he change his name to Michelle?

"And you smell like a Fourth Avenue saloon at two in the morning."

It slowly dawned on me that the brown bear sleeping at Mike's hearthside was getting his own revenge on humankind.

"Hey, Lady," I said, "Just sit down and I'll explain it all. No need to get upset 'till there's something to get upset about. If you still want to shoot me after I finish, I'll hold still and give you an easy target."

She plopped into a kitchen chair and fixed me with her "This better be good." stare.

After I had calmly and, I thought, quite clearly recounted the events of yesterday, Liz sat quietly and stared at me for half a minute. The she stood, leaned across the table and completed the interrupted kiss, adding a little for good measure.

"Ben, you're just not intelligent enough to come up with a story like that on your own, and you've never been able to lie with a straight face anyhow; you're off the hook—for now. And, that bear had good taste in perfume, if I do say so. See if you can find out what brand it used."

Feeling a little cocky at having so easily escaped Liz's wrath, I felt that I was entitled to at least one snide remark in return.

"Oh, no, Liz, I wouldn't want you to start using another brand of perfume. I rely on the different scents to tell my ladies apart in the dark."

I waited, expecting a sharp retort of some sort, but Liz finished preparing her pitcher of iced tea without comment. Then she carried it over to the table, smiled her most seductive smile, and slowly poured it into my lap, ice and all.

When I returned to the kitchen table after the necessary quick shower and fresh clothing, Liz had it set for lunch, the tea replaced with coffee.

"Liz…" I began, hoping to undo some of the damage that my big smart mouth had caused.

She raised her hand in the motion of a cop halting traffic.

"You'd better quit while you're ahead, Buster, unless you wanna' try it again with hot coffee."

I reached into my pocket and extracted a fresh white handkerchief, carefully impaled it on the fork near my plate, and silently waved it in unconditional surrender. Her response was a wet kiss on my forehead and an innocent smile. We finished lunch in a companionable silence, I helped her wash and dry, and we relocated to the living room sofa.

I knew that Liz wasn't actually all that jealous, that this teasing game we sometimes played was really a confirmation of the fondness we felt for each other. But she did seem to enjoy emphasizing the point once in a while, usually to the detriment of my dignity.

"Ben, I spent a lot of yesterday researching the Bureau's latest innovations in technology. Thought maybe they had finally built a Dick Tracy Radio Watch, or some such gadget for discreet emergency communication."

I had hoped the conversation would move in a more romantic direction, but her tone of voice remained businesslike.

"We have some locator beacon stuff, but it's not easily portable. Mostly used for planting in vehicles, boats, or planes so we can track them."

She reached for her shoulder bag and hauled out a device that resembled a medium sized three-cell flashlight.

"The closest I could come was this. The government is in the process of requiring all commercial aircraft to be equipped with an ELT—an Emergency Locator Transmitter. The commercial aviation model can be activated manually or by impact, but it's usually bolted onto the airplane and is too heavy to carry. This one is much-modified." She handed it to me.

"The ELT is now in 'flashlight' mode. Push the switch to 'On' and the flashlight bulb will come on dimly, then fade out in ten seconds or so as though the batteries are dying. If you switch it off, then twist the end cap hard to the right, you're in ELT mode. The beacon will activate on a hard impact. Or push the flashlight switch forward while in ELT mode and you've manually activated the beacon."

I fumbled around with the device, trying to figure out the switching without accidently triggering the beacon. It was a little heavy for a flashlight, but reasonably portable in an AWOL bag or backpack.

"Who would be listening on this frequency?" I asked.

"It will be monitored as a distress band by most aircraft and aviation control facilities once the government's fully implemented the program. Right now there aren't many in use."

"What else do I need to know?"

"The bad news, the emitter is pretty well line-of-sight. If you're in an elevated exposed location, the signal can be picked up a long way out. If you're in the bottom of a narrow valley, a plane would have to be flying right over your head. And remember, the battery is only good for about 48 hours.

"I plan to put a light plane in the air near your location every day about four in the afternoon. If we get a beep, I'll be notified and come looking for you."

I arose to object, she pushed me back onto the sofa.

"Sit down and shut up. We're doing this my way. That still leaves you swinging in the wind for the 24 hours between flyovers, but at least I'll know when and where to look for the body."

I pondered over the subject for half a minute.

"Honey, I appreciate the trouble you went to coming up with this gadget; I know I've sorta left you hanging when I take my trips to the boonies. It's selfish of me I guess, but to be honest, I never thought much about your concerns when I was out of touch. Just figured I'd just tell you about my trip when I got back."

I was feeling ashamed and a little guilty by now, more so as I recalled our emotion-wracked evening a few days ago.

"What can I do to make it up to you?"

She stood, pivoted, and plopped herself down in my lap.

"For tonight, forget all about dangerous missions and close calls. Take me out to a movie."

As my mind stumbled over this abrupt change of direction, she added, "A drive-in movie. Let's go to the Sundowner and park, neck, and cuddle like teenagers—whatever you think you can get away with. Then you can buy me a burger and a shake, and we'll come home and make out!"

I grinned like an idiot, savoring the coming evening like a teenager with a sure thing.

Although drive-in theaters might seem unsuited for Alaska, with its long days and freezing nights, they were popular at that time. In the summer, the long wait for darkness increased the sales at the refreshment stand, and it gave the young folks an excuse for a later curfew. In winter, you hung the speaker inside a front window and a small electric heater box on a separate window. Interiors were thus kept snug and warm without having to idle the engine to heat the car.

I pulled into the movie lot at the corner of Fireweed and the Seward highway and chose a well-centered spot near the screen. John Wayne entertained us with his classic "Rio Bravo", balancing some good gunplay with a couple of fine duets by Ricky Nelson and Dean Martin. We enjoyed the movie and all the other activities that Liz had mentioned; I thought we did quite well for old folks.

CHAPTER 28

Young Ben

I decided to begin my survey of suspicious mines starting with the Debby Lee near Talkeetna. Early Monday morning, I was on the road toward Talkeetna, figuring to visit the remote cabin on Montana Creek where Gordon Hitch and his family made their home. About three years ago, Hitch and his girlfriend, a pretty little cheerleader type, had been involved with a group of political dissidents—terrorists, in fact—who had attempted to trigger a nuclear incident. The pair had abandoned the group after it became plain that its plan might involve death or injury to countless local civilians.

I had actually made myself an accessory to a federal crime by allowing the couple to escape after the plot was broken up. And I had later compounded the felony by faking information that they were now living in southern Mexico with no intention of ever returning. My fall from grace was partly because I had taken a liking to Hitch, but more probably because the girl, Sal, reminded me of another girl—one on whom I'd had a deep crush during my high school years. In April of last year, Sal had presented Hitch with a son, one they had named Benjamin Theodore Hitch.

I hoped my namesake and his parents were getting along well. They lived in a formerly abandoned half log cabin, half dugout, on the south bank of Montana Creek. Hitch supported his family by trapping, fishing, and panning out gold-bearing gravel after spring runoff. I'd had misgivings, been sure that loneliness and the bare-bones lifestyle would prove too much for the young couple, especially after the arrival of young Ben. I hadn't counted on, or even known about, the nearly invisible colony of bush-dwellers spread thinly through the foothills near Talkeetna. Some were running from the tax man, others hiding from husbands or wives, who probably didn't miss them a bit. A few were wanted back in civilization, or thought they were, for youthful indiscretions or for dodging the draft. And some just wanted to be away from nosey neighbors who disapproved of growing one's own pharmaceuticals in a basement or garden shed.

Whatever their reasons for living off the map, they seemed to look after each other and use their personal abilities and talents for the benefit of their neighbors. I knew of a midwife, a moonshiner, a marijuana specialist, a prospector, a mechanic, a disenchanted minister, and a former proctologist, all living within a day's call if their skills were needed. I could certainly see why the proctologist wanted a change of scenery, and I never asked the others.

In any case, I had felt better when Hitch and Sal told me about this group of self-exiles who never worried about politics, war, or crime—just about getting along in their shadow community.

Of course, I'd never mentioned any of this to Liz. Once, back in 1967, Liz had looked away when I decided to deliver justice instead of "due process". The fact that the subject of that justice had recently taken a few shots at her may have influenced her thinking at the time. But she had been pretty well "by the book" since the 1967 confrontation on Portage Glacier, and I didn't want to load-test either her professionalism or our relationship.

CHAPTER 29

Beach Bum Brown

I parked my truck under the trees a mile or so beyond the turnoff to Talkeetna and walked another half-mile to a nearly invisible Jeep road leading toward Montana Creek. The forest was in full summer growth, and the trail narrow with no sign of recent use. I followed it a mile to the creek and turned left, followed a trail upstream for about 15 minutes, and stopped about a hundred yards from the Hitch cabin. I hello'd the cabin, a good practice when the folks you're visiting don't expect visitors, and was answered by a male voice, "C'mon in!"

I hadn't seen Gordon Hitch for six months or so, and had to do a double-take when he waved me in from his chair on the front porch of the cabin. He was still tall and lanky, but the long brown beard which had made him look like a denizen of Dogpatch was gone. In its place was a neatly trimmed "Robert E. Lee" beard which gave his face a fuller and a more mellow, mature look.

"Who are you, and what have you done with my friend Hitch?"

"Ask Sal", he replied. "She said if she had to live with a bush rat, she wanted one whose whiskers wouldn't scratch her in tender places. Besides, she just naturally likes cuttin' hair and trimmin' shrubbery." He stood and offered his hand.

"How you been, Mister Hunnicutt? I know you haven't been staying out of trouble—that's not your style."

"I try, Hitch. I honestly try. But people keep asking me for simple favors, and durn few of 'em turn out to be all that simple. This trip, I'm looking into a few mining operations, just to see if they're legit. One of 'em is the Debby Lee, which according to my map is a couple of miles from here— and all up-hill, naturally."

"And I hope you figured on overnightin' with us. That's a mighty light pack you're totin' if you expected to sleep on the mountain."

"I did sorta hope you'd put me up," I replied. "Needed to check on young Ben, and maybe run off with his mother when you weren't looking."

"Well, there's times I'd help you on your way, but then would come Ben's feeding time, and I ain't equipped for that. You had lunch?"

"I heard that, Gordon Hitch!" I looked over to see Sal standing in the doorway, young Ben on her hip and a dab of flour on her left cheek. I relieved her of Ben and kissed the flour off her cheek.

"Good to see you folks again—you're all looking mighty healthy. And this young cub's getting big enough to send out in the woods to hunt down his own dinner. But what did you do to Hitch—he almost looks respectable now?"

She smiled a private smile and returned to her kitchen.

Young Ben looked me over carefully, yanked on my ear a few times, and rubbed sticky hands over my lower face. Finding nothing but ugly exposed skin, no comforting beard to pull or search through, he puckered up and reached out toward his daddy. Panicking at the idea of being stuck with a bawling baby, I hastily passed him over to Hitch. Young Ben filled both hands with beard and, feeling secure again, snuggled into position for a nap.

"C'mon inside," invited Hitch. "We'll talk a bit while lunch is readyin'."

As I started to hang my pack on a peg on the outside wall, he noticed and added, "Better bring your pack inside too. We got a couple of porkies hanging around here that'll chew up anything with hand sweat on it."

I complied, unhitching my shoulder holster and hanging it across the pack before hanging the whole rig on a high peg, well out of reach of a curious young Ben.

After a satisfying lunch of left-over moose roast sandwiches, and a desert of raspberry preserves on pilot bread, Hitch and Sal cleaned up while I, the privileged guest, walked outside and looked over the grounds. The couple had done a nice job of clearing and civilizing the place without introducing any hint of modernism. The low brush had been cut back for about 50 yards, as had the smaller trees; the remaining older established trees towering over the clearing giving the area a park-like atmosphere. No animal larger than a weasel could approach without being observed, and the entry trail dead-ended at a large deliberately fallen tree which would bar entry to any wheeled vehicle.

The wood pile was stacked high around two sides of the cabin where it would provide additional protection against the violent winds which sometimes invaded the area. It was carefully separated from the cabin walls by about 18 inches to discourage the immigration of insects and rodents seeking food and warmth. The rear of the cabin merged into a dugout in a small knoll, and furnished the bush equivalent of cold storage. I could see a small garden plot located to be easily visible from the front window. I guessed that unwelcome foraging animals soon added themselves to the family food supply.

His chores done, Hitch called me back inside and we sat at the table, oilcloth wiped down and secured in place by cups and a coffee pot. Sal and young Ben disappeared into the blanketed off sleeping area, from which soon issued the slurping sounds of a well-enjoyed meal.

Hitch poured our coffee and we settled back in our chairs, I trying to think of a way to approach my subject without making him feel like an informer.

"Hitch, you ever get up to the Debby Lee mine in your travels?"

"Yessir. Old man Brown knows a lot about the world, but he don't know beans about machinery. Whenever he has a breakdown, he shows up here with sack full of fresh-killed grouse and asks me to help."

"He have a big enough operation to need a lot of machinery?"

"Well, he's got a claim at the bottom of a long, wide ravine that used to have three streams feedin' down to where they merged into one. Two of 'em are long dry. He scrapes the beds of the dry creeks and hauls the gravel over to the live creek. He's got a long

143

sluice box and a small rocker set up there, and washes out the gravel. He uses a small foreign-made tracked rig to move the dirt. As far as I know, the only other machine he uses is a little putt-putt generator for light work or to charge the battery on the earth mover."

"Why would he use a foreign-made machine? Aren't parts hard to come by?"

Hitch laughed. "He uses it 'cause it was there when he won the mine. Won it in a poker game long before I came here. And, as far as I know, he only needed parts one time. Had no problem getting them."

"When was that?"

"Five or six months ago, I'd guess. Mice or red squirrels had gotten under the engine cover. Those little critters like to gnaw the insulation off of wiring, and when he tried to start it up, it shorted out and burnt up his electrical system. I rewired it with no trouble, but the ignition cabling was fried too—he ordered a new set from the factory and I put it in. Runs fine now. And I added some screening to keep the varmints out." He looked at me accusingly.

"Mister Hunnicutt, is somebody trying to pin something on old Beach Bum Brown?"

"Beach Bum?"

"That's what we call him—he don't mind."

"How come?"

"It's like this. Old Brown was originally from the Lower 48. He came up here to get away from hordes of people, crowds of tourists, and miles of traffic. He likes the mountains, likes being by himself, and likes the feeling of getting something for nothing when he pulls gold out of the creeks. 'Course, it ain't for nothing— you know that. Makes you old before your time.

"But a couple of times a year, he gets a yearning to go back to where there's warm sun and hot sand. He cashes in his placer and takes off for a week, or however long his money lasts. Cleans himself up to respectable. Cooks himself tan on a good girl-watching beach, gets waited on in plush hotels, stays about half-mellow. Generally, his money runs out just about the time the crowding gets to him, and he starts remembering why he went to Alaska. He digs out his return ticket and comes back to his mountain."

We sat in silence while I absorbed what Hitch had revealed.

"Brown's timing seems to work out pretty well," Hitch continued. He gets that sun fever about every five or six months, and he works his claim at a rate that tops off his sun-fund at about the right time."

"His gold all in dust and nuggets," I asked, "or does he smelt it into bars?" Hitch chuckled.

"I told you how he is with machinery. If he tried smelting gold, wouldn't a stick on his place be unburnt. Naw, he and I take our placer to town together. Cash it out at Cambridge Assay. He gets more small nuggets than I do, so gets a better price 'cause they like it for making jewelry. You've seen those gold nugget watchbands the pipeliners are so proud of?

"But," he added with more serious overtones, "you ducked my question Mister Hunnicutt. Is the law looking at him for something?"

"Mister Hitch, I can honestly tell you that, as of this second, old Beach Bum Brown is not suspected of anything. Long may he prosper!" I recovered my coffee mug and raised it in mock toast to old Brown.

CHAPTER 30

Fire in the Hole!

Gordon Hitch had supplied me with all the information I needed to eliminate the Debby Lee mine from my short list of suspects. That had saved me a grueling trek through the foothills, and had given me time to renew my acquaintance with my namesake, young Ben Hitch. By the time I left, he had accepted me as an honorary uncle, albeit an odd one, handicapped by a bald face. I did take advantage of the offer of a bed for the night, only a pad in the corner of the main room, but much more satisfactory than a rock ledge on the mountain. The breakfast was good, once I became reaccustomed to the idea of powdered eggs and reconstituted milk. Shades of Korea! I resolved that my next visit would include a stock of fresh edibles to enliven the Hitch diet.

I called Liz as soon as I arrived home, letting her know I had shortened my trip and that she was welcome to visit for the evening. She begged off, being the duty on-call agent for the next two nights. That left me with two lonely nights to sit, think, and plan; activities in which I had absolutely no interest.

Always one to put off a disagreeable chore as long as possible,

I decided to take the next 48 hours off and visit friends down on the Kenai Peninsula. Plenty of time to plan my next mine inspection when Liz was free to add her thoughts and advice—and, I had to admit, her advice was usually pretty good.

I debated whether or not to call the mysterious phone contact number that Jack Ito had given me, and to update him on my progress. I decided not, since all

I could really give him at this point was a report on my lack of progress. I'd wait until I had something more tangible.

I threw my summer sleeping bag in the truck, extra socks and underwear rolled up inside, and struck out for Cooper Landing early Wednesday morning. My carefully restored antique Sharps rifle was also aboard, as was my Winchester hunting rifle. I wanted to practice a little extra-long range shooting with the old Sharps buffalo thumper, and had brought along some carefully hand-loaded 45-70 cartridges. The 338 was along because my visit with Mike had reminded me that I hadn't checked its zero in the last year or so.

Being mid-week, there wasn't a lot of traffic. This was just as well, since the Seward Highway was in various stages of "improvement", all of which led to long delays with impatient drivers stacked up at several different construction zones. The projects included blasting to straighten out dangerous curves, and a good bit of bulldozer work widening the road to add passing lanes. According to the planners, the road straightening, slow vehicle turnouts, and new passing lanes would eventually enable a 60 MPH speed limit and a two hour trip to Cooper Landing and its salmon fishing.

About half way up Turnagain Pass, traffic had its first stop. Signs warned of imminent blasting, and I could see orange-suited workers climbing down from rocky outcroppings stringing the electrical wires that hooked into the main firing wire. After a 20 minute wait, the screech of a horn, and shouts of "Fire in the hole!", a rippling thump—more felt than heard—shook the truck. The rockface which was the center of attention crumbled outward and downward in a cloud of dust; dozers moved in to clear the rubble from the roadway.

Contrary to scenes from current movies, blasting was not intended to literally blast the obstacle out of the way. Holes were drilled in parallel rows across the rock face, explosives (usually a mixture of ammonium nitrate and fuel oil) were pumped into the holes, and each row was set to detonate a few thousandths of a second after the row ahead of it. That way, each tier of rock was broken loose and slightly moved when the next one blew. Less explosives, less noise and shock, and the rock mass slumped into a pile which was easily moved clear by the big Cats.

The Cats worked busily, and in a matter of 15 minutes the lane was cleared for traffic. For lack of any other mental exercise, I laid bets on how far I would drive before seeing the first car pulled over with a flat. Freshly blasted rock, called "shot-rock", was left with sharp unworn edges which raised havoc with thin, worn tires. A lot of small chunks of shot-rock were left in the traffic lane after the dozers did their work.

The first cripple was pulled out onto the shoulder within a mile, an old VW bus with a somewhat "hippie" look. To my surprise, I recognized it as belonging to a shooting acquaintance, who I remembered only as "John". He was a quiet man, a meticulous experimenter and handloader, who was often found at Bill Fuller's gun shop and shooting range in Cooper Landing. I pulled in behind to offer help, but could see that John and his companion had things well in hand. John was stowing the bad tire, and a woman was brushing off the jack and lug wrench before doing the same.

"Hey, Ben, too bad you didn't find us earlier—you could have done the dirty work."

"John, you deserved to do a little work, going on the road with that sorry excuse for a tire. Heck, you could retread it with a big rubber band."

We shook hands and he turned to introduce me to his partner.

"Jan, this is a shooting friend, Ben Hunnicutt. Ben, my wife Jan."

Jan, a big capable-appearing blonde woman, stared at me as she absent mindedly dusted the grime from her hands. She suddenly reached out and shook my hand with a no-nonsense grip.

"I think we already know each other," she said. Puzzled, I stared at her for few seconds; a light slowly dawned on me, and I took her hand in both of mine.

"John, nearly 20 years ago this angel of mercy made my life bearable for many long months in a San Francisco hospital. I don't know how you got hold of her, but don't ever let her go!"

"Well, thanks, Ben. I wasn't sure whether to keep her around or not, but on your say-so, I reckon I will. Going to Fuller's?"

"Intend to, if I don't pick up a flat too. See you there."

After only one more delay, I pulled in behind Bill Fuller's shop in Cooper Landing to find Bill, John, and two locals that I didn't know, lounging around the shooting bench, firing an occasional shot and swapping tales. It being a week day, I was surprised at the crowd—and a little disappointed. Serious precision shooting requires concentration and accurate recording of the results, both difficult to achieve during a general bull session. I decided to wait for better conditions, asked the whereabouts of Jan, and joined her in the small house across the driveway.

Jan, Betty Fuller, and another lady were discussing quilts and quilting, a subject as far from my understanding as Greek literature. Jan immediately closed the conversation and introduced me, explaining our long-ago connection and the remarkable coincidence of today's encounter. I had intended to chat for a few minutes and return to the shooting bench. Jan, however, began to entertain the ladies with tales of the Wounded Warriors vs. Letterman Hospital. That triggered other memories which I felt obligated to reveal, and between us, we used up an hour recalling almost-true hospital stories. Jan had been there much longer than I, of course, and some of her memories were less amusing than mine. I was able to see that I was talking to a truly dedicated lady, one who seemed to be able to empathize with every patient, and still remembered those she had lost. The other ladies seemed to have enjoyed stories of the escapades of the patients and the frustrations of the hospital staff, so I confined myself to the comedic side of my stay there.

Eventually, the sound of gunfire slackened, and I could see the guys moving inside the shop for post mortems, excuses, and alibies. I excused myself and let the ladies return to their sewing exercises. I uncased my 338 at the bench after walking out and setting up a fresh target at 200 yards. I didn't really expect the zero to have changed since I had last fired the Winchester, but a couple of years of knocks and bumps in the hunting field might conceivably have caused the scope to shift in its mounts. My first shot out of the clean cold barrel was a hair low, the second two about two inches higher. I tweaked the elevation adjustment and fired a group of three. The spotting scope showed them comfortably clustered two inches above my aiming point, which would allow shots out to nearly 300 yards without having to allow much for bullet drop. This was fine with me—I personally believed that, in the interest of a clean, merciful kill, most hunters should not attempt to shoot any animal beyond 200 yards.

I went inside the shop to join whatever argument was in progress, and to clean the rifle while the bore was still warm. One of the strangers was gone. The other, a husky man in work clothing, and sporting a walrus moustache, was harassing John about the use of paper-patched bullets. I couldn't imagine a bullet needing patching, or why one would choose paper to do so, so I just listened and hoped to learn.

It turned out that, in the era of the buffalo hunters, some makers loaded their cartridges with bullets wrapped in paper to reduce bore leading. Mike Lineman, the owner of the moustache, was of the opinion that if paper-patching was the thing then, it might work now. John felt that if the practice was dropped nearly a hundred years ago, there just might have been a good reason, and he really didn't want to waste his time finding out. Fuller, the gunsmith, was of the opinion that, to make paper-patching work, the rifle's chamber would have to be specially reamed, and they didn't do 'em that way anymore. Sitting on the battered sofa and listening, I fell asleep—never learning the final decision, if any.

After lunch, I finally got around to doing some long-range work with the old Sharps. Bill Fuller watched with interest, he having restored the rifle as a gift to me back in 1967. The farthest target available was a steel gong something over 500 yards up the side of a mountain, and the old girl rang it consistently when I did my part. Bill had described that particular Sharps as a rifle with a soul—it had fitted together easily, operated smoothly, and it shot where it looked. I told myself that one day I should tell Bill how it had taken out a terrorist armed with a modern sniper's rifle, but that incident was still classified by the Nike missile people. The story would have to wait.

CHAPTER 31

Hard Luck Stan

After the other shooters had loaded up and departed for home, I lingered over a last cup of coffee. Mike and Bill were still discussing bullet casting, so I awaited a lull in the conversation.

"Hey, Bill, are you familiar with the mining activity near Moose Pass?"

"No more than I pick up from coffee shop gossip," he said. "You gonna take up prospecting as a sideline instead of living fat on Uncle Sam's bounty?"

"Naw—that sounds too much like work. Just checking things out for an interested friend."

Mike chimed in, "I do a lotta jeeping around near Crown Point, Falls Creek, and Ptarmigan Creek. What do you need to know?"

"Anything going on up there that needs heavy equipment—anybody actually living on their claims and working them seriously?"

Mike reflected for a moment. "Not since 'Hard Luck' Stan Snider got pissed and finally pulled out last fall."

"Hard Luck?"

"Yeah. He filed on one of the old Falls Creek claims that had lapsed when the owner missed his annual assessment work."

I gave him a questioning look.

"Well," he explained, "once you file a claim, you've got to do a certain amount of work each year to keep it valid. Doesn't have to be actual mining—replacing corner posts, maintaining the access road, repair of structures, all count. Feller skips it, or forgets to report it, the claim is open for someone else to file on." I nodded and he continued.

"Stan was pretty smart. He saw that there was a power plant and a ball mill already set up. Nobody generally goes to the trouble and expense of hauling heavy equipment into the back country until he knows there's good pay waiting. Reckon Stan didn't ask why the power plant and the mill were broke down, and why nobody had bothered to fix 'em.

"So the first season, Stan builds a shack beside the creek to live in, another for his tools and gear, and renamed the mine the Katy Bee, for an old girlfriend. When he returned the following spring, not much was standing. Looked like the creek had ice-dammed during the winter, and when the spring thaw came, so did a flood that wiped out both shacks. Old Stan was a quick learner. During the second summer, he rebuilt further up on the plateau, out of reach of the creek. Still hadn't got around to looking for gold."

"Been me," I said, "wouldn't have been any third summer."

"And me," said Bill. "There's gotta be a better way to make a living."

"Like drinking coffee and BS'ing in a gunsmith's shop," I added.

"There was a third summer," said Mike. "And Stan found that the creek hadn't bothered his place a bit. It was the avalanche coming down from the Ptarmigan Lake side that ripped everything to hell. Now nobody can ever say that Stan was a quitter. He went to town and bought a well-used piece of earthmoving equipment, some French brand made in the Far East. He used it to dam and dike around Falls Creek until it was pretty unlikely that the stream could reach his structures, and he rebuilt them out of reach of the slide zone. By fall, he had worn out the earth mover, hauled it to town to get the running gear rebuilt.

"Made one last trip to the mine just after we had the worst week of windstorms in 30 years. Everything was gone except the iron balls from the mill and the truck chassis and engine that had been the power plant. So "Hard Luck Stan Snider" decided to quit the mining business—I heard he's living in Chugiak now, working as a barber." Mike looked at me with a challenging grin.

"So I guess the Katy Bee is up for grabs if you want it."

"Bill," I said, "I think I'll stay the night in your loft if you'll have me. I'm gonna hike up and look at the Katy Bee tomorrow just to see if Mike's lying and the creek's littered with nuggets.

Early the next morning, I parked the truck in a graveled area at a railroad siding just south of the Falls Creek bridge. Since I expected to return in a few hours, I took only a light pack with rain gear and a jacket, lunch, and my rifle. The two-track jeep road led around an inhabited cabin and upward, generally following the creek but high on its right bank. Eventually the stream bed became a deep gorge with many small falls and pools, while the trail moved higher up the wall of the gorge. The track was walkable, but its left rut had become a watercourse during rains and runoff, and was so much deeper than its mate that I doubted that even a Jeep could navigate it without tipping over.

Although I kept half an eye out for bear or bear sign, I was caught completely by surprise when a family of spruce grouse exploded from under my feet. The flash of adrenaline hit my gut like an electrical jolt, leaving me with a ready rifle and nothing to shoot. Three of the younger birds settled on a low spruce branch a dozen feet away, glancing stupidly around to see what had spooked them. I stood until my nerves settled, put the rifle back on Safe, and wished I had a rock to throw to teach them better manners.

I finally broke out of the bush onto the shallow marshy valley that cradled Falls Creek just before it took its dive down into the gorge below. Sure enough, there was the old truck chassis and engine and a pile of broken timbers, both on my side of the creek. Kicking through the lumber, some fresh and some old, gray, and rotting, I saw dozens of rusty iron balls about the size of tennis balls. A movement up the slope on the left side of the valley revealed a fat black bear lying in the sun and raking blueberries into its mouth with both front paws. High up on the divide on my right, a mountain goat with her kid was trotting up and out of sight toward Ptarmigan Lake in the next valley.

It appeared Mike Lineman was right—there was no sign that any mining worthy of the name was going on here. And, as pretty as the scene was today, it would not be a comfortable place to set up a bogus mine and simulate mining. I was winded from the two-hour, uphill hike, so climbed up onto a sun-warmed boulder and enjoyed a scanty lunch and a short nap.

The walk downhill to my truck was easy and adrenaline-free, as I was expecting the grouse family's little surprise party. I made a short stop at the Jockey Club in Moose Pass, hoping to have a beer and pass the time chatting with irascible old Dwayne Nadine, proprietor and bush pilot, but was told that he was flying some tourists over the glacier fields west of Seward.

I tried to think of some other pleasant way to waste time but, recalling the probable construction delays between Summit Lake and Anchorage, decided to head toward home. A good decision, I found, as traffic on Turnagain Pass was stacked back to the parking area on top. I pulled off, shut down the rig, lowered the windows, and remembered my first trip over the pass almost 20 years ago. I had come from Anchorage, driving an old GI sedan through a violent wind and rain storm along Turnagain Arm. And swearing that, if this was any sample of Alaska, I wanted to be somewhere else. When I drove up the pass and broke into sunny skies, fluffy clouds, and the surrounding green mountains, I had pulled over and parked in this very spot. I had sat in the sun and absorbed the quiet grandeur, listened to the music of the many clear streamlets trickling down from the snow fields above, and had fallen in love. That was when I knew that when this 90-day assignment and my forthcoming tour in war-torn Korea were over, I would find a way to return and experience this majestic land.

My reminiscing was interrupted by the sound of starters grinding and vehicles starting up, traffic beginning to move downhill through the construction zone. I waited for the last to leave and hooked up behind as tail-end-Charlie. The delay had been caused by another blasting session. When I approached the area where heavy equipment had brushed away the blasted rock, I slowed and threaded my way through, careful to avoid the small chunks of jagged shot-rock that remained. The flagman noticed and grinned, giving me a thumbs-up. He and his buddies probably wagered on the number of flat tires than a particular shot would produce.

I got home in the late afternoon and called Liz first thing. She was barely home from her office, and I wanted to catch her before she started cooking.

"I'm just back from the Kenai," I said. "After I clean up a bit, I'll take you out to dinner."

"Why don't you just stay there?" she asked. "I'll bring up a pizza when I come."

That sounded like it could be the beginning of a comfortable evening, so I put a few more bottles of Moosehead in the refrigerator and had a quick shower and shave. I heard Liz come in just as I finished dressing, swished a bit of mouthwash, ran a brush through my thinning hair, and went out to meet her in the kitchen. She was already slicing up the pizza, but tipped her head up for a kiss as I walked by to fetch a beer from the fridge.

"How was your stint as Duty Officer," I asked. "Any national emergencies?"

"Pretty boring. How was your visit with Bill and Betty?"

I gave her the gist of it, adding the story of meeting my old Letterman nurse, Jan, and finding that she had been attached to my acquaintance John for quite a while. I opened the beer, kissed her on the neck as I walked by to the sofa in the big room, and plopped down in readiness for a relaxed evening.

"Oh— forgot to mention. I took another mine off our list this morning. Now, there's just the Little Nel, and we can be reasonably sure that's the one we're looking for. At least, if Jack Ito's theory is on the money."

"Oh? Good. How did you manage that?"

I told her of my conversation with Mike Lineman, and my subsequent visit to the site of the Katy Bee. Instead of the congratulations I expected, I received an icy look, the one I called the gun-barrel stare.

"Dammit, dammit, dammit! Don't you ever listen?"

I threw up my hands in puzzlement.

"Liz, what's ailing you now? In half a day, I clear up a question that needed answering, and I thought I'd done something right for a change. I..." She slapped a palm over my mouth, a pepperoni-smelling palm, I noticed.

"Ben, who knew you were up on that particular mountain, or when you'd be back?"

She removed the palm and awaited an answer.

"Well, Bill or Mike Lineman mighta guessed."

"Guessing won't cut it, my little idiot. You could have called me, you know, before you left the Fuller's."

"Well, I..." The palm clamped down again

"I know. You didn't want to worry me. Or, more likely, you just didn't think about it." She paused. "It's not just bad guys, you know. You can break a leg up there, get bear-bit, get shot by some crazy prospector, or fall off a cliff. And tell me this—did you have that very expensive and sophisticated emergency locator beacon with you?" The palm relaxed.

My glance at the closet door was sufficient answer. That was where we had left it after she had demonstrated its use. The palm slapped down again, and with much more force than I really thought necessary. She stared into my eyes for a few seconds, then slowly removed her hand and went into the kitchen.

I waited a few moments; there was silence. I followed her into the kitchen and found her quietly nibbling on a slice of pizza.

"You'll have to get yourself another beer," she said. "I'm drinking yours." She took a swallow to make her point. "Try the pizza. It's pretty good."

The fire-breathing dragon had disappeared, and in her place was the self-contained, dignified lady I knew and loved. I stood, gazing at her and trying to understand the mood shift. She stood, took my face between her hands, and planted a long pepperoni kiss on my unsuspecting lips.

"Ben," she said, "I just remembered something. I remembered my mother very seriously trying to educate me on the subject of men. She said many things, most of which I've ignored."

She kissed me again, more lightly this time.

"But one thing she said was the most important. She said to never take up with a man and try to change him. She said that, in the first place, it probably wouldn't happen. And most important, if it did happen, he'd be a different man and I wouldn't want him anymore. And I like you the way you are; stupid, stubborn, inconsiderate, and..."

I cut her off with a long Moosehead kiss, which blended well with the pepperoni.

"Now," she said, giving me a slightly pained look, "I'm gonna tell you why you keep walking the edge of that cliff." I stepped back, not in the mood for personality analysis, and not really feeling that my risk-taking was that far out of line.

"Perk," she said.

"What?"

"Sergeant Perkins. When you first told me about him, you said that the worst part of your sorrow was never being sure you would have had the courage to do for him what he did for you. I think that every time you short-cut common sense, every time you push your luck or give in to an urge to take a chance..."

"I'm subconsciously testing myself to see if I measure up?" I walked over and plopped onto the sofa, pondering the matter.

"I'm not sure I agree with you," I said, "but I won't say you're dead wrong. I may not always stop and weigh all the factors before I make a move, but I don't just jump into unknown waters either. If my subconscious is taking a hand in what I do, it's pretty darn subtle about it."

"And you know," I added, "a hundred Alaskans take to the bush or the mountains alone every day—it's not all that dangerous."

"Yeah," she replied, "and the 99 smart ones let somebody know where they're going!" I had no reasonable answer, so changed the subject.

"Liz, we oughta let Ito know what's happening now that we've eliminated two of the three mines. Can you call his magic number from a secure FBI phone at your office? Tell him about my plans for Monday? He might want to get ready for a visit, knowing I intend to stir the pot a little. He'd want to be in on the grand finale, if there is one. Or, he might want to prepare himself for the news that his entire theory was just hot air."

She agreed, and we passed the remainder of the evening on more pleasant matters.

CHAPTER 32

Go Around!

Liz and I had decided that, if the weather held, I would head up to Eureka the following Monday and look over the Little Nel. I'd ask around the Roadhouse to pick up as much background as possible, and would drive or hike into the hills Tuesday. I would have the ELT in my pack, activating it only if things went to hell and I needed backup or rescue. Liz would have a light plane in the air each day, listening, at around three or four in the afternoon, probably flying out of the small Eureka airstrip. If I had not returned or been heard from by noon Friday, a search party would be sent in.

We added a sort of code; if the beacon was steadily sounding, I was already in trouble—come looking for me ASAP. If I switched it on and off several times, send back-up the following morning; I was going to trigger some sort of engagement with the bad guys, if any.

It was mid-August, and the weather—generally fickle this time of year—was holding nicely. Sunny and 60 to 70 degrees in Anchorage, which meant sunny and 10 to 20 degrees cooler at Eureka with morning ice on the water bucket. My  pack was heavier than I liked, as it included a medium weight sleeping bag, the ELT, more food than I usually carried, my Zeiss 10X40 binocs, rain gear, and a pair of pistols. My old standby, the Colt 45 automatic, would ride in its GI chest holster while I was in the field, or in the specially made pouch inside my leather flying jacket. The little Smith 38 snub-nose, my "lucky" gun, fit nicely in a pocket or in my right boot top. The same skilled gentleman who had crafted the gun pouch inside my jacket had enlarged the shaft of my boot for the same purpose.

The Winchester 338 rifle and a few extra cartridges would come along as bear insurance. If I were ever eaten by a bear, I didn't intend it to be for lack of fighting back.

I drove across the Caribou Creek bridge near Sheep Mountain, climbed out of the Matanuska River Valley, and continued up onto the high rolling tundra toward Eureka. The owner of the Eureka Roadhouse, whom I had met on a near-disastrous man-hunt two winters ago, seemed like the most logical source of information. I pulled my Ford pickup up to the big window fronting the dining area, shut it down, and went inside. As I turned to the right to pick a booth, I saw a beckoning hand about half way down the aisle. Hal, the proprietor, waved me to the empty seat across from him.

"You bringing more entertainment for us this trip?" he asked.

"Hope not. I'm getting old—doubt I could survive another adventure like the last one."

"I heard about the grand finale," he said. "Did that gal really blow her old man's brains out and kick him off the bridge?"

"Well, it wasn't quite like that. But that's about the way it panned out. She was something else again."

"I see you've got your camper rebuilt and mounted," he said, glancing through the window at my truck. "Reckon I won't make any money off you this trip."

"You might. I'm hanging here for a few days. If I can get some coffee going right now, you might make a quarter off that."

Hal raised a hand and a steaming cup of coffee appeared before me in a few seconds. I took a sip and set it down to cool a bit. I told Hal I needed to take a look around the mining areas in the upper Nelchina country and wondered about access from the Eureka side.

"During the past few years," he said, "a few folks have actually built seasonal or year-round homes in the foothills between here and the mountains. The roads they cut in are drivable most of the year. Some of the miners have extended the roads even further so they could drive closer to their diggings with equipment and supplies. It's still tough to get anything but a cat all the way to the mining area, but they drive their pickups as far as possible and they've bladed out a sort of community parking lot at the end of the road. There are several well-used trails from there to individual mines."

"Can I get to the Little Nel mine that way?" I asked.

"Yeah, but you have to go around or through a bunch of other claims to do it. The Nel is pretty isolated, but there's a trail to it."

"Any problem crossing the other claims?"

"Generally, no, if you don't mess with their equipment or start panning out their sluice boxes. Only a few miners seriously work their claims anymore; a few others use 'em for summer homes or hunting camps, and one or two live there all year, just to be away from people." He thought for a few moments, reached for a napkin and produced a ballpoint.

"I'll sketch out a rough map that ought to get you to the Nel. And I'll mark off one claim you'll want to walk around. It'll cost you an extra mile, but, believe me, you'll want to walk around it."

In about five minutes Hal had produced a very respectable map showing the road net, trails, and approximate claim locations. One was heavily outlined and labelled "Jodo".

"That's old Joe Dobrynski's claim. He doesn't even like birds to light on his claim. Afraid they'll fly off with a grain of his gold, I guess. Anyhow, there's a big sign says 'JODO, Keep the Hell Off' and an arrow pointing to a detour to the right that says 'Go Around'. Good advice, I'd say."

By this time, it was nearing noon and I was looking forward to a hot roast beef sandwich, Eureka style. I ordered, offered to buy Hal one of his own lunches. He declined my offer, leaving me room to make a crack about the food being so bad even the owner wouldn't eat it. His feeble grin told me he had probably heard it many times before.

Hal was wrong about not making any money off me. After lunch, I took a long hike across the tundra and around the lake behind the lodge, enjoyed the bracing air, and worked up a good appetite for the evening meal. After enjoying the meal, which I figured I had earned from my healthy walk, I retired to the snug bar at the rear. Hal had always poured a generous shot, so the bar and a bunch of nearly-true hunting stories kept me and several other stool-sitters busy until an early bedtime.

I was up pretty early the next morning, largely due to a couple of locals dropping by for breakfast. Their presence didn't bother me, but they were of the young school that believed in demonstrating their stud-hood by buying the biggest, loudest one-ton four-wheel-drive diesel pick-up trucks available. And, somehow, they had convinced themselves that the trucks burned less fuel and lasted longer if you never shut them down. I lay in my homebuilt camper listening to the rumble and clatter of a monster truck idling on either side, their diesel exhaust fumes beginning to seep into my breathing space.

I gave up, got up, dressed, and moved my truck away from the stud-rigs. Breakfast was taken as far from the yakking truck drivers as I could arrange; they finally left in a cloud of stinking black smoke, and I took my coffee at leisure.

The air was crispy clear and in the high forties when I fired up the Ford and drove west toward Glennallen. I found a well-maintained dirt road about where Hal had said it would be and turned north, hoping it would stay this good all the way to the end. During the first five miles, following the earth's contours but gaining altitude all the way, I passed a few side drives leading to various residences tucked back into the foothills. They were of typical farmhouse construction, neatly painted and with the typical ranch house clutter of pickups, snow plows, and assorted broken machinery scattered about.

As the homes thinned out, the road deteriorated accordingly, seemingly kept in barely good enough repair to be usable. It skirted around low-lying boggy areas, many made more boggy by drivers who assumed that horsepower and momentum would always overcome mud. Their efforts to dig themselves out afterward usually left an impassable morass. The road crested ridgetops which presented a view of a rolling sea of tundra off to the right, and rising foothills leaning against the craggy mountains silhouetted to the left. As it led into the foothills, it diminished, reduced by washouts, ruts, and potholes to a Jeep trail. Finally, it ended on a rocky flat overlooking several small valleys and stream beds.

Two pickups were parked near the rim of the flat area, both facing back down the track in a ready-to-go attitude. A battered surplus military Jeep, still wearing its olive drab war paint, was covered by a tightly tied tarp and parked the same way. I turned the Ford around and parked facing back—if it was local custom, I thought, there was probable a good reason, and I might as well go along with it.

Out of curiosity, I walked over to the Jeep to see if the bumper markings were still legible. They were: a "2" and a triangle followed by "16FA" on the off-side and "B-1" on the driver's side. Shaking off the memories of decades past, I got out the sketch map that Hal had provided and chose the trail that should eventually lead me to the Little Nel mine.

The trail, more than a footpath but less than a Jeep track, skirted the high edge of a wide valley in which were a complex of smaller valleys and gullies. The trail afforded a view of many square miles of mostly open country, green vegetation following many of the stream bottoms and small gullies. Raw earth and rocks showed in places where extensive placer and hydraulic operations had once stripped the surface bare. I could see signs of old diggings and a few shacks scattered throughout the area, but nothing indicating current activity.

I passed several trails which branched off the main track and probably led to claims in the valley bottom. Finally, I reached the spot Hal had warned me of; the track kept straight on, but a sign pointing to a side trail read, "Go Around!" I fully intended to do so, but the main track seemed to lead up and over an outcropping which provided an inviting panoramic view of the entire valley. I had stepped forward a few paces, binoculars in hand, when the sharp smack of a bullet striking rock, followed by the echoing boom of a high-powered rifle, drove me into the dirt as though I were back on Hill 672, in Korea.

CHAPTER 33

The Diggings

I lay there quietly for 30 seconds or so, then looked around to see where the bullet had gone. A roundish rock, about 36 inches in diameter and with a flat face, was 20 feet to my right. A fresh white scar and smear of rock dust was plastered almost in its center. Other older bullet scars hinted of previous warning shots—and they were pretty well centered also.

I very slowly stood up and retrieved my binoculars. As I stood, trying to grasp the situation and decide what I should do next, I faintly heard the double "click-clack" of a bolt action rifle chambering a fresh round. I raised my hand in farewell, retreated to the side trail, and went around.

I never knew whether old Joe Dobrynski was guarding a real treasure-trove of gold, or if he just got his jollies by scaring the bejabbers out of passing hikers. I decided it would not be polite to go down and ask him.

Hal wasn't kidding when he said going around would cost an extra mile; it was mostly uphill, and I was winded when I reached the point where the bypass trail rejoined the main track. There I

saw another set of signs facing the opposite way and another round rock spattered with bullet marks. I wondered how old Joe ever got any work done if he spent all his time guarding his borders.

The next sign of civilization was a square four-by-four post set in the ground beside the track. It had a Mason jar lid nailed upside down on the top with an upside-down glass jar tightly screwed down on it.

Inside the jar was some paperwork which I guessed contained information regarding a claim. "Hard Times No. 2" and "NE" were stamped into the wood of the post. A few hundred yards further down the track, a small weather-beaten shack came into view. Recalling the reception I had received at the last claim, I stopped and looked the place over. When I noticed smoke coming from a battered tin chimney, I decided to take a chance.

"Hello, the cabin!"

After a few moments the door swung open. I had expected to see some scruffy old man with a weathered face and shaggy beard, possibly with a shotgun in the crook of his arm; instead, I saw a man in his thirties, short haired, clean shaven, and wearing clean khaki trousers beneath a wool plaid shirt. He beckoned with his left hand, his right holding a large book with his thumb marking his place.

"C'mon in. Coffee's hot!"

My morning's drive and walk having taken me well into what my stomach claimed was lunchtime, I happily obeyed and secretly hoped there was a little something to accompany the coffee.

Despite its shabby outward appearance, the interior was as nicely appointed as any gentleman's hideaway. Sheet rock had been added over extra insulation, the floor was carpeted, nearly full bookcases covered about half the walls, and a few good paintings and prints hung in between. A very small kitchen occupied an alcove in the rear and a matching alcove, curtained off, probably contained a bedroom.

I unslung my rifle and pack, leaned them against the wall, put out a hand and introduced myself. My host did likewise, seated me at the small kitchen table and poured a cup for each of us. His name was Robert Higgens, his vocation, professor of literature at the University of Alaska in Anchorage. My eyebrows must have shot up at this revelation, as he laughed and began to explain.

"Oh, I'm a gold miner too, just not an enthusiastic one. I bought this claim a few years ago from an heir of the original owner. Liked the location, the peace and quiet, and the fact that I could work the gravel one or two days a week in the summer and find enough gold to pay for groceries. I mostly read, write enough to stay in the good graces of the College, and work the stream when I run low on money." He made a sweeping gesture toward the books and paintings.

"I brought this stuff in a little at a time, made the interior comfortable, left the outside shacky to discourage thieves." He grinned. "Of course, the kind of people who would rob miners' cabins probably wouldn't know what to do with books anyway."

"I wondered when we shook hands," I said. "Not many professorial types have calloused hands and a red neck from working out in the sun."

A mouth-watering aroma began to make itself known. My thoughts were distracted as I looked around for its source. Higgens noticed and apologized.

"That's multi-critter stew. I turned the heat up when I heard your holler—should be ready in a minute or so."

"Thanks. Didn't want to be rude, but that 'whatzit' stew tripped all my hungry switches at once. What's in it?"

"You might not want to know," he said. "Basically, whatever wanders by when I have a gun handy. I'll pop a grouse, rabbit, rock chuck, parka squirrel, or caribou. Chop it up and throw it into the stew pot with some seasoning and a few vegetables—let it simmer and add to it when it gets low. I hardly ever have to do any real cooking, and it keeps me going pretty well."

We both took generous helpings without seriously depleting the large stew pot, and I came back for seconds. A more tasty and filling meal wasn't to be had outside of the Club Paris steakhouse.

"What brings you to these diggings?" he asked. "You don't have the look of a prospector, and the good claims are all taken anyway. Hunters generally stick closer to roads and trails that make it easy to haul out their meat. You're not Fish & Game—I know all the local 'fish and feathers' people."

"I'd guess you'd say I'm sort of a government man," I answered, not wanting to stray too far from the truth. "This watershed, between the two mountain masses, has been mined since before WW1. Has its ups and downs, but somebody always seems to be working it. My boss wants me to do an informal survey to get an idea how many claims are being seriously worked, how many are hobby or recreational claims, and how many are abandoned."

"Well, if you expect to walk to each one, you'd better be carrying rations for a month. If you can accept word-of-mouth from a guy who lives here, I can tell you about most of 'em."

"Talking beats walking," I replied. "Be grateful for any info you can give me, especially if it saves hiking. And I don't need any more Winchester detours if I can avoid them."

"Yeah, I heard the shot a while ago. That's when I put the coffee on. If I'd heard two or three, I'd have gone to check if anybody was hurt."

"Well, that would have been kind of you, I guess; ever have to do that?"

"Only once. Feller got upset about being shot at. Went onto the Jodo to root the old man out. There was a bit of gunfire—the intruder came back out a little on the shaky side; said he crawled around in the rocks for an hour and never laid eyes on old Joe. But every time he paused to rest and look around, a bullet kicked dirt or rock chips on him. He finally figured out that the old guy was playing, could have popped him at any time—said he slung his rifle, held up both hands, and got the hell off the Jodo."

"Now I know that talking is better than walking!" I said. "Let's talk."

Higgens went over to one of his book shelves and pulled out a roll of maps. He thumbed through them and extracted one, which he flattened out on the table.

"This may be worth a thousand words," he said, weighting the corners with various pieces of tableware. "Pretty well shows the whole watershed, and I sketched out the claims when I was considering buying the Hard Times.

"Now the next two claims up from me are the Jolly Boys." He pointed to a pair of rectangles penciled on the map. "A pair of brothers named Jolly acquired them—named 'em Jolly Boys Number One and Two. About ten years ago, I'm told, one Jolly brought a woman to his claim. Wife or girlfriend, nobody knows. In any case, she was the catalyst for an argument that led to a gunfight. One Jolly died, the other ran, and the woman took their stash of gold and disappeared. The claims are abandoned, but someone was looking them over last summer."

He moved his finger over to another site and gave a thumbnail description of its status, not nearly so interesting as the Jolly Boys' tale.

Claim by claim, Higgens located and described the other mining operations on his map. None was of particular interest to me, of course, until he got to the Little Nel, but I made notes for appearance' sake, and in case of future need.

"Now, I don't know much about this one," he said, pointing at last to the Nel. "Vacant until about two years ago, and appeared to have been long abandoned. A party helicoptered in last year, looked it over for a day, and left. Came back a week or so later and started setting up for business. I never did see 'em do any sampling or pick work—it was like they knew in advance there was pay. Anyhow, they brought in a couple of prefab buildings and tool shed, a sort of crude tracked earthmover, and they've been there ever since."

"Big crew?" I asked.

"Not really. The few times I've seen 'em were just when I was hiking around hunting or looking for new scenery. One guy in charge. Never told me his name—didn't tried to run me off, but kept a tight eye on me while I was passing through. Another man, really fat, looked Asian or maybe Alaskan native; seemed like he was doing the dirty work. Some women's clothing hanging on a clothesline, but I never saw 'em."

"They doing any mining at all?"

"Not much that I could see. But they don't seem to ever leave the claim—all their supplies and groceries come in by helicopter, usually about every two weeks. The little draw that their creek runs through leads into some nice woods and on up into alpine country, but they hardly ever wander out of their claim area."

He stared at me thoughtfully. "Something about the Little Nel interests you, Ben. What did you say you did for the government?"

I side-stepped his question with one of my own.

"Who belongs to the three rigs I saw parked at the end of the trail?"

"The Jeep's mine. The pickups to some of the other claimholders hereabouts. I don't know which. You didn't answer my question."

"Ain't gonna," I replied. "I like your Jeep. It served in the 2nd Armored Division with me, Germany, 1955. I might even have known the lieutenant who used it. Damn' small world."

"OK," he said. "Be coy if you must. As to the Jeep, I picked it up from a homesteader who was calling it quits. No idea where or when he bought it. I liked it because it has character, and it has the personality of a stubborn old veteran—it'll try anything you ask of it, and generally gets the job done." He gave me a queer look.

"How would you know that a particular lieutenant used it?"

"The bumper markings. The '2' and the triangle stand for the Second Armored Division. '16FA' is for the Sixteenth Field Artillery Battalion. 'B-1' indicates that it was assigned to the Battery Commander of B Battery, 16th Field Artillery Battalion, 2nd Armored Division. They were a 155mm towed artillery outfit stationed at Baumholder, Germany, during the Cold War. I knew a few of its officers, including a first lieutenant who had B Battery at one time. Of course, the Jeep could have been transferred between any number of units, but it pleases me to think that Dick Gulick may have ridden in it."

I reached for my pack, slinging it and my rifle, and shook hands again with Higgens.

"Thanks again for the chow and the hospitality. And that info about the gold diggings hereabouts will save me a lot of time and hiking."

"If you're nearby come evening, feel free to drop by and bunk on a warm floor. I doubt you'll make it back to your rig by then— the Nel's a good hour or two from here and I have an idea that you're especially interested in it for some reason."

I didn't answer, but smiled, clapped him on the shoulder, and pointed myself back toward the trail.

CHAPTER 34

The Little Nel

The trail more or less paralleled the valley floor, keeping high enough on the valley wall that I could look down on the various shacks, some simple and some quite elaborate, that marked the claims. The decades of mining work that had stripped the vegetation and top soil from much of the valley bottom left the signs of human activity easily visible. The Nel, according to Higgens' map, was the last claim at the head of the wide valley. It was bracketed on the north and south by the flanks of the mountains which formed the valley, and on its east by the rising terrain at the head of the valley. After an hour and a half of hiking, I was within sight of my goal.

One of the pre-fab houses that Higgens had mentioned was about 75 yards from the tree line which formed the north border of the claim. A similar, but smaller, structure sat a little to the south of the main building, a roughly made storage or tool shed located slightly beyond it. I saw a dilapidated sluice box and a small rocker near a little creek which tumbled out of the bush and joined the larger stream which watered most of the claims in the

valley. A Terracoupe earth-mover sat idle near the tool shed, and the outhouse a hundred yards further to the south. There was no sign of activity and no smoke issuing from the chimney pipe of either house.

I decided to approach the site through the woods, probably due to some lingering infantryman's instinct to remain in cover as long as possible. I moved up to my right, entering the brush and, almost at once, stumbled onto a partly overgrown trail leading uphill from the mining site. I turned downhill toward the tree line, stopping as I stepped out of the trees and into the open, facing the house. I could now see why there was no chimney smoke; a large propane tank was mounted behind each pre-fab, neatly solving the problems of firewood, cooking stoves, cabin heat, and other such Boy Scout-related chores that come with camping in the wild. All their needs must be delivered by helicopter, I thought—no wheeled vehicle large enough to haul those propane tanks could navigate the inbound trails.

"Hello the house!" I called. There was no reply. I waited a decent interval and began walking down toward the building. When I was about half way, the front door opened and a man stepped out pulling on his jacket.

"Howdy. What can I do for you?"

I could see that his shirt was unbuttoned beneath the jacket, and an untidy bulge hinted at a handgun stuffed in his belt above the right hip.

"Just passing through—hoped maybe your coffee pot was on. I've walked a bit today, and it's getting late."

"Sorry, buddy. You woke me from a nap, and the stove's cold." I could see that the nap part was probably correct—his hair was mussed and he was barefoot.

"Any place I could lay my sleeping bag for the night? Doesn't have to be warm, as long as it's dry."

"Sorry again. My, er, wife and I pretty well fill this place, and my helper over yonder," he waved toward the smaller building, "has his wife with him too." I glanced toward the second building and saw a very obese man standing in the doorway. There was a flicker of motion in the window behind him.

"There's no one working the next claim to the west," he continued. "Maybe you could use the shack there. Just stay clear of my place. We don't need tourists here." He stepped back inside and closed the door.

As I stood and thought about the conversation, I had an odd feeling I had seen the man before, that I should know him. His appearance was quite ordinary with the exception of a bushy head of very black hair and a high intellectual-appearing forehead. He seemed average in height, maybe a tad lazy if he was napping when he should have been digging, but nothing special

170

enough to ring my bell. I turned about and made my way back up the trail, scouting the area in preparation for my spying activities later in the evening.

Actually, there was nothing in the man's actions to make me suspicious. Living out here in the boonies, it would be normal to greet a stranger with caution and a pistol within easy reach—especially if one had several women in his care. Firing up the coffee pot on no notice would be an annoyance, and I couldn't blame him for balking at that suggestion. And with women to care for, why let a stranger sleep in your midst?

But one thing had triggered my suspicion—there was absolutely no sign that any mining, hard rock or placer, had been done in months or years. The Little Nel was the only operation that had not been eliminated from the list of suspects furnished by Jack Ito, and it had ordered and received Terracoupe parts from Vietnam. And, if they were importing and reconfiguring gold for resale, they really wouldn't need to mine their own. I needed to get a close look at that Terracoupe…

Terracoupe-- that was it! The miner I had just met reminded me strongly of the proprietor of the "Womack Brothers" Terracoupe dealership in Anchorage. The resemblance was close enough that he might well be the other Womack.

My reflections distracted me enough that I almost walked into the side of a crude log shack half covered with brush and moss. The tin roof was rusty and pulled away from the structure in places. The log walls were still stout, but had shifted with time and weather so that the heavy door was jammed shut. The shack was only about six feet square, and there was no window to give any clue as to what might be inside. A hint developed, however, when I noticed a faded sign over the door stating in no uncertain terms, "No Smoking Dammit".

I was pretty sure that I had come upon an old dynamite storage magazine, probably one left over from the hopes and dreams of a much earlier prospector. Circling the structure, I found a stack of rusty hand tools leaning against the back wall. Extracting an old drill point from the weeds and grass that had grown up around it, I moved back to the door and found a good pry-point. Using the drill as a crowbar, I found it easy to move the latch bar and pop the door open.

My guess proved correct; two cases of Du Pont 40% Dynamite lay in the far corner, one case full and the other half empty; a roll of fuse and a box of blasting caps were stored on one of several wood shelves nailed to the wall above it. The shack showed no sign that it had been entered for years, although nesting material from some sort of rodent family was scattered about. When I checked out the explosives, I found the caps dry and apparently serviceable, the orange coated safety fuse the same.

The dynamite was another matter. The eight inch sticks had been carelessly tossed into the opened box, some having had their heavy brown oiled paper coverings punctured or torn. The lower portions of the box itself were darkened and the wood appeared oil-soaked—but I knew it was not oil that had caused the discoloration. The manufacturing date stamped on the end of the wooden dynamite box was "AUG 20 1953", about the time I was drifting around in a hospital ship in Inchon harbor.

Dynamite is really nothing but liquid nitroglycerine soaked into an absorbent material, clay or other similar binder, to give it body and to blunt the extreme sensitivity of pure nitro to shock or rough handling. Storage in an excessively hot place, such as a tin-roofed shack exposed in summer to 18 or 20 hours of sunshine a day, can cause nitroglycerine to leach out of the binding material and form drops of pure liquid. Pure nitro is extremely hazardous to handle, subject to detonation by the slightest disturbance. Not wanting to take any chance of being in the vicinity if 75 pounds of dynamite detonated, I very carefully backed out of the shack, gently closing the door and propped it with a chunk of rock. Marking its location in my mind as a good one to avoid, I moved on up the slope and found a small sun-warmed clearing that allowed a discreet view of the Little Nel, below.

I napped away the afternoon, my snooze interrupted once by the buzzing of a light plane traversing the valley at about 500 feet. I assumed that it was Agent Nichole's pilot listening for anything that might sound like an emergency transmitter sounding off. About ten minutes later it returned, flying in the opposite direction and a thousand feet higher. I had to admit that it felt good knowing that someone was monitoring my travels, and that there might actually be the possibility of back up if I got into real trouble.

I put off my supper until eight PM—later would have been better from a tactical viewpoint, but hunger forced the issue. 'LURP' rations, short for 'Long Range Patrol', were filling enough, but were not all that appetizing when eaten cold. I topped off with a jumbo Baby Ruth candy bar, the closest thing to an energy bar that I had available, drank a healthy slug of water, and waited for dusk. There would be no true darkness on this clear summer night, but somewhere around one AM the light would fade until one couldn't quite read a newspaper outside. When the night finally got as dark as it was going to, I stripped my pack to the bare essentials, slipped on my leather flying jacket with the GI 45 and spare magazines in inside pockets, and made sure the little 38 was secure in the shaft of my right boot. I cached the rifle and the remaining items from my pack under a tree several hundred yards uphill from the dynamite shack. I had gone part way down the hill when I remembered the ELT, cursed my carelessness, and went back to retrieve it.

CHAPTER 35

You Kill Him, Please?

I decided to come into the camp from the opposite side of the valley, figuring I could check the tool shed and the Terracoupe without exposing myself near the inhabited buildings. That required going around the head of the valley and into the woods on the far hillside, adding 45 minutes to my hike. 'Oh, well', I thought, 'It'll be 45 minutes darker when I get there.' The walk was uneventful and I found the wooded area on the south side of the claim to be nearly identical to that on the north side. It even had its own trail leading upward. As I descended, I nearly fell into a partly shored up cave entrance, loose rock and brush pushed into its mouth, hiding it from below. I guessed it to be part of earlier diggings, perhaps the original discovery hole which had caused the first prospector to stake the Little Nel. I could come up with absolutely no reason to examine the cave. Indeed, I could not recall a time in my life when I had come up with any reason to enter a cave— any cave, anytime, anywhere.

I continued down the hill and out into the open area, careful to keep the tool shed between me and the nearer pre-fab. The shed

 was a simple open fronted affair, the open side toward the other buildings, and was no more than eight feet wide. I moved around to the front and inside, keeping an eye on the helper's living quarters in the small cabin. There was little light, but I could see and feel well enough to determine that shovels, picks, sledge hammers, and other tools for manual labor were hung or propped against the back wall. A

chain saw hung on each side wall, and a number of fuel cans sat on the dirt floor. All the tools looked and felt rusty—very little work had taken place on this claim if these were the only tools on the site. I moved out to the Terracoupe parked a few feet away. I was on the side exposed to the helper's quarters now, but felt that the dark silhouette and shadows of the shed and the machine would conceal my movements.

The digging machine mirrored the condition of the hand tools. Its track cleats were rusty, and grass had grown up through openings between them; there were no tracks in the dirt indicating any recent movement. As I pondered my next move, I became aware of a flicker of movement near the larger pre-fab. I spun around, not sure whether to run for the brush or freeze in place. A figure had been moving from the cabin to the outhouse; it came to a halt, hesitated for ten seconds or so, turned and walked slowly in my direction. Still unsure what to do, I eased the small 38 out of my boot. I certainly didn't want to shoot anybody—after all, I was the trespasser. The figure had not yelled a challenge or called for help. Maybe the sight of my revolver would keep him or her quiet until I managed a graceful escape.

"Sir," a female voice called out in a loud whisper. "Is OK. I need talk to you please, Sir."

I could see her well enough to make out that she was alone and carrying nothing. I slipped the 38 back into my boot and waited.

"Come behind shed," she said, taking my arm and leading me around the structure.

"You policeman?" she asked. I shook my head.

"I need policeman." She pointed back to the larger quarters. "I not wife. He keep us here like slave. Cook, wash clothes, screw. Bad country," she waved at the horizon, "Can't run away."

"Other girl too?" I asked.

"Yes. Was 'nother other girl. I think they kill her, then bring this girl. I never see first girl go. They tell girls they need cook for mining camp. Real good pay. Bring us in chopter, never pay. Lock us when chopter come with food, whisky, cooking gas." She pointed toward the small cabin.

"He big fat pig. Bad to girl. Beat and make much pain. I think he kill."

Looking at her slender, small boned frame and delicate features, I hazarded a guess.

"You girls are Vietnamese?"

"Yes. Fat pig Vietnamese too." She looked into my eyes and asked very quietly and sincerely, "You kill him, please?"

I was too full of conflicting impressions to respond to her somewhat logical and very polite request. If these guys were actually connected to the gold smuggling operation, I was ready to believe the worst of them. I had my suspicions based on the lack of industry on the site and based on the fact that I didn't like the Womack brother, if indeed he was. The testimony of this girl, if true, was all I needed to persuade me to revert to my nasty self—the one who preached "Justice, not due process."

On the other hand, I might have just stepped into the middle of some sort of lover's quarrel, one that could get me hurt, or cause me to harm the innocent victim of someone else's wrath.

"I must talk again to you and to the other girl before I do anything," I told her. "Is there any way we could meet and talk tomorrow? Maybe make a plan?"

She was quiet for a long time. I could understand her problem if her story was true. If all the two men could find to do was hang around their dwellings and harass the women, the only private place was probably the outhouse. And it seemed unlikely that the two girls and I could meet in the john unnoticed.

"Boss man Judd like blueberries. I think maybe some blueberries ripe on hill." She pointed toward the north slope where I had found the dynamite shack and had taken my afternoon nap.

"I ask him if Linh and I go pick berries tomorrow. Meet you there. Tell all."

"Will somebody come to guard you, or to watch for bears?"

She gave a contemptuous laugh. "Quan, the pig, too fat and lazy climb hill. And boss Judd no care—bear get girl, he just order another girl."

"One more question. Do these men dig any gold from this place?"

"I never see them work; just when something break and need fix. They lazy. Would starve in Vietnam if can't steal."

"OK,' I said. "I'll go now. Wait for you on the hill tomorrow morning. If you cannot come, put something red on the clothesline where you hang wash. Understand?"

She nodded, touched my arm for a moment, and started back toward her previous destination. She stopped and returned.

"My name Nhan," she said, turned back and resumed her interrupted journey to the outhouse.

I was getting more nervous by the minute, expecting someone else to heed the call of nature and spot us while taking their nocturnal stroll. As soon as Nhan left me, I made a stealthy retreat along the route I had come, not breathing easily until I was under cover of the woods. I circled back around the head of the valley until I was on familiar ground near the dynamite shack on the north valley wall, well hidden by the tangle of young spruce and birch trees.

I wasn't sure boss man Judd Womack, if it were actually he, would buy off on the berry picking scheme. It was a bit early in the season for blueberries, but if there were any, that's where they would be, ripening on the sun-facing north slope of this hill. All I could do was wait and watch, while keeping out of sight of the men below.

I stayed in the shelter of the trees where my small camp stove couldn't be seen from below and cooked up my first warm meal since Bob Higgens' multi-critter stew. The army rations weren't quite as good, I had to admit, but they filled my hunger space adequately. Even the powdered freeze-dried coffee hit the spot.

I finally got around to thinking about what I should do tomorrow. If I didn't find the girls' story plausible, should I just leave and report my findings to Jack Ito, letting him handle the situation as he saw fit? And then what if they told their boss that I had been here, and what questions I had asked? Or, if they actually were trafficked women, what might happen to them after I left? It seemed a bit cowardly, passing the buck to people who weren't on the spot, and who weren't personally involved, to make decisions affecting these girls' lives.

If I did buy their story, should I try to spirit them out of the valley and back to Anchorage, reporting the situation and letting Ito do his thing? Womack evidently contacted his people in Anchorage by radio—I had seen the antenna strung behind the house. As soon as the girls were missed, Womack would radio his people to shut down the Anchorage operation. There would be nothing to find when the Terracoupe shop was raided. It would take me a day to walk the girls out, and half a day more to get to Anchorage, or to a reliable phone. Plenty of time for other-brother Womack to fold up the work in the shop.

I had been puzzled at the lack of activity at the mining site—no trace of mining, no trace of gold being smuggled in or being smelted into bars. An hour ago, while climbing up to my mini-camp, it had struck me like a slap on the head. The gold scheme needed a mine to account for the gold, but that was strictly for accounting purposes—the gold could be processed anywhere. And I guessed it was being smelted and molded in that small room at the rear of the Terracoupe shop—the room where the other Womack had been so busy when I visited him. After that, it could be taken to the point of sale or storage with paperwork showing it as the product of the Little Nel mine. I was sure that a detailed investigation would reveal that the same group of people owned both the Womack Brothers shop and the Little Nel mining claim.

In any case, it became apparent that I couldn't risk the Vietnamese girls' lives on a bad guess. I'd have to somehow silence the radio and get the girls out. I'd have to do so without hurting anybody—unless they proved that they needed hurting. If the two men were complete innocents, I'd let Jack Ito come here, apologize, and pay the damages.

CHAPTER 36

Berry Picking

I slept away the remainder of the night, having somewhat readjusted to a sleeping bag and ground sheet. Last night hadn't been quite so pleasant, the memory of my comfortable camper still in my mind as I scraped away marble-sized rocks and twigs that felt like golf balls after the first hour. Not knowing at what hour the berry pickers might be on the trail, I was up pretty early. To while away the time, I pulled out my binoculars and scanned the mountains and hillsides all around me for any signs of life. I saw a red fox single mindedly seeking out mice or voles in clumps of grass along a stream, a single stray caribou moving over the far ridgeline, and any number of ravens. I turned about and viewed the highest slopes of my own hill, but saw no movement. I was about to lower the binocs when a gray-brown twitch at the corner of an alder thicket caught my eye. I focused carefully and was eventually able to make out the form of a mountain grizzly just rising from a sunny spot and looking about.

It was an old bear, lean and rangy, its coat scraggly, faded, and bare in spots. It moved like an old man, slowly and stiffly,  stopping to sweep a few crowberries or blueberries into its mouth with an outsized paw. I doubted that the old bear would make it through the coming winter—it obviously hadn't put on any fat for hibernation, and didn't appear in good enough condition to hunt caribou or dig out marmots. I marked its location and direction of travel. The last thing I needed in my life now was a hungry bear. Or so I thought.

It was nearly noon when I saw the girls leave the mining site and begin their climb up the trail. They were carrying small plastic buckets and moving slowly. Nhan matched her pace to that of a second girl who was moving like the old bear, stiffly and carefully. While they were climbing, I kept watch on the site. Nothing stirred until the fat Vietnamese, Quan, left the smaller pre-fab and waddled out to the outhouse, scratching and yawning.

I whistled softly as the girls came within hearing, and they altered course toward the clump of brush that concealed my little camp. Linh was slightly smaller than Nhan, and I began to understand why she had walked so slowly. Quan must have abused her constantly; she had vivid bruises and swellings that were obviously done within the last 24 hours, and older injuries that must have spanned weeks. As small-boned as she was, I couldn't believe she didn't have broken bones or worse. My earlier ideas on giving the two men the benefit of a doubt faded away—a man who could condone this kind of treatment was as bad as the one who inflicted it. Someone was going to pay.

"This Linh," said Nhan. "Your name?"

"I am Ben", I said. "You had no trouble?"

"Only trouble if no berries. What you need to know?"

"When does the helicopter come again?" I asked.

"Four days," she said, holding up four fingers.

"Why does Quan beat you?" I asked, turning to Linh.

She shrugged. "He get drunk, he beat me. He don't like food, he beat me. He can't screw, he beat me. He have 'nother girl before me. I think he kill her, put in hole in mountain. When he drunk, he say he do that to me."

I thought about the old cave on the south slope, the one that looked as though rocks and brush had been pushed around to hide it. I didn't want to think about what might be inside.

"Nhan, what kind of radio does Judd have in the big house?"

She framed her hands into an imaginary box the size of a desk typewriter.

"Black radio, work by battery."

"Does he have any other way to talk to people outside?"

"I think no. One time battery die. Judd cuss. Radio dead and can't tell chopter bring more battery. Take two chopter trips bring new battery. Now have many battery."

"OK," I said. "I need to think about things. You pick berries, but stay close. A bear is near top of hill." I pointed up toward the area where I had last seen the grizzly.

I had planned to just grab the girls and start walking back toward the Hard Times and Jodo claims until we reached my truck. A fast run to the nearest phone, then to Anchorage where I'd stash the ladies and join Liz for the raid on the Womack shop. All this after I had somehow silenced the radio, of course—which I hadn't yet figured how to do. Linh's condition quickly vetoed the first plan. She'd never make it back to the truck walking, and I certainly wasn't man enough to carry her all that way. Linh's only way out was by air— by helicopter, to be more specific. It appeared that I was going to have to test Liz's ELT after all.

The girls were evidently finding some berries. I saw them busily working the low brush in a clearing a hundred or so yards away, staying in plain sight of anyone who might be watching from below. That was good, in that it accustomed the men to having the girls away from the mine site without suspecting them of mischief. 'Anything to lull them into a sense of unsuspicious routine,' I thought, because my next moves would definitely disturb their routine.

I was beginning to feel drowsy, whiling away the hours in my sheltered spot in the sun while the girls worked. I was determined not to fall asleep; while I was concentrating on not doing so, a gentle hand shook me awake and pointed to two pails of berries.

They had a reasonable number of berries in their pails, although many were just short of being ripe. I feared that Linh would pay a price for the not-so-ripe harvest; it seemed like the kind of thing Quan would welcome as an excuse to abuse her again. To my pleasant surprise, the girls had a remedy. The sat on the grass and switched most of the greenish berries around so that Nhan's bucket held most of the rejects. Nhan explained.

"Boss Judd get pissed off at green berries, but maybe no hit me. Quan see green berries, hit everything near."

"Now we must plan," I said. "Nhan, when does Judd first leave you alone in the house after he wakes?"

DON NEAL

"I make him coffee first thing. If he no want screw, he drink coffee, go outside to craphouse. Maybe stay ten, fifteen minutes."

"When does he go out again?"

"Don't know. Sometime stay house all day."

"How about Quan?" I asked.

"Mostly sleep until noon. Linh up early, do woman work. Fat pig do nothing."

"OK, now is the hard part. Before we can run, we have to break the radio. Break it good. Nhan, is there an axe or hatchet around the house?"

"Small axe," she replied, spreading her hands about 18 inches apart. "In tool box."

"As soon as Jud gets in craphouse, you get axe and break radio. Smash good."

I brought my arms down like a logger cutting wood.

"Then you and Linh come to this hill. Fast. I will be here. I will not let them catch you." I pointed to the scope-sighted Winchester leaning on my pack.

"We will wait on this hill, maybe all day, all night, until my friends come in helicopter, take us out. You bring warm clothes tomorrow."

They looked at me doubtfully, probably doing what I was doing—thinking of all the things that could go wrong with my simple plan. Then, in a show of faith that both flattered and embarrassed me, they each stood, gave a short bow and a weak smile, and set off down the trail swinging their berry buckets.

By now the sun was starting to skate down the horizon and I reckoned it was time to ready the ELT for use. I intended to wait for a plane flying the valley on the same course as the one I had seen yesterday afternoon. I would switch on and off alternately and hope our hastily devised code was understood. Several hours later, the plane made its pass; I fired up the ELT when it was nearly above me, turned it off, then on several times, and turned it off just before it cleared the valley on its return flight. I caught a waggle of its wings just before it disappeared from view.

I slept little that night, spending most of the night picking holes in my plan, and asking myself what would happen if...

CHAPTER 37

The Bear

I was up early, not knowing for sure what time Judd took his morning stroll to the outhouse. It was absolutely essential that I be lined up and ready to cover the two women on their escape to the brush. I didn't plan on killing anyone, but was quite willing to discourage any pursuit. Joe Dobrynski's technique should work fine. With luck, my rescue squad would come zooming in fairly early to take the weight off my shoulders.

At precisely 0816, I watched the boss man leave his quarters and stroll toward the outhouse. An hour earlier Quan had opened his door clad only in shorts, peed into the dirt in front of his doorway, and disappeared. I figured he was back in bed.

Thirty seconds after the outhouse door had closed on Judd, Nhan popped out of her door, dropped a hatchet, and trotted toward the wooded hillside. Linh slipped out of the smaller house and joined her. They both carried small bundles and wore the "pajamas" so prevalent in their native Vietnam. Rather than racing hell-bent for freedom, Nhan had slowed to match poor Linh's limping gait. It turned out that they had plenty of time—

 Judd used up his 15 minutes and more before emerging from the seat of ease. He took his time ambling back to his house, hands in pockets and probably whistling to himself. By the time he reached the door, I had the girls high up in the woods near my spike camp and had seated myself in a spot that allowed me to observe the claim site through a gap in the foliage.

Judd hesitated at the door, reached down and picked up the axe that Nhan had dropped. He looked at it in puzzlement, opened the door and entered. Ten seconds later he ran out the door, wildly looked about in all directions, and began shouting. Although I couldn't make out the words from a quarter-mile away, I could hear his voice echoing across the valley. He shouted toward the smaller house. Apparently getting no answer, he ran to it and disappeared inside. I could hear nothing more until he reappeared, dragging fat Quan who was struggling to pull on his clothes as he stumbled out the door.

There were a few minutes of animated discussion with Quan mostly listening. Judd and Quan returned to their respective houses, both emerging in a few minutes carrying rifles and ammunition pouches. The rifles appeared to be US issue M16's. Judd made his way to the south side of the valley, while Quan reluctantly plodded toward my side. I could have shot them both with the 338, but that seemed a bit drastic—I thought if I could take them more peacefully, I'd have a lot less explaining to do.

I called the girls over, told them what was happening, and moved them to a thick clump of dwarf spruce and willow which lay several hundred yards east of the uphill trail. I fished the little 38 revolver from my boot and showed it to Nhan.

"Can you shoot this?" I asked. She looked doubtful. I swung out the cylinder and extracted the five cartridges. Closing it, I pulled the trigger several times, snapping the hammer on empty chambers.

"Now you," I said, handing the gun off to her. She waived it around experimentally, pointing it at various parts of my body in the process.

"No!" I snapped. I took it from her and handed it back with the muzzle up, making it a point to exaggerate my avoidance of pointing it at any of us. She looked ashamed and turned her body so the muzzle of the pistol was aimed at a tree trunk. I nodded in approval and indicated she should snap it as I had. She did so, but the stiffness of the double action trigger mechanism made it impossible for her small hands to hold it steady as the hammer fell. The gun twitched and jerked each time she pulled the trigger.

"Wait," I said. I retrieved the 38 and slowly demonstrated cocking it and then squeezing the trigger. The hammer fell after only a few ounces of trigger pressure. I repeated this several times and returned it to her. Holding the 38 with two hands, she pulled the hammer back until it clicked. She aimed it at a tree and touched the trigger, breaking out in a delighted smile when the hammer fell with little disturbance of her aim. I showed her how to hold the weapon with both hands while cocking and shooting, and watched her practice until I was sure she wasn't apt to harm anyone but her target. I reloaded the cylinder and handed the gun back to her.

"Only shoot when close," I said, stretching my arms apart like a bragging fisherman. "Not when far." I walked ten feet away, stopped, and shook my head. "This is too far."

Having taught a three-day safety and marksmanship course in five minutes, I hoped it was all for the best. I motioned the girls to be quiet and applied my efforts to locating fat Quan. At the rate he was moving when I last saw him, he should be getting close, but not dangerously so. I assumed that he would take the easiest path up the hill, and suspected I would hear him panting long before I saw him. As far as he and Judd knew, the Vietnamese were alone and would be no threat if encountered.

I intended to surprise Quan and take him prisoner, wait for Judd Womack to come looking for him, and do the same. Even if I were all wrong about gold being smelted in the Anchorage shop, the provable human trafficking charges should justify any harsh treatment that the pair might suffer. After that, we'd just wait for the FBI team to swoop in and scoop us all up. I had the ELT beacon broadcasting steadily now, which should guide them straight to us.

I moved slowly and quietly along the hillside, keeping under cover and searching for Quan. He must have stayed low on the hill, I thought, not wishing to enter the trees from fear or laziness. I found myself 50 yards from the decrepit dynamite shack and turned uphill to avoid it. My attention was focused below, where I expected Quan to appear at any time, and I never saw the half-rotten log that rolled under my foot. I twisted in the air and fell heavily, rolling another ten feet down the hill before stopping against a moss-covered stump. I cursed loudly, disgusted with myself and forgetting my need for caution.

I heard an exclamation and the clack of a bolt going home. There was a torrent of automatic weapon fire, most of which ripped chunks and splinters off the dynamite shed. Quan must have thought someone was hiding inside, and didn't much care who. Recalling the crate of super-sensitive explosives inside, I yelled a warning.

"Quan! Cease fire—there's dynamite in that shack!" I heard the sound of a fresh magazine being snapped in place. Quan shifted his aim to the sound of my voice and a swarm of bullets cracked, snapped, and buzzed around me. At least two were effective—my rifle was jolted out of my hands, its walnut stock shattered at the grip, and I felt a numbing blow to my chest, under my left arm. I had to get the hell out of there before he reloaded again and dumped another magazine in my direction. The girls were to my right as I looked up the hill, and were well concealed. I dug my only remaining weapon, the old GI 45, from inside my jacket, snapped the safety off, and made sure the chamber was loaded. Putting it on safe again, I started moving straight uphill. My warning about the dynamite shack had given away my presence—Quan would be alert now for a possible armed enemy.

I needed to get clear of him long enough to check my wound, but didn't want to rest too soon—shock or blood loss might prevent me from rising again. I deliberately made as much noise as I could, hoping to keep his attention until we had bypassed the girls' hideaway. Quan was moving very cautiously, still not sure who or what he had engaged, so I stopped behind a tree and pulled up my jacket. Apparently, the bullet had taken out a section of rib and spun off without penetrating into any vital areas. The long gash where the bit of rib had been ripped out was bleeding profusely and the numbness induced by the impact was starting to wear off. I wiped up some of the blood on a handkerchief and left it on the ground for Quan to find. Unbuttoning my shirt, I pulled its tail out of my trousers, twisted it up and wadded it over the wound. Zipping up the leather jacket seemed to compress the wad of cloth enough to stop most of the bleeding.

I gave a groan or two which I hoped Quan could hear, and started up the hillside again. I didn't know how much of a tracker Quan might be, so I made it a point to leave blood spots at obvious places. I needed to keep his concentration on me—if he stumbled onto the women, he'd be holding all the cards in our deadly game. Another 50 yards and I held up, watching behind and listening for his movements. I didn't see him, but his laboring breathing told me he was close.

The wound in my side was making itself felt, the pain worse and my strength ebbing. We had neared the upper fringe of the wooded area, the trees thinning and clumps of alder beginning to appear on the open slopes ahead. There was enough fresh blood seeping from the tear in my side that I no longer needed to lay a false trail—droplets were falling every 15 feet or so. A crackling thump behind, punctuated by an expletive in Vietnamese, told me Quan was close behind. He evidently had more stamina than his appearance indicated.

The trees were left behind and there was only tundra ahead, dotted with irregular clumps of alder, head-high and ranging in size from ten to 40 or 50 feet. I had to make it to the cover of the first clump of alders before Quan emerged from the trees, otherwise I'd be caught in the open, a sitting duck. Quan couldn't miss forever, despite his spray-and-pray marksmanship—even a blind hog finds an occasional acorn. I took off uphill in a ragged trot, half expecting a bullet at any time. Reaching the first alder patch exhausted but more-or-less alive, I dropped behind it, swiveled around, and peered through the branches for my pursuer. He barely showed himself, hesitated, looking left and right, obviously shy about exposing himself to whatever armament I might have. That was good thinking on his part; if he followed me up to my alder patch, I fully intended to abruptly stand up and shoot him in the face with my 45.

I rested in place while I could, willing him to do the same. Instead, he faded back into the woods and began moving to his left, staying pretty much under cover of the vegetation. I realized that he intended to flank me, probably moving several hundred yards to the left before resuming his climb. If he moved steadily and watched to his right, he stood a good chance of spotting me hiding behind an alder clump or moving up the slope between clumps. If he got above me, he could work his way down and force me into the open for a clear shot. Despite his very unmilitary appearance, I had a hunch that Quan had once been involved in some serious armed encounters. At least, to my gratitude, no one had ever taught him to shoot straight.

Since he had some way to go before he began his climb, I resumed my ascent in an attempt to stay above him. Moving from patch to patch, like working my way through a maze, I gained altitude, but always looking to my left in case he overtook or passed me. Another nerve wracking ten minutes of climbing and crawling and I was forced to stop and rest. I was very tired and leaking badly.

Looking again to my left and a little higher on the slope, I caught a movement. It was mostly hidden between two alder patches, so I shifted slightly and put my binoculars on it. My old friend the starving grizzly was half lying on a dead animal of some sort, worrying at it with one paw. Focusing more sharply, I could see that it was an old mummified caribou carcass, probably from last year. It was mostly stiffened hide, so desiccated and stripped of flesh that even the ravens had rejected it. The old bear, a boar it appeared, suddenly heaved himself up from his disappointing meal and seemed to test the air. The sun had warmed the day to the point that a whisper of upslope wind was building—the bear stood on its hind legs and sampled the wind again, showing definite interest in what it brought.

It suddenly dawned on me what message the wind was bringing to the old boar. Quan was probably walking straight up the hill below the bear in his attempt to outflank me. I circled the large alder thicket I was using for cover and stopped at the top edge, from where I could see the bear clearly. He dropped to all fours, moved to where he could see anything approaching from below, and waited expectantly.

I actually thought of shouting warning to Quan, but quickly reconsidered. Not only would it probably get me killed—I had little faith in Quan's sense of gratitude—but it might get the old bear killed also. And I knew in my mind that Quan, if arrested and taken to court, would probably serve less than five years for what little criminal activity could be proved. I again fell back on my old motto, "Justice, not due process," and decided to let nature mete out the justice.

I watched Quan skirt the alder thicket separating him from the bear, carrying the M16 at hip level. He was watching his footing, eyes downcast, when he came in view of the bear, some 30 feet away. His version of precision marksmanship had not changed—keeping the rifle at hip level, he began to hose down the hillside in the general direction of the bear. Two things occurred almost simultaneously, combining to mark the downfall of fat Quan. The M16 jammed after a dozen shots, as they tend to do if not frequently cleaned, and one of the bullets, possibly a ricochet, hit the bear. I saw the bear flinch, and I could see Quan futilely working the M16's operating handle as the bear charged.

When the bear smacked into its assailant, both the rifle and its owner went spinning through the air. The bear was on Quan before he could regain his feet, swatted him twice in the chest, and crunched its jaws into his left shoulder. Quan began to scream as the bear chewed on his shoulder; this seemed to annoy the bear. It slapped Quan casually across the face with its right paw, then became even more annoyed with the blob which was now hanging on the paw. He licked and chewed it off. It looked to me like the blob consisted of most of Quan's face. Quan was still trying to make sounds, small animal sounds, which the bear ignored as it began to feed.

CHAPTER 38

In Your Ear!

I quietly and slowly withdrew, leaving the bear to enjoy his meal, and worked my way back down the hillside trying to ignore the increasing pain in my left side. I tried to reassemble the thoughts and plans which had been so thoroughly derailed by the events of the past hour. When would my rescue party arrive, or would they? Did the ELT work as advertised? Where was Judd Womack, and what was his reaction to the gunfire that he must have heard? Would my bear make it through the winter now that he had a nice, fat carcass to feed on for a few days? I shook my head to clear my muddled mind. How had that last question inserted itself? Had I lost enough blood that I would crash before reaching the girls?

The last was answered by two voices—that of Nahn as she grasped me by the shoulders and lowered me to the ground, asking if I was all right, and the voice of Judd Womack telling her to get the hell away from me, which she ignored.

"Who the hell are you? Where's Quan? What was that shooting about? What are you doing around here anyway?"

 All I really wanted right now was for somebody to plug the hole in my side. Nahn, seeing the blood and the ragged hole in my leather jacket, was trying to do just that, and I was resisting. The 45 automatic was back in its pouch inside the jacket, and Womack would surely see it if she unzipped and removed the jacket. I finally decided it was better to lose the gun than to bleed to death, so allowed her to remove the

jacket. As she was doing so, I pressed her hand to the shape of the gun. She hesitated for a moment, and rolled the jacket up as she removed it, I rocking from side to side to assist her without revealing the gun to Womack.

"Answer me, dammit. Did Quan do that?" I nodded.

"Where is he then?"

I waved in the general direction of the hill behind me.

"Did you shoot him?"

I shook my head.

"Dammit, talk to me, man. Nodding and waving won't get it. I want answers."

"I was just passing through. Talked to one of your women and found out that they're slave labor. Wanted to help them get away. Your man tried to stop me, shot me." I let my head wobble and slumped as though I was about to pass out. Nhan was still trying to access my wound to staunch the bleeding.

"Get away from him!" barked Womack, shoving her to one side. He knelt in front of me, jabbing the muzzle of the rifle against my sternum.

"What were you two doing on this claim?' I asked. "You sure weren't mining for gold. It's illegal to file a claim if you don't intend to mine." I didn't really know whether or not that was true, but I needed to get him talking. My eye was on the folded jacket with the 45 inside. The gun was loaded with the safety engaged. If I could get a hand on it, the safety could be snapped off and the pistol fired in a second, through the jacket if necessary.

"None of your damn' business," he answered jabbing me again with the rifle. I flinched and cried out, exaggerating, trying to impress upon him how helpless I was.

I had discovered long ago how difficult it is for a person to concentrate on two things at once. When one is poised to shoot, as Womack was at this moment, his own talking can be a distraction. When the time for action comes, it takes a second to disengage the brain from the mouth and to refocus on the business at hand. I wanted to start a conversation that required a train of thought that might occupy him for the second it would take me to grab my 45. I knew the odds were against making it, but I saw zero options. If he killed me, he would kill the girls to cover his tracks. I had to take the chance.

"You know," I said, "if you hadn't let Quan kill the first girl, you could probably talk your way out of this whole thing. But when they find her in the cave, you'll go down as an accessory to murder—Quan will talk his head off to get a deal."

I could see his mind working, and the dawning realization that he would now have to get rid of Quan also.

"Look," he said, "Quan got drunk and did the girl on his own. I never told him to kill her or to hide the body. If he said I did, he's a liar. The son of a bitch is uncontrollable when he gets to drinking, and I couldn't keep him sober." He nodded toward Nhan. "I treated the girls right. We were gonna pay them well after we shut down for the winter. Lots more than they would have got working the rice paddies in Nam. Besides that..." At this moment I snatched the M16 muzzle with my left hand and shoved it skyward, my right diving under the jacket and scrabbling for the 45. I located it, but my hand fell on the slide instead of the grip. By the time I had desperately shifted my hand in an attempt to grab the butt and snap the safety down, Womack had discovered that my left arm was weak, so weak and that he could push the barrel down and into my gut with no strain at all. He began doing so, grinning and levelling the rifle muzzle very slowly, so that I could see the inevitable coming.

As I braced for a bullet in the belly at close range, I glimpsed Nhan slowly and deliberately cocking my little 38. Womack, intent on enjoying my futile efforts to push the rifle away, didn't seem to notice her until she plugged it into his right ear. There was a muffled report, the M16 came loose in my hand, and Womack folded like a sack of sawdust. I was spattered with left over bits of Judd Womack and my ears were ringing from the shot. I gave up; everything was taken care of and there were no more bad guys to worry about, so I faded out.

When I woke, the ringing in my ears had changed to a thumping rhythm that seemed somehow familiar. Nhan and Linh were plucking at my clothing, fear on their faces, and pointing to the two helicopters that hovered above their former home in the valley. I motioned toward my binoculars and Linh brought them to where I lay. A quick look showed that they were definitely official birds, probably stuffed with government agents, and were hovering, worried about an ambush. After I reassured the ladies, we had to wait another ten minutes for the bosses to decide that landing was safe. When the birds were down and their noisy engines shut off, I reached under my bloody jacket again, this time finding the right end of the 45. I fired three shots into the air in about three seconds, waited five seconds, and fired three more. I instructed the girls to move up into a clearing where they could be seen, and wave toward the landing party. Then I faded away again.

I woke with more people plucking at my clothing, this time to remove it. Men with FBI jackets and SWAT gear were milling around, scaring the hell out of the Vietnamese girls, picking through my pack, and exploring the general area. A pair of medics had me pinned down, half naked, and had an IV going in each arm. My head was resting on something soft, warm and familiar. I looked up into the concerned eyes of FBI Agent Elise Nichole, armed, flak-vested, and dressed for battle, holding my head in her lap, and tenderly stroking my brow. There are definitely worse ways to wake up.

"Liz", I whispered, tell your crew to stay clear of that old shack just down the hill. It has old leaky dynamitestored in it."

Liz called one of the agents over and passed the information. I could tell by her demeanor and by the reaction of the agent that Liz was the Agent-in-Charge of this operation. I had not seen her in her "trail boss" mode before, and she made me proud.

While we were close enough to keep the conversation private, I briefed her on my activities here, and of my suspicion as to where the gold was being processed. I told her of the supply helicopter being scheduled to arrive in three days, and of the radio being smashed to prevent warning the gang of my visit. I did not have the time or the inclination to go into details about the young Vietnamese girls and their activities, except to demand that they be taken care of and that they be kept in Anchorage, not passed to the immigration authorities. I also mentioned that Linh had been badly beaten, and that she should be examined for internal injuries in Anchorage—and that Nhan be allowed to stay with her as a companion.

While I was talking to her, the medics did something to my IV's, and I began to feel sleepy again. I asked if Nhan and Linh were nearby, and they were ushered over to where I lay. I introduced them to Liz; at first, they seemed uncertain of the lady in fighting armor, but soon sensed the connection between us and relaxed a little. I took Nhan's hand and softly said "Thank you." The last thing I remember saying to them was that Liz would look after them.

CHAPTER 39

The Raid

It was the afternoon of my first, and I hoped, my last day in the hospital, and I was in a heated argument with Liz. She had used the coded telephone number given me by Jack Ito, and he had been located and had called back on a secure FBI line. He ordered that the planned raid on the Womack shop be delayed until he arrived in Anchorage, which he said would be the next day. My dispute with Liz revolved around the fact that I intended to be in on it.

"Dammit, Liz, they've put back all the blood I lost, and put a patch on the damaged rib. The doc says the rib is gonna hurt like hell for a month or so, no matter whether I'm in bed our out. No reason I can't just follow your and Jack's people in and watch what goes on."

"Oh, yes there is. I'm in charge of the FBI contingent on this raid, and I say you can't."

"But I'm not in the FBI."

"Then why did I lead two choppers and a SWAT team into the wilderness to pull your sorry butt out?"

"'Cause you missed me?"

The trace of a smile showed through. "Maybe. I wish that guy Quan had missed you too. If that bullet had steered left after hitting the rib, instead of to the right, you'd be dead and the Vietnamese women would still be servicing those animals. But I won't authorize you to be on my team, Ben. You wince every time you breathe hard, and your left arm is nearly useless. You already had three bullet holes in your stubborn hide; this makes four, and the scars on your torso look like an Alaskan road map."

"All right for now," I said, "but I'm out of here tomorrow, and I'm still gonna try and work my way onto that raid."

"What do you mean, you're out of here tomorrow? The doctor won't clear you to check out for at least another two days."

"Honey," I said, smiling and taking both her hands in mine, "I did a little searching through the rulebook. Did you know that a hospital can't keep a person in against his will?"

I felt her hands and arms go rigid, then limp as she withdrew them from my grasp.

"Stupidly stubborn, or stubbornly stupid." She stood and stalked out without another word.

Jack Ito did arrive early the next morning. He must have been in the air most of the night, but you wouldn't have known it by his appearance or his demeanor. He first checked in with the FBI and introduced himself to Liz. Liz took him back to the office of the SAC and introduced him to Monk, who did everything in welcoming him but kiss the hem of his robe. Ito conferred with Liz and Monk for an hour; then he and Liz went to the hospital to see me. I wasn't there.

A taxi had dropped me at my home off Rabbit Creek Road, and I was drinking a Moose Head and heating a bowl of chili when the phone rang. I answered and held the phone away from my ear, expecting an enraged Liz to open fire on me. Instead, the quiet voice of Colonel Ito said, "You're home. Good. We'll be there shortly." He hung up without further comment and I went back to my beer and chili.

When Jack and Liz arrived, I ushered them in and offered beer and chili. Liz silently refused and ducked a kiss on the cheek; Jack shook hands and nodded enthusiastically. I took it that his overnight flight didn't include much in the way of food. When we were finally sitting at the kitchen table, two eating and one sulking, I made my report to Jack. I made it in much more detail than my briefing to the FBI, and, with the added chore of answering Ito's questions, it took the better part of an hour.

"Now," I said, when the beer, chili, and my report were all finished, "I need a few things done after this mess is cleaned up."

Jack's eyebrows went up—apparently, as a full colonel of Intelligence, he wasn't used to people telling him how they wanted things done.

"Get someone in that cave to the south of the site. I think you'll find the body of the girl that Quan killed. If not, it'll be in another cave or shaft nearby. We need that to show the seriousness of their crimes, and to remove any doubt that Nhan's shooting of Womack was justified." Liz finally spoke. "We're on it now."

"OK." I turned to Jack.

"The Vietnamese girls are without doubt illegal aliens, smuggled in to be trafficked like slaves. If they choose to stay in this country, I'd like them given some kind of legitimate status, maybe as refugees needing asylum, and a head start in some appropriate community. They took a big chance, even if it was in helping me help them. And Womack was in the process of gutting me when Nhan stuck my pistol in his ear. Saving the life of a government employee must entitle her to something."

He scratched his head in thought, smiled—"I think I can handle that. What other miracles would you like me to pull off?"

"Get me in on that raid. I assume it's coming off tonight or tomorrow?"

"Tomorrow at ten in the morning. Our watchers say everything looks normal at the shop, so we are assuming that no word of your escapade at the Little Nel has leaked out yet. But getting you in would really be a miracle. Agent Nichole here has absolutely forbidden it, and I can see that crossing her would qualify me for hazardous duty pay."

Liz looked happy for the first time since she had arrived. I spluttered and sought for excuses to have my way, but ground to a frustrated halt. Jack raised his hand.

"May I suggest the rarest thing to be found in an interagency squabble—a compromise?"

Liz and I both turned our heads and gave him our strictest attention, I with hope, and she with suspicion.

"Ben, you ride in with us, but you stay in the car with the back-up while we go in. When the shop has been found clear, you may join us and be an interested spectator while we search the place."

He spoke with such finality that Liz and I simultaneously nodded agreement without further argument. I marveled; my old friend and drinking buddy, Jack Ito, really sounded like a colonel now.

"Now Liz," I began, speaking with the entitlement of the walking wounded, "there are a couple of things I'd like. First, there is a red Ford truck sitting at end-of-road up behind Eureka. Since it was driven up there on a government mission, may I ask the government to get it back to me?"

I switched my attention to Jack.

"Sir, while in my hands, my favorite hunting rifle was hit by one of Quan's bullets and the stock shattered. I'm sure the FBI salvaged it from the scene of the shootout, and I'd like the stock replaced—at your expense. You seem to have infinite funds at your disposal.

"And as to expenses, you will be delighted to know that I have decided not to charge you for the round of 38 Special ammo that was fired into Judd Womack's right ear, since I did not personally fire that shot."

I was picked up at eight the next morning and delivered to a briefing room in the Federal building. There were two groups in attendance, a half-dozen FBI personnel led by Agent Liz, and as many unbadged but proficient-appearing people under Jack Ito. All were armed and armored, most carrying small hand held radios.

The briefing took twenty minutes, discussing radio call signs, rules of engagement, what if's, and plans B and C. Three people from the FBI would enter the back door and three from Ito's group, the front door, at precisely ten o'clock. Two from each group would remain outside at each door, and the last from each group would remain in the back-up vehicle with special weapons, the base radio, and me.

After the briefing, both groups relaxed and intermingled as casually as though they were about to attend a ball game. I noticed a few women in Ito's group, although they were sometimes hard to pick out beneath the flak vests and weapons harness. Those who were easy to pick out were usually worth the effort.

I found a soft chair in an unused office and sank gratefully into it. The doctor was right—that damn rib wound hurt no matter what I did, but I wasn't about to let Liz know. She'd start worrying, and a worrying Liz was not comfortable to be around. Besides, she didn't need any distractions until the morning's work was done.

I was itchy to get this operation under way, mainly because there needed to be some point at which I could say, 'OK, the job's done, finished, and we can relax and come back into a real world with real people.' I thought back on my travels since I had first been accosted by Kioko in the airport bar. The secret exchanges of information with Jack, the clandestine meeting with him up on the Kivchak River, my trip to the cabin on the banks of Montana Creek to confer with Gordon Hitch, the climb up to the Katy Bee mine site where 'Hard Luck' Stan Snider had striven in vain, and finally the trek to the Little Nel through the mining country above Eureka—they all seemed like clips from Dorothy's search for the Wizard of Oz. At least the final scene would play out in a real building, in a real town, with real people arresting real criminals. And maybe even finding real stolen gold pilfered from the vaults of a real nation which was fighting for its life.

My thoughts were interrupted by the command, "Saddle up!", and the designated dozen commenced the noisy routine of buckling, tying, pulling, and testing their gear and weapons. By a quarter to ten the small convoy was deployed in its assigned positions, my vehicle parked across the street from The Womack Brothers' business with a clear view of the front entry. I sat in the front seat, the two guys with me sat in the back, relaxed but alert, one wearing a radio headset, the other maintaining a constant watch in all directions, his head swiveling like a radar search antenna.

The radioman came alert, responding to an incoming call with, "Yes ma'am." He repeated it twice more, and when he clicked off I asked him what was happening. He hesitated before replying, finally letting a grin break loose.

"That was the AIC, Sir. She said you were shot up from a previous engagement. Said to look after you well, because if anything happened to you she'd have my ass. I don't think you were supposed to hear that last part." Both men laughed, meanwhile keeping their eyes glued to the front entry way. I saw Liz, Jack, and two men preparing to break the door down if necessary, but the door swung inward at a touch. They entered, circled the counter, and disappeared into the back room. I sat watching the front counter, waiting and expecting to hear gunfire, and fully intending to rush the building if I did, despite strict orders to the contrary. The little 38 Smith, well-cleaned, was back in its usual place in my boot.

It was less than five minutes after entry when the radioman touched my shoulder.

"All clear, Sir. You can go in now." He added, "Please watch your step and don't fall down or anything; the lady wasn't kidding." Surprised at the smoothness of the raid, and the lack of violence, I very carefully walked over and entered the shop.

CHAPTER 40

Gold is Where You Find It

The "other" Womack brother, was handcuffed to an exposed water pipe, and appeared calm but worried. Cuffed to another pipe was a small wiry man, probably Vietnamese, who was stoically staring at the wall. The team members were methodically searching the shop, checking drawers and cabinets, and the boxes and crates on shelves along the walls and up in the storage loft. Ito watched for a while, turned and addressed Womack.

"You and your brother are joint owners of this place and a gold mine called the Little Nel, near Eureka." Womack nodded. "Where do you keep the gold that your brother sends in from the mine?"

"I melt it down and sell it to gold dealers. The proceeds go to keep up the equipment and pay the help."

"May I see where you process the incoming gold?"

Womack shrugged and indicated the handcuffs. Jack made a sign and one of his team unlocked Womack from the pipe, cuffing his hands behind his back afterward.

Womack led us to the smaller room within the shop, nodding toward a small electric furnace and some small ingot molds on a workbench. I examined the equipment closely; it had been obviously used for gold, as tiny bits and droplets were present in the work area. There was no raw gold to be seen, however. All we could do was to wait and hope the searchers could turn up something incriminating.

I motioned Jack to follow me and walked out onto the main floor.

"Jack, I saw some fine grains of gold on the cross brace below the bench vise. It looked like the metal sawdust you get when hacksawing steel, but was definitely yellow. If the gold coming in from Nam is in large ingots, it would have to be sawed into smaller pieces to fit in that little furnace. Have your guys look for a power hacksaw of some sort." He nodded without comment and went to pass the word among the searchers. I sat down on a wooden packing crate and tried to ignore the inexorable increase in pain along my left side.

Another ten minutes of fruitless searching, and there was an exclamation of discovery from a searcher in the small room housing the smelting furnace. I walked in just as a power miter saw was being dragged from the back corner of an under-bench storage cabinet. It was a compact model, much lighter than the "chop saws" generally used by carpenters, and was fitted with a metal cutting blade. Close examination disclosed bits of gold jammed between the teeth of the blade.

Liz had joined us as we looked at the saw. I could see we were all thinking the same thing; we had found indicators, but nothing close to the proof required in a court of law. Not that I was sure Jack needed a court of law. I went back out into the main shop and began examining the crates and boxes of parts that the search team had pulled away from the wall. Lifting and sliding some of the heavier containers triggered the pain in my shoulder and side again—I became more careful as I worked my way along. Everything I looked at seemed to be what it was; nuts, bolts, springs, brackets, pistons, ring sets, and about everything else needed to build a Terracoupe.

I opened the cover on one box that contained replacement teeth for the backhoe bucket. They were neatly wired into a bundle of five, the bodies painted the pea-soup green which seemed to be standard for the Terracoupe, and the cutting edges left bright. The next box was actually a sturdy wood crate with a hinged top. It contained six cast iron or steel track cleats for the machine. They were preserved against rust or damage by having been dipped into a plastic which hardened leaving a thin, black rubbery coat. This coating had to be peeled off prior to installing the part. The cleats were irregularly shaped and weighed about five pounds each. I partly lifted the crate to move it out of the way, cursing the pain in my side as I did so.

The similar crate next to it also contained six cleats, packaged and preserved in the same manner. I moved it aside to reach the next one, flinched and cussed again. The pain had struck again, and worse. The third crate contained only five cleats. As I started to move it aside, a voice from the corner of my mind signaled, 'Whoa, something's not right.' The box with five cleats weighed about the same as the one with six. I picked up the five cleats, one at a time to examine them. The center cleat took an effort to lift; it was at least twice as heavy as the others. I called Liz and Jack over and showed them two identical crates, one containing six cleats and one containing five.

"Lift this one," I said, pointing to the first crate, "then lift this one." pointing at the second. Jack cautiously lifted each, commented that they felt about the same. Then he counted the cleats in each and his face lit up in a broad smile. He went into the crate containing five and took out the cleats one by one as I had, stopping and hefting the center one. He handed it to me. I took out my pocket knife and peeled back a square inch of the black coating, revealing the yellow luster of pure gold.

The Vietnamese, who was still handcuffed to the water pipe, spat out something that sounded like "To su cha may!", and turned his face toward the wall. I found that I didn't much mind being cursed as long as I didn't know what was being said.

Running down the remaining gold cleats was no big problem; a crate of five with one gold cleat weighed as much as a crate with six iron cleats, gold being nearly two and a half times as heavy as iron. Every crate containing only five cleats, contained one of pure gold. The smugglers had gone to some lengths to make the crates weigh nearly the same; all would seem normal if no one opened the containers and noticed that some held only five. The only other factor likely to have given the scheme away was the fact that there were enough spare track cleats in the warehouse to replace all the tracks on two dozen Terracoupe earthmovers.

While the raiding party was still treasure hunting, I quietly made my way out to the back-up team vehicle and collapsed on the front seat.

"You OK, Sir?" asked the radioman.

"Fine, just a mite tired. Don't worry—she won't be chewing on your ass."

I popped two pain pills and settled down for a nap.

When I woke in a hospital bed the next morning, the doc had an X-ray made of my left side, looked it over, and gave me a dirty look.

"What have you been doing, idiot? You popped loose everything I did to stabilize that chopped up rib. Now you're going to stay in this bed for at least 48 hours if I have to strap you in. Give me any flak and I'll call your girlfriend."

He having invoked the ultimate weapon, I surrendered. After more shots for pain, and the resulting long nap, I called the FBI offices and spoke with Agent Nichole. I held the phone away from my ear while she fired her broadside; when the smoke cleared, I asked if she or Jack could come by in the evening and brief me on the results of the day's work. They both arrived after what passed as dinner and pulled up chairs. Before he began to fill me in, Jack produced a small unmarked bottle containing a rose-tinted beverage.

"Your after-dinner cordial," he said, pouring some in a hospital glass and offering it. He produced another glass and poured a portion for himself.

"Sorry, Liz," he said. "This is a special thing." She gave a questioning look, but said nothing; Jack and I touched glasses and drank.

I was puzzled for a moment—the sweet but slightly spicy wine touched off vague pleasant memories which I couldn't quite pin down. Then my memory flashed back to Kyoto, Japan, and I realized that this was the excellent plum wine that I had been served by Amami and Kioko during our visit to their Geisha house. Jack smiled as he watched my face light up with pleasure at the taste of the wine, and the memories accompanying it.

"Kioko had a flight through Anchorage this afternoon—she left this for you with her warm regards. There were two bottles; I'll send them home with Liz when she goes." He raised his eyebrows. "I assume you two see each other on occasion?" I assured him that we did.

The raid had been a success on all fronts and enough evidence had been uncovered to piece together the entire plot. The search had been made easier by Agent Liz's idea of furnishing each searcher with a small magnet. Most items that resembled steel but were not attracted to the magnet turned out to be disguised gold.

Paperwork found at the shop had led to half-dozen bank accounts and several safe-deposit boxes loaded with cash or small gold ingots. The Womack brothers had been CIA contractors in Vietnam, and had developed many shady contacts in Saigon. The two Vietnamese had been among those contacts and had connections to the group which had initially planned the looting of the treasury. After they arrived in the States, they had set up a lucrative sideline; they smuggled Vietnamese women into this country with false promises of jobs and good pay, and of eventual legal status. Nhan and Linh were only a few of the many who came, and were sold or leased out as prostitutes, cheap household help, or full-time mistresses.

There was now enough justification to raid and shut down the Terracoupe plant in Nam, locate their remaining stashed gold, and probably to track down the people who set up the enterprise. The Womacks had kept careful records, including names and dates, under the assumption that they were far from Vietnam and its official scrutiny.

I was satisfied with the results of our labor, or would be when my truck and rifle were back and running. Jack said that his bosses, who must have been on a stratospheric level in government, were pleased, and that the government of Vietnam was deliriously happy at not having to admit that the nation's pocket had been picked. I felt quite happy that my thrashing around had achieved so much, but sobered a bit when I thought of one loose end.

"Jack, Liz, has anyone told the local Womack that his brother and the man Quan were killed on the mountain?"

"The local brother's name turned out to be James, and no—he still thinks that both were arrested and are jailed separately. We're playing them against the deceased—you know, the old 'whoever deals first gets the best deal' scam. I, or someone, will tell him when everything is tied up tight."

"Which reminds me," said Liz, "you didn't give us much detail about Quan getting charged by the bear. Could you have saved him?"

I carefully considered my answer. "I doubt it. I would have had to show myself, and he was hunting me with an M16. He'd shot me once, and it didn't seem smart to give him another chance. Besides, my priorities for saving people don't include those who have beaten and murdered women."

"Justice, not due process," she said thoughtfully. "We checked the cave, Ben. Two nearly mummified bodies were there—Asian females."

"Then I'm happy about the bear eating Quan's face while he was still using it."

I changed the subject. "I'd like to see Nhan and Linh again before they disappear into the system. Could you arrange that?"

"Done." said Liz. "Linh is in this hospital having her injuries taken care of. Nhan is staying with her. They're waiting outside to see you; probably be in here as soon as we leave. Colonel Ito somehow wangled them into the country as refugees seeking asylum, so they'll have a protected legal status now."

"Thanks, Jack," I said. "Maybe that'll make up for some of the ugly things that have happened to those poor girls." I reached out and shook his hand and Liz leaned over for a departing kiss.

A few minutes after Liz and Jack had left there was a timid tapping at the door. I motioned my visitors in and marveled at the changes I saw. They were dressed in new clothing of the current style, and I could see the pleasing results of some minor hair styling and a touch of makeup. Linh wore a cast on her upper left arm, and still walked with a slow limp. Their wary, suspicious expressions had faded to mere traces of caution. I sensed that they now believed things might actually get better for them—but they weren't going to count on it just yet.

"You are beautiful," I said, motioning them to sit by the bed. Nhan gave a flicker of a smile.

"Thank you," she said. "We feel good. Feel clean. Linh have crack in bone, small hurts all over, but now better. Want to thank you for help us."

"I need to thank you for saving me," I said. If you hadn't poked that pistol in Boss Judd's ear, we would all be dead."

"Sorry about ear," she replied, "but you say get close. I get close."

Linh interrupted to speak to Nhan, a long stream of Vietnamese, and gave me a questioning look.

"Linh want to know what happen Quan and bear. Say she want to know all."

I told Nhan, and in detail, thinking she could censor the account as needed for Linh's benefit. Nhan turned and translated to Linh. Linh pondered for a few moments, her face, upon which I had never seen a smile, began to soften. Like a rose unfolding to the morning sun, a beaming smile spread across what was now a beautiful face.

"Quan, he bear poop now!"

CHAPTER 41

Friendly Persuasion

It had been over a month since I was released from the hospital, my truck had been returned, my rifle was being worked on, and I had just verified that my body functioned in all respects. Liz was in my kitchen scrambling a batch of eggs, and I could smell fresh coffee. It was a bright Sunday morning in October and all was right with the world.

Yesterday I had received two registered letters: one contained a US government check for $40,000 for unspecified services, and a grandly official letter effusively thanking me for those (still unspecified) services; the other, a matching check from the government of Vietnam, and a similar letter which included a small Vietnamese medal. I had immediately deposited the checks, happy to see a more-than-comfortable bank balance once again, and had dropped the medal in a desk drawer. Whether I ever wore it would probably depend upon who won the war.

"Hey, Liz, do you wanna drive north and have lunch at Eureka this afternoon? The leaves and tundra up there should be splashing orange, yellow, and red all over the place."

"I have to go to the office this afternoon," she said. "You go ahead if you want to. I'll see you later on—for dinner at my place if you'd like."

"Wow, the lady's cooking me breakfast and dinner in the same day. Wonder what she wants?"

"Don't get too uppity, Buster, or you'll be eating cold beans for a month. As for what I want, I've got it. Weeks on end without worrying about you being

208

hung up on the side of some mountain, and me not even knowing where to look for the body. Think you can keep it that way for a while?"

"Liz," I said, "that bad feeling you had about this job turned out to be too right. Maybe I'll pay more attention to you next time."

"Yeah—sure you will."

"After taking that bullet, I'm happy to rest in the lap of luxury for a while. I'd forgotten how nasty it feels to get shot—think I'll try to avoid it in the future. I guess I'll just goof off around here for the afternoon. Meet you at your place around five?"

She nodded as she dumped half the scrambled eggs on my plate, sat down, and served herself the other half.

The eggs were done right; allowed to harden a bit in the pan before being chopped up, rather than being homogenized. This allowed the bacon bits to add just the right amount of flavor and the yolk and white to be tasted separately as one ate. At least, that was the way we did it in the south, so it had to be right.

"And by the way, I never thanked you for the ELT unit—it worked well and I won't mind hauling it around on my next trip to the boonies."

"Well," she said, "don't count on a SWAT rescue next time. You were on an official mission, so I had no problems. But if I tell Monk that I need to rescue my boyfriend who decided that he wanted to paddle from Whittier to Juneau on a hollow log, he may not be so cooperative."

"Oh, he'll be OK," I said. "I sent a letter to your DC offices just praising the hell out of his boys and you for their cooperation, efficiency, bravery, cleanliness, loyalty, reverence, and anything else I could think of. I think Jack did the same. When all that comes down through channels, he'll be our slave forever."

I did just what I promised, goofed off around the house until 4:30. At five, I was at Liz's door, and by seven I was comfortably stuffed with meat loaf, butter beans, and mashed potatoes. By 8:00, I was feeling romantic, and by 8:01 Liz had fended me off and suggested a late movie. My disappointment was somewhat eased when she suggested the drive-in—I had very good memories of our last trip there. This evening might turn out to be as nice as the one tucked away in my memory. The movie was called, quite appropriately, "Friendly Persuasion".

--- THE END ---

AUTHOR'S NOTES

Military-oriented readers may have stumbled a bit in those chapters involving the Korean War. The Phonetic Alphabet in use by the Army at that time differed from the one in use today. The change came with the creation of NATO, and was designed to make the system more user-friendly for our allies. For lovers of military trivia, WW2 and Korean War GIs used the following:

Able	Jig	Sugar
Baker	King	Tare
Charlie	Love	Uncle
Dog	Mike	Victor
Easy	Nan	William
Fox	Oboe	Xray
George	Peter	Yoke
How	Queen	Zebra
Item	Roger	

ROGER was also used in phone or radio communications to indicate "message received".

OVER meant "your turn to talk".

OUT indicated that the conversation was terminated and you were going off the air.

SAY AGAIN meant "repeat your last transmission".

The Air Force liked the term, *WILCO*, which meant "I will comply". The Army had little use for it, since it was assumed that, if one received an order, one would most assuredly comply.

The R&R camp described in Ben's interval in Japan is a composite of several that were set up for battle weary troops. The luxuries described may not have been available at all camps, but the benefits to morale were as great.

The Japanese terms used in the chapters about the Geisha world may not be universally accepted; these terms vary between the various districts and islands of Japan.

The shenanigans described in the chapters concerning Letterman Army Hospital may have been slightly exaggerated, but occurred at some military hospitals within the system.

The Kivchak Fishing Lodge is a product of my imagination, and that's too bad because I'd like to go there some time.

If any reader decides to search out the valley of the Hard Times, Jodo, Jolly Boys, and Little Nel gold mining claims, don't bother—it doesn't exist. But if one enjoys such explorations, the Kenai Peninsula of South-Central Alaska abounds in countless old mining sites, most of which are accessible to a determined day-hiker.

The Falls Creek claim (renamed the Katy Bee by Hard Luck Stan) does exist. I once owned it.

ACKNOWLEDGMENTS

Thanks to my friend Lance Trasky for the loan of the Purple Heart shown on the back cover, one of three he obtained the hard way.

My thanks to my "test readers":
Kara, Marge, Deborah, Mary and
a pair of Cheryls.
(All ladies, you'll notice; they treat me more kindly than men.)

And a very special thanks to my friend of many years, Dr. Nhan Tran, who inspired the Vietnamese connection.

Without the guidance and encouragement of Debi Gordon of First Edition Design Publishing, you would not be reading this. Many thanks, Deb.

ABOUT THE AUTHOR

Don Neal, author of the Ben Hunnicutt novels, is a retired soldier. Reared in Suffolk and in Surry County in southern Virginia, he dropped out of the College of William and Mary and enlisted in the Army after the Chinese entered the Korean War in late 1950. His 28 years of service encompassed nearly the entire Cold War, taking him to Japan, Germany, Korea, and Alaska. He has served in the Infantry, Artillery, Armor, and Air Defense Missile branches. His last ten years of service were with the Nike Hercules Air Defense Missile units protecting the Anchorage and Fairbanks population and military centers against Soviet bomber attack during the Cold War.

He and his family have lived in Anchorage, Alaska, for over 50 years. His hobbies include military history and the research and study of antique and historical firearms—with an occasional foray into drag racing.

His four novels reflect Alaska as a Territory, then as a raw new state before it was transformed and modernized by the discovery of oil and the building of the Trans-Alaska Oil Pipeline.

www.ingramcontent.com/pod-product-compliance
Lightning Source LLC
Chambersburg PA
CBHW022047240626
47154CB00007B/2609